Stan Barstow was b
in the West Riding o
married and has a s
After working in the
industry, mainly as a
became a full-time writer in 1962.

His first novel, *A Kind of Loving*, was published in 1960. Since then he has published three volumes of short stories and eight more novels, including *A Raging Calm, Joby, A Brother's Tale, Just You Wait and See*, and most recently, *Give Us This Day*. His work is read and studied widely in schools. He has been published in the United States and translated into nine European languages. The Open University has conferred on Stan Barstow an Honorary Degree of Master of Arts.

He has won The Royal Television Society Award for Writers on two occasions and The Writers' Guild and BAFTA Awards for his television dramatisations, notably *Joby, A Raging Calm* and for Winifred Holtby's *South Riding*.

A Kind of Loving became a feature film (director John Schlesinger) and a ten-part television serial. *A Brother's Tale* was also televised in three episodes.

Author photograph by Neil Barstow

Also by Stan Barstow

A KIND OF LOVING
THE WATCHERS ON THE SHORE
THE RIGHT TRUE END
THE DESPERADOES
THE GLAD EYE and other stories
JOBY
A RAGING CALM
JUST YOU WAIT AND SEE

and published by Black Swan

Ask Me Tomorrow

Stan Barstow

BLACK SWAN

This is a work of fiction. The characters and incidents in it are imaginary.

A BLACK SWAN BOOK 0 552 99184 8

Originally published in Great Britain
by Michael Joseph Ltd.

PRINTING HISTORY
Michael Joseph edition published 1962
Corgi edition published 1974
Black Swan edition published 1990

This book is set in 11/11¼ pt Mallard
by Colset Private Limited, Singapore.

Black Swan Books are published by Transworld Publishers Ltd., 61–63 Uxbridge Road, Ealing, London W5 5SA, in Australia by Transworld Publishers (Australia) Pty. Ltd., 15–23 Helles Avenue, Moorebank, NSW 2170, and in New Zealand by Transworld Publishers (N.Z.) Ltd., Cnr. Moselle and Waipareira Avenues, Henderson, Auckland.

Made and printed in Great Britain by
Cox & Wyman Ltd, Reading, Berks

For Gillian

1

Zero Hour was seven-fifteen and by seven Wilf was sitting about the living-room simulating calmness with the help of the *Yorkshire Evening Post*, whose usually bright and newsy paragraphs were to him, this evening, persistently blank and uncommunicative. The string orchestra on the wireless was playing something by Grieg, the sound coming through thin and tinny, interrupted by bursts of crackling atmospheric. After one particularly obliterating charge Wilf got out of his chair and bent over the shabby walnut-veneered cabinet and fiddled with the controls, watching the indicator move over the names of obsolete stations of the 'thirties. He was conscious that the set was giving of its best and fretfully impatient that at this big moment in his life he might be let down by something outside his control. The wireless was one his father and mother had bought before the war and it had long since ceased to be a source of entertainment. Ousted by television – their latest set, on which Wilf's brother Harry was making the hire-purchase payments, dominating the room in its twenty-one-inch glory – it was switched on for time checks and little else. Some women used radio to give them background music during the working day; but Wilf's mother couldn't abide music while she was busy about the house.

Pots chinked in the scullery where she was finishing the washing-up. As he turned from the radio Wilf glanced at his father who sat upright in his chair, in shirtsleeves and waistcoat, on one side of the hearth. He hadn't spoken for a long time, sitting there, his dark eyes resting on the fire in the blackleaded grate. He was several years older than Wilf's mother and had married fairly late in life. There was in his personality a silent passivity that had passed on to neither of his sons. It was not, however, the calmness of a quietly contented man, but more the deliberately willed quiescence of one who limited communication with an exasperating and disappointing world, erupting into rare volcanic rages when it tried patience too far. There was a layer of deep, unfathomed bitterness in the man that only his silence made tolerable. He sat in silence, the smoke wisping upwards from the smooth uncrushed cylinder of the half-smoked cigarette held delicately in his heavy fingers.

Wilf threw the nervously pulped butt of his own cigarette into the fire as his mother came through from the scullery, drying her hands on the damp tea-towel which she then hung neatly over the rail of the wire-mesh fireguard which had enclosed the hearth since he and Harry were small children and Harry, one night with a banked fire glowing red in the grate, had fallen with both hands on the hob. He wore proud boxing gloves of bandages for weeks after that and their mother bought the fireguard for a couple of shillings from a woman down the street who was moving house and, her own family grown, had no further use for it. The Cottons retained it now as something absorbed into their habit of life, the mother employing it as a useful airer for towels and the underclothes of the three men of the house.

'Has our Harry come back yet?' the mother asked rhetorically, for it was obvious he wasn't in the house.

'Not yet,' Wilf murmured.

Harry was out on some errand down the village. He had promised to be back – promised his mother, that is, not Wilf, who had deliberately made no special point of asking him to be in. He'd been gone nearly an hour and there was no sign of him.

'He's goin' to be messing about till he misses it,' his mother said as she glanced at the alarm clock on the mantelpiece.

'Perhaps he's settled down to listen somewhere else,' Wilf suggested. He half hoped that this was true, anticipating the self-consciousness his brother's presence would impose on him.

'Well he should make an effort to be at home for once,' the mother said. 'It's a family occasion.'

It was, in some ways, Wilf thought, a village occasion. There would be many wireless sets tuned in tonight to a broadcast which had no particular attraction other than its being the result of the activity of someone known to the listeners. The sudden small local fame that had come upon him both irritated and gratified him. He wanted passionately to be 'somebody': to be discussed and respected by the knowledgeable in the literary world beyond the village that he read about in books and magazines and caught the pungent scent of in the magazine sections of the *Sunday Times* and the *Observer*; but the interest of local people, whose curiosity was for something unusual in their midst, mostly embarrassed him, emphasising to him his differences and smiting him with a self-consciousness that he was afraid might cripple his future work. The gratification came with the knowledge that his people, among whom he so often felt alien, respected achievement even in a field strange to them. His mother, for instance, was, he knew, deeply proud of him, yet he was at times exasperated beyond patience by her inability to comprehend a mind and imagination which could roam beyond the confines of the village, the pit and the home.

The clock said ten past seven. Wilf, as excitement grew in him, wished he were alone, in a room of his own, so that he could savour the occasion to the full, critically and absorbedly, without the distraction of trying to assess the reactions of others.

'Last minute as usual,' his mother said, still on the

subject of the absent Harry. 'He'll be late for his own funeral, that one.' How her mind could dwell on and be satisfied with the trivialities of daily life! Her hands, as though unable to be idle for a moment, plucked a man's vest from the fireguard. She held it to her cheek to test it for any last trace of dampness. Her agitation finally provoked her husband into speech.

'Sit yersen down an' stop natterin',' he said. 'Our Harry 'ull come if he wants to, an' stop away t'same.' He turned his heavy square head slightly towards his younger son. 'Tune that wireless in, Wilf, an' turn it up a bit.'

Wilf did as he was told and the sound of the string orchestra shrilled out into the room. As he sat down he reached from the table the copy of the script which the BBC staff in Leeds had sent him, remembering how almost ill with excitement he'd been on the morning their letter arrived to say they were holding the story in the hope of finding a place for it in their programmes. Here now, in the script, was the nearest his words had ever come to the coveted state of print, and the producer's letter had been the first indication from the outside world that those words, put haltingly on to paper on the card-table in the temporary solitude of his and Harry's bedroom, could be more than a private indulgence. The money, though useful, hardly mattered. He would have given them the story if necessary.

There was the sound of someone moving in the scullery. Wilf fancied it had been preceded by a tap on the back door, and as his mother, turning in her chair, said, 'Here he is now . . .' their next-door neighbour looked into the room.

'I'm sorry to bother you,' she began, her trailing hand tapping on the other side of the door as her head appeared. She'd come, she said, to ask if Mrs Cotton had such a thing as a cup of sugar she could let her have till tomorrow. As Wilf's mother got up hurriedly to the cupboard, Mrs Lewis advanced into the room, explaining how she had happened to find herself without this basic commodity, her voice, the loudest on the row, battling with the last bars of the string orchestra's music. At any other time Wilf would have turned the volume down out of common politeness, but now he swore under his breath and sat doggedly unmoving as the music ended and the announcer closed the recorded programme. Mrs Lewis was a notorious borrower: a cup of sugar, half a dozen potatoes, a couple of eggs, half a bottle of milk – hardly a day went by without an emergency call. Wilf's mother pushed the cup into the woman's hands. Mrs Lewis had never had her needs met with such alacrity and as though sensing this and feeling that the incident somehow lacked balance she began again to explain in detail why she needed to recourse to borrowing sugar from a neighbour at seven o'clock on a Thursday night.

As his mother fluttered agitatedly, wondering how to make the other woman vanish into the ground, Wilf, his head craned closer to the speaker to hear the opening announcement, said, in a voice as loud as their neighbour's, 'Would you mind, Mrs Lewis – there's something I 'specially want to listen to.'

Mrs Lewis, cut off in mid flow, let her mouth drop open slightly. 'Oh, well,' she said. 'I didn't mean to—'

'It's our Wilf's story, you see,' Mrs Cotton explained. 'It's just coming on.'

The crackling hum of the wireless was broken by the announcer's voice: 'This is the BBC Home Service from the North of England. We present "Man in the Dark", a short story by Wilf Cotton, read by Tom Baxter . . .'

'Oh, aye, I should ha' remembered,' Mrs Lewis said. 'Only I thought it was on the telly an' ours is broken down. Anyway, we haven't had a wireless for a long time. Ours had got past it an' Jack said he didn't see any sense in payin' out good money for a new 'un when we'd never use it anyway. I mean, there's everything you want on the telly now, isn't there? All t'sport an' football results an' everything. Jack said he didn't even need t'wireless for checking his pools, an' that war about all it war used for . . .'

Wilf groaned audibly. 'Blast the woman,' he said under his breath. 'Blast her, blast her, blast her.'

'Mrs Lewis!' his father said all at once. 'Will yer either clear off out or else sit down an' shurrup.'

The woman broke off again in mid-sentence, her eyes widening as they darted to Mr Cotton's inscrutable face. He didn't look at her. His eyes were fixed once more on the fire. It was as if he hadn't spoken at all. Wilf's mother, anxious that her neighbour should not leave under the propulsion of what might be construed as rudeness, narrowed her eyes and, nodding her head slightly as though in conspiracy, gently pushed Mrs Lewis to a straight-backed chair. The woman lowered her body until her fat little buttocks were poised on the edge of the seat. She sat there, oblivious to the wireless, darting quick little glances about the room, nervous under the restraint imposed upon her tongue, until eventually a foolish little smile lifted the corners of her mouth. It was as though she had suddenly realised that the taciturn Mr Cotton, whom she hardly heard speak except to pass the time of day, was not to be taken seriously in his abruptness and she would be silly to let his words upset her. Wilf's mother, quick to notice the other woman's expression, was pleased that she had given her time to consider before going home to report the exchange to her husband, a man given to quarrelsomeness.

Wilf had almost forgotten her presence. He was following the story in his script, noting the occasional newly revealed clumsiness in the writing and one point where the reader had changed the word order of a sentence to make it come more easily off the tongue. Of the reading in general he had hardly any criticism apart from the dialect in the dialogue exchanges, which was more true to the Lancashire border country than to the miners' Yorkshire. He let the script rest on his knee and closed his eyes to listen with pleasure as the voice reached the climax and, beautifully paced, slid over into the dying fall of the story's end. In the moment of silence that followed he reached out and switched off the set, opening his eyes to look directly at his father's impassive profile. He knew that his mother would speak first, but it was his father's reaction he wanted. For his father, more than any other person Wilf knew, was 'The Man in the Dark', a man whose life had been that of the pits for nearly forty years, who had himself experienced the bitterness that younger men knew only as a legacy handed down to them. Men like Ronnie Betley quoted it with glib ease in time of dispute. Men like his father had lived it.

But it was Mrs Lewis who, having heard perhaps one word in ten, and that misunderstood and quickly to be forgotten, took the silence as a cue for speech and pronounced the first verdict.

'Well, wasn't that nice! Fancy havin' what you've written broadcast on the wireless! I'll be putting on airs living next door to a real author. Don't you think your Wilf's clever, Mrs Cotton? Aren't you proud of him?'

The story's brief trance was shattered for Wilf. He squirmed under the woman's idiotic blather, anticipating it as the first of many similar comments he would be forced to endure in the next few days. He wanted badly now to have the opinion of someone who *knew*, someone whose criticism he could value. But he knew no one, working in complete isolation, this event the first breach in the confining fence of rejection slips. It was a breach that it was up to him to widen and of a sudden he felt gripped by an enormous confidence in his own ability. He had heard his words tonight as perhaps thousands of others had heard them, and he wasn't ashamed. He got up, possessed by an urgent need to be alone, to think and weigh the situation. As his mother answered Mrs Lewis with every seriousness he went to the foot of the stairs and took down the warm raglan overcoat in grey tweed, bought out of the BBC's cheque, and put it on.

'I'm going for a walk,' he said.

'Well if you run into our Harry tell him I'll have a word or two to say to him when he comes in,' his mother said.

'It doesn't *matter*, Mother,' Wilf said, glancing at Mrs Lewis.

'I think it does. I think it's a pity when a chap can't take an interest in his own brother's achievement.'

'He's probably caught it somewhere else.'

'Aye, an' he'll catch it here when he gets back. You can bet he's got himself holed up in some pub or other and forgotten all about it.'

Wilf let the subject drop. 'I'll see you later, then. So long. Cheerio, Mrs Lewis.'

He went out the back way, making a call at the lavatory before leaving. The lavatories were brick-built, three to a block, standing in the long yard that ran the length of the row. As he opened the door, whose upper edge was saw-trimmed into a repeating pattern of points and three-quarter circles to give a little ventilation, he was careful not to rub against the wall, because the whitewash was flaking off and easily adhered to one's sleeves. The lavatory was whitewashed every year, either he or Harry giving it a new coat in the spring. They were of the tippler type and as a small boy, just graduated from his personal portable sanitary arrangements inside the house, Wilf had nursed a real fear of falling down the vertical shaft and being lost for ever. And for a long time after, as he grew older, if he happened to be enthroned in there when the pressure of water released down the drains from the houses became sufficient to operate the mechanism, the sudden surge and thump of the tippler board would cause him to grab at the seat with both hands as a gust of warm air rose up to caress pleasantly his bare buttocks. He locked the door and returned the key to the hook just inside the scullery. Most of the more particular families locked their lavatories. The Cottons started doing it after a morning early in the war when Wilf's mother, going out at dawn, had surprised a soldier coming out buttoning up his battledress blouse as though he'd spent the night there. She found it hard to reconcile the pool of dried vomit on the floor with his fresh young face and polite good morning, but from then on the door was locked.

Wilf went down along the backs of the houses and through the brick-floored entry into the street. Parkinson Street had been named after William Parkinson, a director of the colliery company and a JP in the district about the turn of the century, when the houses were built with the profits from coal. A special tile had been let into the brickwork on one of the houses in the middle of the street, with on it A*1901*D. Though they consisted of only a living-room and a scullery and two bedrooms and had no hot-water system or indoor sanitation, the houses in Parkinson Street were of a slightly superior standing to most of those in nearby terraces because their front doors did not open directly on to the pavement, being separated from it by a six-foot width of earth and a waist-high brick wall. A few optimistic spirits up and down the street tried to cultivate wallflowers or snapdragons in these 'gardens' but mostly they were left to the grass, which would grow anywhere. Here and there dark-green privet struggled dispiritedly behind the walls. There had never been much through-traffic and the street was a reasonably safe place to play. As a boy, with his brother Harry and different friends, Wilf had helped set up many a game of street cricket, chalking the wickets on the wall and bowling across the width of the road. They used a bat cut from a flat board and only a soft ball, yet it was never very satisfactory because of the proximity of the houses, especially the Leaches' house almost directly opposite their own. No sooner had they started than an upstairs window would slam up and Mrs Leach's dust-bonneted head appear to remonstrate with them:

'Yer young feniens, yer at it agen! You break one o' my winders an' I'll skin ye alive, the lot of yer!'

Mrs Leach was a real damper on the enjoyment of street games. They'd had the feeling that she was constantly poised behind the bedroom curtains, watching for signs of some misdemeanour. She had died before Wilf reached his teens, failing in health quite suddenly, until all at once she was gone and the undertaker's men were struggling the pitch-pine coffin out through the front door to the waiting hearse. They were interested in murder about that time, their fascination having been aroused by a volume of celebrated murder cases which Wilf had uncovered on the sociology shelf of the public library. All the classic cases of violent death were in there: Jack the Ripper, the Seddons, Crippen, Buck Ruxton, and the rest. Murder to them had a strong flavour of gaslight, antimacassars and overfurnished rooms, and recalling little Mr Leach, always in strong contrast to his big, domineering wife, as he stood on the pavement in black suit and bowler hat, his moustache drooping in the damp air of the funeral morning – a figure straight from the pages of *The Gallows' Walk* – they had wondered how long it would be before the police made the arrest. When nothing happened they decided to investigate themselves and there were, initially, some wild suggestions for breaking into Mr Leach's house to search for poison and other evidence of his guilt. Common sense and caution ruling this out, they settled for observation of Mr Leach's movements, which was a boring business since he hardly left the house on weekday evenings. Their reward came, however, one Saturday afternoon when they followed their quarry into Calderford and saw him meet a woman on a street corner. They trailed the couple from shop to shop and through the market, then to a tall Victorian terrace house behind the railway station, where they went in.

Hunger finally terminated the boys' watch but they went home convinced that they had discovered one of the vital elements in the case: the other woman. It robbed the affair of some of its flavour of secrecy and intrigue, and marked the beginning of a definite decline in their interest, when Mr Leach's lady friend, a plain-faced plump young woman, began to visit him openly in his own home. It seemed she was a niece of the late Mrs Leach and it wasn't long before Mr Leach married her, in the opinion of the street perhaps a trifle soon after the funeral of his first wife, but, it seemed, quite legitimately and above board. Six months later a removal van was at the door and they were gone – some said to Sheffield, others Birmingham – and not heard of again.

Les Roper was the third in the trio of amateur sleuths, the only one of their pals to be let into the secret of 'Mr Leach's crime'. Les was dead now, killed – after National Service in Cyprus during the troubles – on his motor-bike when returning one wild rainy night from his girl friend's house in Barnsley.

On nights like this, when he walked with no set purpose except to escape from the warm, stifling atmosphere of home, he could hardly step into the street without disturbing the past. Almost every object he saw had its associations: the Leaches' house, which would always be the Leaches' house to him, though another family had lived there for years past; the lamp-post on the corner of Parkinson Street and Syke Terrace where they had played on winter nights and on which, one time, they staged a mock lynching that came perilously near to the real thing and sent poor badly-done-to Peter Pendle, who wet the bed and himself until into his teens, home with a clothes-line burn halfway round his neck. In the corner house at that time lived old Davenport, a widower without a family. He had seemed to them to have always been old and alone. He walked out of his back door late one night and across the yard to the lavatory where he shut himself in and ended it all by drinking a bottle of corrosive disinfectant. People wondered why, if he had to do it, he hadn't committed the act in the comfort of his own house. Wilf later saw it as a sense of fitness in the old man: a mark of respect for a home which the police found spotlessly clean and tidy when they entered to look over his effects.

Looking back, Wilf saw himself as a boy no different from other boys. He had played, run, fought with the rest. He was perhaps a little brighter at school than many, but not as clever as some. When a scholarship at eleven took him to the grammar school in Calderford he felt little sense of movement away from his class. For scholarship boys were common enough and by no means all of those he associated with during the next five years were studious youths, happiest when grappling with algebra, physics, geometry and French. And of those who worked diligently there were few who saw these formative years as a gateway to a new world of culture, knowledge and achievement. The highest most of them looked was to a teaching position in a local school, with short hours and long holidays. For the rest there was a vague idea of some job without physical labour, outside the pits which had claimed their less fortunate friends, who were bringing home wages two years before they themselves stepped out of the classroom to face the world. And as time passed by some of them, in their eight- and nine-pound-a-week clerking jobs, looked at the free-spending friends of their boyhood and wondered who were the fortunate ones, pondering upon the curious reversal of values in the post-war boom years when the prestige was less in what you did than in how much you were paid for doing it. The white collar had become the symbol of economy, the black fist the sign of plenty.

For Wilf, a wages clerk at Bronhill, where his father and brother both worked underground, the restlessness was not long in making itself felt. But to him it was only partly the unease of seeing at first hand those less intelligent than himself taking home wage packets twice as heavy as his. What nagged more and more was a dissatisfaction with his life as a whole, which grew with a dawning awareness of a world and values outside the village and the knowledge that the opportunity given him, and which a few boys he knew had been cute enough to grasp, he had largely wasted. Too late he remembered the interest in history which he hadn't bothered to develop beyond the immediate requirements of test-papers and exams; too late he recalled the French and Latin which, he knew, with more study on his part, would have opened up to him their fascinating worlds. Not too late, though, was he reminded, in the most superficial but nevertheless for him decisive way, of a natural facility in English Language and Literature. It had needed little conscious application for him to cope, rather more than adequately, with these complementary subjects at the level required. But it took a casual visit to the cinema several years later to begin to show that, in his case, this facility had been the sign of a latent talent for something beyond the parsing of sentences and an ability, after previous instruction, to write a two-hundred-and-fifty-word essay on Shylock's reasons for demanding his pound of flesh.

He'd gone to see a film – not a very good film but one which featured an American actor whom Wilf, at that time, greatly admired and whom a girl younger than himself had told him he physically resembled. In this film the actor played the part of a writer. He hadn't done any good work for a long time and found the company of a bottle more congenial than that of a typewriter. But towards the end of the film he made an impassioned speech to the woman he loved in which he told her all that writing had meant to him, all that writing was. It was a good speech, lifted straight out of the original novel, which was by a better writer than the one who'd done the screenplay, and Wilf left the shabby little cinema and walked home through the sooty rain of the Bronhill night with it ringing in his ears. He tracked the novel down in the central library at Calderford and read it and others by the same author. Along with them he devoured every book about writing he could find. He was away. And by the time he realised just what he'd taken on it was too late: writing, the need to express the throb and quiver of life on the page, had become part of him. There came a time when he felt almost ashamed of the casual hit-or-miss way he had stumbled on what had by then become the biggest thing in his life, and he thought that this must be one of the factors which cut him off from the giants, who had surely felt in the grip of a God-given destiny from early in childhood. But it in no way lessened his determination and the deep and basically unshakeable conviction that some time, though it might be a long time in coming, he would make his mark.

In the meantime there was a life to live, a living to earn . . .

2

The room he shared with Harry was small. A narrow sash window overlooked the yard. There were two single beds and a chest of drawers and room for hardly anything else. They hung their clothes in a curtained-off alcove. In the alcove also were a suitcase in which Wilf kept his manuscripts, the secondhand portable machine on which he typed them, and a collapsible card-table with a worn green baize top. When he wanted to work he set up the table and sat on the end of his bed. Between the bed and the wall was the narrow three-shelf bookcase which held his small library. Along with the Concise Oxford Dictionary and Roget's Thesaurus there were several books about writing, including L.A.G. Strong's *The Writer's Trade*, E.M. Forster's *Aspects of the Novel* and H.E. Bates's *The Modern Short Story*. The rest were mostly fiction. He read avidly, feeling all the time that life could never be long enough for him to cover all he should read. For while his contemporaries were constantly adding to the numbers of published books, there was behind them the huge heritage on which they were based. He had made sorties into the picaresque worlds of Defoe and Smollet, adventured in Dickens, but by no means exhaustively, and been led by a new series of paperbacks to Emile Zola, whom he found overblown but admired for his brutal energy in *La Bête Humaine* and the power of his narrative sweep in *L'Assommoir* and *Germinal*. What giants they all were! And how thin and puny his own work looked beside theirs. He had lately discovered the nineteenth-century Russians and thought that perhaps the most sheerly impressive novel he had ever encountered was *The Brothers Karamazov*, which he was reading just now.

But he was in no mood for Dostoyevsky tonight and as he undressed in the cold light of the single electric bulb which shone without shadow on the blue distempered walls he glanced idly over the books on the shelves, reluctant to start anything new. When he got into bed it was with Robert Liddell's *Some Principles of Fiction*. He had read it through more than once but could always browse in it and find something to interest and stimulate.

He heard the back door thud as someone entered the house and a few minutes later Harry came upstairs. Wilf could smell the beer on him before he glanced briefly into his bright dark eyes.

Harry returned Wilf's glance. 'Now then.'

'Now then.'

He wasn't drunk but there was just enough more of his usual carelessness of movement to cause him to feel the smallness of the room. He stumbled passing the foot of Wilf's bed and, not troubling to save himself, fell across his own where he turned on to his back with his feet touching the floor. He put his hands behind his head and relaxed.

'It's a good job we're both thin 'uns or we wouldn't have room to turn round in this box.'

Wilf went on reading. Harry wasn't expecting any answer.

'I wonder how far we are off the top of the council housing list nowadays . . .'

'You know mam only had our names put down for the sake of it,' Wilf said without looking up. 'You'll never persuade her to move now. Three times the rent, and two sons of marrying age.'

'Ah,' Harry said, looking up at the ceiling, his eyes half closed against the glare of the light.

'Anyway, you might have the room to yourself before long.'

Harry lifted himself on to one elbow. 'You're not thinkin' o' gettin' wed, are you?'

'No, but I might buzz off somewhere . . . I feel like climbing the walls sometimes, sticking round here.'

'Don't we all,' Harry said. 'Don't we bloody-well all. Where you thinkin' o' going to – London?'

'No, not so far. But far enough to be able to do what I like without wondering what other people will think of it.'

'Have you said anything to the Old Lady?'

He'd never mentioned it to anybody, never having crystallised his vague desire to escape into anything like a definite resolve. Even now he had no real plan, nothing more than an intensification of determination brought on by hearing his story broadcast.

'No. Why?'

'I just wondered. Summat's rubbed her up the wrong way. She hadn't a civil word for me when I came in.'

'Well you know what that's all about, don't you?'

'Damned if I do.'

'She's narky because you didn't come in earlier.'

'Oh, that's it . . . The big occasion . . . How did it go, anyway?'

'All right, I suppose,' Wilf said, deliberately offhand. 'I'd've liked it better if Mrs Lewis hadn't come in to borrow some sugar just as it was starting.'

'Silly old bitch . . . I'm sorry I didn't get back in time.'

'Oh, that's okay. There was no obligation.'

Harry flopped back across the bed and closed his eyes. 'I was down at Ronnie Betley's. We got talking and I hadn't time to walk back up. They had it on, though.'

'Oh, you did hear it, then? I thought you'd missed it when you asked how it went.'

'I meant did you think that chap read it right, an' all that. I'm no judge of these things. Ronnie an' his missis said I'd to tell you how much they enjoyed it.'

'Oh?'

'Aye. Ronnie said it war about time somebody started to tell outsiders what it's like to work in t'pits for a living. Me . . . I reckon they can think what they like as long as the brass is right.'

He struggled up into a sitting position and tugged at the knot in his tie. 'Ronnie said he'd like you to pop down one night an' have a natter. He says he's got one'r two ideas you might be able to use.'

'I'm not going to peddle Ronnie Betley's propaganda for him,' Wilf said. 'If he wants to preach the cause he'll have to do it himself, not through me.'

'Propaganda? Cause?' Harry stopped struggling with his tie and stared at Wilf. 'What the hell are you talkin' about? There's only one cause round here and that's our rights. It's Ronnie Betley's job to look after 'em. He's the union secretary, in't he? An' a bloody sight better secretary than old Cuthbert ever war an' all.' He got up off the bed and began to undress.

'Cuthbert used to settle trouble. Ronnie Betley makes it. That's the difference between 'em.'

'The difference between 'em,' Harry said harshly, 'is that Cuthbert got soft in his old age an' Ronnie Betley's got some fire in his belly. There's two ways o' settlin' trouble. One's to get your own way an' the other's to let the other bloke have his.'

'There's another way,' Wilf said. 'Compromise.'

'Aye, compromise. You can nearly hear old Cuthbert sayin' it. Compromise an' moderation. An' what did it get 'em all before the war, eh? Standin' about on street corners without a couple of ha'pennies to rub together an' no grub in the house.'

'You think Ronnie Betley wouldn't let you all stand on street corners if it furthered his ends? With him it's the cause for the sake of the cause. It's not a struggle at each stage for the righting of a separate injustice. That's the weak-kneed socialist philosophy of people like Cuthbert and my father. What Betley and his like are working for is a complete change of system, for absolute power. It used to be the shout that everything would be all right when the pits were nationalised.'

'Well it isn't, is it?'

'No, but you can raise hell about it when you feel the need to. What some of you blokes don't seem to see is that if ever Betley and his crowd get complete hold of the reins you'll have to keep your mouths shut and do as you're told.'

Harry pulled on his pyjama trousers and said through a huge yawn, 'What the hell do you know about it anyway? You've never done a day's work underground.'

It was the last infantile dismissive retort from a man in a man's world to one who was a slightly contemptible, if necessary, appendage to the real business of earning a living.

'Your skill in argument astonishes me,' Wilf said. 'Ronnie Betley must rub his hands every night when he thinks about you all.'

'Oh – Ronnie Betley,' Harry said.

'No, not Betley, his wife,' Wilf said. He watched Harry's head turn and his heart beat a little faster. Beer usually made Harry amiable but their little argument could have counteracted that.

'What d'you mean by that?' Harry said.

'She'd make a more acceptable bedful, wouldn't she?' Wilf said deliberately. He was drawing his brother out, but warily, waiting for confirmation of a hunch he'd had for some time now. A moment passed as Harry pulled his undervest up over his head.

'I've seen you talking to her on the street,' Wilf said. 'You want to watch it, Harry. Your eyes give you away. I hope you don't look at her like that when Betley's around.'

Harry dropped the vest and smoothed back his short dark hair with both hands. The upward lift to his arms tautened the skin over his ribs. His chest was smooth, hairless and white. He wasn't deep in the chest but there was an indication of a dogged, wiry strength under the light covering of flesh and muscle.

'You see too much,' he said, reaching for the other half of his pyjamas.

Wilf felt himself relax as the moment of danger passed. He waited while Harry took off his wrist-watch and wound it up reflectively. He hung it by the strap from a small picture-hook driven into the plaster of the wall between the two beds. He had something on his mind. Wilf waited.

'He'll be in the same bed as her just now,' Harry said, almost to himself. 'An' he's probably got his arse turned on her.'

'It's his privilege.'

'Aye, man, but what a waste.'

'He's not a man to cross, Harry.'

'No, an' he's not the man to give her all she wants,' Harry said. 'I'm sure of it. Least, sometimes I'm sure of it. Most times I can't make up me mind whether she's starved and lookin' for a bit on the side, or if she's just a cold-blooded teaser. One thing I do know: when she crosses her legs an' shows you her stocking tops it's no accident.'

'In other words, she knows why you go down there.'

'She's a good idea.'

'And what about Betley?'

'Aw, he gets so carried away with what he's sayin' he hardly knows she's in the same room.'

Wilf looked at the wall without seeing it, occupied with a mental picture of June Betley's long legs carrying her along High Street. She and Betley had no children and her breasts were still firm and high. She bothered with her appearance, using make-up skilfully, and had her hair set often. But you couldn't call her pretty. On the other hand prettiness was often insipid and June Betley was far from that.

He said, 'God knows I'm no judge, Harry, and women take a lot of fathoming, but don't you think you could be wrong? I mean about her playing up to you. She and Betley always give the impression of being happy enough together. It could be you're completely wrong and she'd be shocked if she knew what you were thinking about her.'

Harry sat with his shoulders bowed, looking at the floor between the beds. He turned over what was in his mind for a while longer before lifting his head and looking past Wilf.

'I know things about her that even Betley doesn't know.'

It came out as a flat statement of fact, not at all boastfully; and as he finished the sentence Harry switched his gaze to Wilf and looked steadily at him as he made no reply. Wilf returned his brother's look, trying to keep any expression from appearing in his eyes. And then he realised that Harry was hardly conscious of Wilf's eyes holding his; he was looking straight through them at Wilf himself. He was assessing him, weighing him. He wanted to tell somebody something and he was deciding Wilf's suitability for the role of confidant. Wilf wondered if he would measure up and felt all at once concerned that he should. He and Harry had not been particularly close for a long time now; not in the way they were as boys. They had common roots, a common background, but no longer common interests. They had grown too different from each other in recent years – or at least, Wilf had become different. For whereas Harry conformed, without realising it, was at ease in his world, Wilf was a renegade, hankering after something different, something Harry couldn't understand. He knew that it sometimes troubled Harry. A writer from outside he would have taken in his stride, for he prided himself on being a good mixer. But one in his midst, his own brother, with whom he'd done all the things that boys do together – it disturbed him, made him uneasy. It upset the natural order of things. It was as though, in some curious unformed way, he felt that Wilf had betrayed a trust.

So he waited, wondering just how far apart they had

grown, until Harry came out of it suddenly, pushing himself up off the low bed. 'I'll show you summat.' He went to the alcove where he bent down and lifted aside the curtain as he felt for the attaché case in which he kept his personal belongings: his union membership and National Health cards, a packet of letters from National Service pals, a few pounds put aside, an endowment insurance policy for five hundred pounds, two or three paperbacked books with lurid covers and contents that didn't live up to their promise. Despite his free and easy manner Harry was a tidy, methodical man with a streak of thrift he must have inherited from their mother. Among the things in the case was a bundle of photographs wrapped in an oilskin tobacco pouch, and this he took out, coming round again between the beds as he snapped the rubber band back on to his wrist. They were mostly groups of young National Servicemen caught off-duty in Germany and Cyprus and Wilf had seen them before. They were of no conceivable interest to anyone who hadn't been there at the time but they illustrated another aspect of their relationship in which Harry had an unspoken superiority. For he, in a reserved occupation, had deliberately sought the adventure of National Service while Wilf, in line for call-up, had been rejected because of an ear infection.

Harry was particularly fond of one photograph showing him sitting on a donkey while a pal dangled a carrot before the impassive animal's nose. He thumbed through the bundle, stopping abruptly to look at Wilf again.

'I've never breathed a word about this to anybody, so there'd better not be a whisper from you.'

Wilf didn't bother to assure him but, rather nettled, half-inclined his head in a slightly mocking gesture of assent. Harry's eyes wavered as though he was having last-minute doubts, then he picked out one of the photographs and passed it to Wilf, face down.

'Just have a look at that.'

Wilf turned it over and slid a little further down in the bed, drawing in his breath and hissing it out again between his teeth. What he was looking at was a picture of a girl curled up in an armchair. She was wearing a pair of brief panties and nothing else. Her hands cupped and partly covered her breasts and her face was turned full into the camera's eye, meeting it with a bold, provocative smile. She was several years younger than he knew her but there was no mistaking who she was.

Harry had gone to his jacket for cigarettes. He took out a packet of twenty Senior Service and lit one, turning back to Wilf as he blew thin streamers of smoke down his nostrils. There was a queer almost feverish glitter in his eyes.

'What d'you think to that, then?'

Wilf felt as if he were holding a stick of dynamite with a short fuse.

'Where the heck did you get it?'

Harry began to tell him, sitting down on the bed again. He'd had the photograph nearly a year. A pal of his had moved to a pit near Sheffield and he'd gone over to spend a weekend with him. They went out on the booze and got in with a couple of press photographers who'd just been on a job. One of them took them back to his flat at closing time. He dabbled in amateur pin-up photography on the side and brought out a huge envelope of pictures for them to see. Harry's first instinct on seeing June Betley smiling up at him from the pile was to blurt out that he knew her; his second, following hard on the first and killing it, was to keep his mouth shut. He curbed his curiosity too for the sake of not drawing attention to that one photograph and later, when the opportunity presented itself, he slipped the picture into his pocket and brought it away with him.

Wilf was looking at the picture most of the time Harry was talking. It was no good comparing it with the kind of thing you got in those little books of nude studies – half-a-crown's-worth of lust and wishful thinking – that were sold in backstreet newsagents' and on the bookstalls of Calderford Market. This was someone they knew. She was flesh and blood first and a monochrome image second. Half the men in the village must, either voluntarily or otherwise, have mentally stripped her naked as she passed by, and prints of a photograph like this would go quicker than a black-market supply of tickets for the Rugby League Cup Final.

He said, 'Well, well, well,' because at the moment, with all kinds of implications running round in his head together with the thought that Mrs Ronnie Betley was by far the most exciting woman he knew and it wouldn't take much persuasion to make him dally with her himself, he couldn't think of anything else to say.

Harry reached over and took the picture back. He gazed at it pensively. 'The bitch,' he said in a moment. 'The teasing bitch.'

'What you're wondering now,' Wilf said, 'is just what took place at that little session.'

'I can imagine,' Harry said.

'But you wished you could have asked.'

'I wouldn't have known if it was the truth or not. He was a bit of a bragger.'

'I always thought she was a Calderford girl.'

'That's where Ronnie met her, but she'd moved to there from Sheffield. I knew that before.'

'D'you think he knows about that?'

'I'm sure he doesn't. He thinks his wife's a lady.'

Wilf grunted, busy extending his theories about the character and personality of Ronnie Betley. Harry put the stuff back into the case and put the case away. He lit another cigarette before getting into bed. He lay back on the pillow, smoking moodily and dropping ash into a small glass dish which rested in his lap.

'Want to know what I think?' Wilf said when neither of them had spoken for several minutes.

'Okay.'

'Well, you can take this for what it's worth, but this is

how I see it. When it comes to union affairs, local government, politics, and influencing men Ronnie Betley's nobody's mug. I might add, as my own opinion, which not many people round here seem to share, that given the circumstances and the necessity, he could also be a ruthless bastard. But that's by the way. Along with all that he's got a streak of naïvety where women are concerned and any determined woman with her fair share of feminine guile could manoeuvre rings round him. Which is where friend June comes in. What Betley is proud of having for a wife is a status symbol: a woman who is sexually desirable but not sexually promiscuous.'

'That's what *he* thinks,' Harry growled.

'Shut up, I haven't finished yet.

'Women like June Betley, with looks like hers and all the appetites to match, are in a tricky position. They never lack a good time but they're not the type men think of as wives. So when a woman like that meets a good prospect she has to make sure he doesn't get frightened away. June might have done the rounds in Sheffield but when she moved up to Calderford she left her reputation behind her, if she had one. She meets Betley, who's obviously a well-known personality with plenty of influence, and decides he's for her. I may be doing her less than justice here because it's possible she genuinely fell for him. But anyway, she makes sure he gets the picture of her she wants him to get, and his being the man he is helps along.'

'So what?' Harry said when Wilf paused.

'Are you with me so far?'

'All the way,' Harry said. 'Maybe the style wouldn't have been the same, me not being a literary man like, but I could have told you all that meself.'

'Okay then, where do we go from here? We'll assume she's got what she wanted only Betley's a bit disappointing at bedtime. She sees you quite often and finds you attractive. She knows you're interested and she can't resist a bit of excitement by giving you the come-on. But you're nobody, Harry, and she's got Betley, who might do anything. And Betley's not the type to stand for any messing about on the side. He'd divorce her like a shot if she once stepped out of line.'

'So she wouldn't mind having a roll with me, but is it worth the risk?'

'In a nutshell.'

The creak of the second stair from the top told them that their mother was coming to bed. Their father had been there an hour or more but she, more often than not, pottered about downstairs till midnight. 'Getting ready for morning,' she called it and it covered a multitude of small activities left over from the day's work: tidying up the living-room, washing the suppertime pots and laying the table for breakfast, perhaps a bit of mending. There was always another job she could find to do. Her whole life was centred on the house and the care of her three men. She rarely went out except to shop in the village, and to the market in Calderford on a Saturday. She never read a newspaper and hadn't been inside a cinema in years. Television had to some extent widened her horizons but her enjoyment was mostly confined to the simple thrill of the give-away quiz programmes and the pageantry of Royal occasions. Nothing she saw provoked dissatisfaction with her lot. She accepted her place in the world without thought of questioning it and was content to do the work to hand, counting herself fortunate that there was enough money coming in and that the poverty and hardship she had witnessed in her youth had not followed her to blight her adult life.

She pushed open the door three inches and spoke through the gap.

'Are you two lads goin' to talk all night? It's time you settled down and got some sleep. You'll be waking your father up next and then there'll be trouble.'

She pulled the door quietly shut again without waiting for an answer.

'Put the light out,' Harry said.

They didn't say anything more that night. When Wilf got back into bed he slid down under the clothes with his back to his brother. He heard the scrape of a match as Harry lit another cigarette. He didn't need to guess what he was thinking about. He thought about his own affairs and before he fell asleep he felt that he'd come to a decision.

3

He walked through the raw January morning across the village to the pit. There was a frost on the grass and the bare thorn hedges. Number one slag-heap, which crouched like the shape of some sleeping monster for half a mile alongside the Calderford–Barnsley Road, was a dark-grey bulk against the lighter grey of sky and the rolling tree-crowned distances of parkland were lost in a thin mist. Largely untouched by the tide of industrialism which had swept across the Riding to north and south, Bronhill and the villages like it had one prime reason for existence – coal. The huddle of weathered plum-coloured brick, the pit-head gear, the slag-heaps, scarred a landscape in many ways unchanged since royal prerogative had carved it into estates for favoured noblemen several hundred years ago. Now coal was the king, the men who worked it the lords of the earth, and they showed their disdain for the feudal past that lay around them by the majorities with which they returned Labour politicians to parliament.

Royal favours can be withdrawn; the whimsicality of princes is notorious. Coal was an exacting ruler and demanded its own terrible price. At one o'clock on a June morning in 1946 the muffled roar and tremor of an underground explosion shook Bronhill out of its sleep. Next morning there were nineteen widows in the village and thirteen fatherless children, six of them in Wilf's own class. The teacher, a young woman from outside the area, and not long out of training college, tried to start the lesson; but the sight of the young bewildered faces before her was too much and she fled weeping from the room. In a village where everyone is either working in coal or serving the needs of those who do, where intermarriage makes family groups large, the deaths of twenty-seven men affect everybody. If it wasn't your own father it could be your best friend's, or your brother or an uncle; if not your own husband, then your sister's or your daughter's. In some cases it was an overwhelming personal tragedy that made the mind reel; like the Williamsons of Syke Terrace, where a father and his two sons died together. Ten men, their bodies irrecoverable, were sealed off in a gallery that would not, in the lifetime of the present generation, be reopened for working. The other seventeen were buried at a funeral to which the entire village turned out. Bands from three collieries, their instruments flashing in the sunlight of a perfect summer day, played *Abide with Me* and *Nearer my God to Thee*, and the women wept and there was no consoling them in their hour of common grief.

It was the sharp clack of steel-tipped heels on the paving stones as he crossed the street, making for the mouth of the lane that would take him the short way to the pit, that brought Wilf out of his thoughts, and he gave a little inward groan as a voice called out to him from behind.

'How's the famous hauthor this morning? Walks straight by his old friends now the BBC's taken him up.'

Wilf stopped and half-turned as Arthur Ryder caught him up. He couldn't escape; they were both going the same way. But fortunately the pit was only a few minutes away and he wouldn't have to suffer the other's company for long.

'Hello, Arthur.' He wondered if his voice sounded as churlish as he thought it must.

But Arthur came on, smiling as if Wilf had greeted him like a long-lost friend.

'Written any good books lately?' he said, the smile fixed like a charm against the malevolent disposition of the world.

'Look under Somerset Maugham in the library,' Wilf said. 'One of my pen names.'

'Ho, ho, ho.' Arthur liked that one. 'Very good. I'll have to remember that.'

Of course Arthur would have an opinion to pass about the broadcast, some criticism of the tale itself or the way it had been presented, to which Wilf would have to listen with every appearance of interest and concern, when in truth he didn't give a hoot for Arthur's opinion on that or any other subject.

But he was saved . . .

'Missed it meself, unfortunately,' Arthur explained. 'I was up at that new bingo school they've started at the Roxy. Terrific success. Packed out. A woman there – I thought she was goinna pass out. She was waitin' ages for one last number for a ten-pound prize. Talk about sweat! You want to come up next time.'

'Never cared for it,' Wilf said. 'I always preferred Snakes and Ladders.'

They walked together along the lane, between the bare, wintry hedgerows, Arthur chattering away without stopping, while Wilf wondered why he should find the other so unbearable when everybody else tolerated him without strain. For it was tolerance, he was sure, on the part of everyone except Arthur's mother, widowed in the '46 disaster, who had brought up her only child in an atmosphere of ever-loving care, and the pale, loose-lipped doting girl who had married him and presented him with a sickly squawling infant whom Arthur, in proud paternity, wheeled through the village streets every Sunday morning in a high brand-new twenty-five-pound pram, a gleaming galleon in chrome and dove-grey cellulose paint that wouldn't have disgraced a royal nursery and was really beyond all reason on Arthur's clerk's wages. One cause of the irritability

Arthur aroused in him, and probably at the root of his dislike for him, was that they were both so much out of place in their surroundings; only he knew it and Arthur did not. Arthur with his fussy neatness of dress, his brilliantined hair with its artificial pushed-in wave, and his Sunday-morning baby-airing promenades, in defiance of all village male custom; Arthur the non-smoker and almost-never drinker, more at home among the middle-age matrons than with the men, never to be found in the village pubs, nor in the Miners' Welfare except on social occasions; superbly oblivious to condescending treatment from men who worked hard, drank hard and talked straight with or without the drink but particularly so when the evening's pints were safely stowed away – Arthur was everybody's cheery friend whether they could stomach him or not, and as happy as a hen clucking contentedly away in its own backyard.

'I suppose they pay quite well for plays on the BBC?' Arthur remarked in a voice that conveyed his interest in knowing how much as well as his desire not to offend should Wilf not wish to discuss the matter.

'It wasn't a play,' Wilf said; 'it was a short story.'

'Oh, well,' Arthur laughed, 'you know what I mean.'

Yes, I do, Wilf thought. But it's not bloody good enough, Arthur. You know the difference between a short story and a play. The county went to the trouble of giving you a grammar school education and its limits were surely not meant to be confined to imparting sufficient knowledge of arithmetic to calculate miners' wages and take an intelligent interest in a bingo game.

'I wouldn't call it overwhelmingly generous,' he said. 'But it makes our weekly wages look sick.'

'If you could write one of them a week you could give up counting other folk's money and count your own, eh?'

'That's right.'

'But then you wouldn't have the security, would you?' Arthur said brightly.

'Ah, the security . . .'

'I allus remember me mam sayin' to me when I passed me scholarship – "Arthur," she said, "I'm goin' to let you take it up because though I can't really afford to keep you at school till you're sixteen, them two years'll make all the difference in your life. They'll mean 'at you can go to work in your best suit if need be, and you'll have a salary instead of a weekly wage. It'll mean 'at you'll have security, Arthur." I used to remember what she said when I wanted to play out instead o' doing me homework.'

'And now look where you are.'

'Yes, look,' said Arthur seriously.

Well, you couldn't blame the mother, Wilf thought. His own mother had reached an almost identical conclusion and she hadn't lost her man and been thrown on to the world to fend for herself. Today was payday and Arthur would stand next to Wilf and quip and joke as he passed across wage packets twice and three times as big as his own, because a miner was a miner and unskilled in any other trade, but a wages clerk could serve any employer of labour. He had security.

They walked on together. 'What do you want out of life, Arthur?' Wilf asked after a silence.

The question appeared to surprise Arthur; probably nobody had ever asked him it before, and reflective talk of that kind was rare in Bronhill. His surprise showed in his quick glance at Wilf.

'A bit of a tall order for this time of day, isn't it?'

'Oh, I know this is the kind of subject you get round to after a couple of pints, if at all,' Wilf said. 'But I'm serious, Arthur. I'm not trying to take the mickey; I want to know.'

'Well, I dunno,' Arthur mused. 'I suppose I want a bit more of what I've got.'

'Which is?'

'You mean what have I got? Well, a good job, the beginnings of a nice little home, a wife and family

. . . Oh, and I'd like to win a hundred thousand quid on Littlewoods' treble chance, but it doesn't keep me awake a night.'

'And that's it?'

'Well . . . yes.'

'You don't walk about with a constant uneasy feeling at the back of your mind that somehow life, real life, is passing you by somewhere else and that next week or next year will be better than today if only you can get to the centre of it and find what you want?'

Arthur shook his head. 'No, I don't. But I think a lot of people do, and I'm sorry for them.'

They had to cross a stile into a field and Arthur, going first, stopped halfway over and looked back at Wilf with a little smile playing about his eyes and mouth.

'Some people spend all their time thinking about what they haven't got. *I* think about what I have got and how lucky I am to have it.'

There was in Arthur's look an element of amused perception of the foolishness of men that was as unexpected as the spark of sympathy it kindled in Wilf. He followed his companion over the stile and clapped him on the shoulder.

'You know what, Arthur? You're a happy man.'

Arthur chuckled. Being held up as a criterion of something pleased him. 'I suppose I am,' he said. 'I don't think about it much.'

Suddenly at a loss before this young man whom he had always regarded with mild contempt, Wilf fell back on facetious banter:

'And to what do you attribute this spectacular success in life, Mr Ryder? Come along now, give the audience the benefit of your experience and superior knowledge.'

Arthur thought seriously about it for a moment. 'Well, I don't think it's got much to do with how much money you have, an' all that, for a start,' he said. 'It's more the way you look at things. You know, an attitude of mind, like.'

'Ah, yes,' Wilf said, suddenly serious again. 'You've put your finger on it there, lad. That's the rub. Perhaps what we need is a psychiatrist each to turn us all into contented puddings.'

4

About eight o'clock that night Wilf went round to the Wardles' house in a terraced street ten minutes' walk from home. The Wardles' front door opened directly on to the pavement. He knocked, knowing that he would have to knock again to be heard over the blare of the wireless-set playing so loudly inside the house that he could almost make out the words of the speakers. He stepped back, hands in overcoat pockets, and looked down the long street, at the twin rows of lighted windows and, halfway down, the blaze of the off-licence, its door constantly opening and closing on customers buying breakfast bread and bacon and cornflakes but probably not overmuch in the drink line, since the people of Albert Street were not given to drinking at home when the noise and smoke and company of the Mitre on the corner and the King's Arms along the main road were to be had for a few minutes' walking.

He clenched his fist and drove it vigorously at the Wardles' door, hearing in a moment the rattle of the sneck before the door opened and a short, thickset, slightly bow-legged man in shirtsleeves looked out.

Wilf said good evening. 'Is Glynis in?'

'Oh, it's you, Wilf. Aye, she's in. Come in, man, come in.'

Wilf followed Mr Wardle inside, closing the door behind him and fighting his way into the light through the heavy dark-green draught-curtain which hung on a rail and shut off in a little rectangular lobby both the street door and that at the foot of the staircase. The Wardles were a fire-hugging family. To go into their house like this, in cold weather, was to find three backs turned to the room, three pairs of feet on the brass fender, three faces slowly toasting in the heat of the huge fire blazing in the high open grate. The fireplace was the focal point of interest in the living-rooms of all these houses but to the Wardles it was like an altar at which they worshipped and the rest of the room no more than a territory into which they made occasional lightning forays for the necessities of life. The draught-excluding curtain was put up in mid-October and taken down at the beginning of May.

'You'll have to get used to giving that door a hammering, man, when we've got the wireless playing,' Mr Wardle said. 'The missis likes a good play and she misses half of it unless it's turned up loud enough to entertain the whole street.' He reached over and turned down the volume as Mrs Wardle twisted her head from the fire and gave Wilf a vacant smile, and Glynis got up and moved towards the table.

'You said nothing about Wilf coming round tonight, Glynis. I thought you were all settled down for a night by the fire.'

'Oh, we hadn't anything fixed up,' Wilf said. 'I just thought I'd pop round.'

'By all means, Wilf, by all means. You don't need an invitation here. You know you're welcome any time, any time at all. You're not too proud to take us as you find us, I know.'

Mr Wardle touched the volume knob on the radio, this time switching off completely.

'Please,' Wilf said; 'don't turn it off for me. You'll miss the play.'

'Aw, it's dead,' said Mr Wardle, pulling down his loose, rubbery lips. 'Not a scrap of life in it. Sending me to sleep an' the missis an' all, it was. We'll try for some music on the other programme in a bit.'

Wilf smiled. He liked to hear Glynis's father talk. He had come north from Wales thirty years ago but the lilt of the valleys was still strong in his voice.

'Did you want to go anywhere special, Wilf?' Glynis asked.

He said, 'No, no. I thought we might have a little walk, and a chat like.'

'I've no need to change or anything, then?'

'No, just pop your coat on and you're fine.'

'Change,' Mr Wardle scoffed. 'Dressed up behind the counter of a shop all day and then changing at night.'

Glynis took no notice of him but said something about washing her face, and went into the scullery. Wilf heard water running into the enamel bowl.

'Ah, well, just a little stroll and a chat tonight, is it?' Mr Wardle waved Wilf to a chair beside the table and Wilf sat down without taking off his coat. He wondered if either Glynis or her father had invested his words with the wrong kind of significance. But the stocky Welshman went on imperturbably, 'A reasonable night out, is it?'

Wilf told him it was turning milder and thawing.

'Well then, I might have a stroll down to the Mitre later on.'

Wilf smiled to himself. So far as he could gather Mr Wardle took a stroll down to the Mitre every night in the year, whatever the weather, and drank two pints of mild ale, rarely more or less.

Wilf's glance crossed with Mrs Wardle's and they exchanged vague smiles once more. She sat in silence on a stool close to the fire, a cigarette with a long ash drooping from her lips. He had once made an effort to converse with her but it was difficult because of her deafness.

Mr Wardle lit the dottle in his pipe, sending out clouds of acrid smoke.

'We listened to that thing of yours on the wireless last night, Wilf. Very good indeed, we thought. Didn't we,

Mother?' he bawled suddenly at his wife. 'That story of Wilf's – on the wireless.'

Mrs Wardle nodded and smiled. 'Yes, it was lovely.'

'Very proud we were to hear the announcer say your name. Twice he said it.'

'I'm glad you liked it.'

'Oh, it does you great credit, Wilf boy. There's not over-much of that kind of thing round these parts. Back home, mind, it's different. We have a long tradition of poetry and culture. Writers are ten a penny. Good ones, too.'

'Yes, I know.'

'Aye, they're a rough and ready lot round here. Fine fellers, though, most of 'em.'

Glynis came into the room brushing her hair which she had recently had cut short in the current fashion.

'Look at her now. Just like a woman, isn't it? You tell her to pop her coat on and she spends half an hour brushing and preening herself.'

'I'll be ready in a minute,' Glynis said. 'I'm not going out looking a slut even if it is just for a walk in the dark.'

'All cats are grey in the dark, love. Haven't you heard that?'

'Who're you calling a cat?' Glynis said equably.

Looking at her from his chair as she laid aside the brush and dabbed powder on her nose, Wilf wondered how she could be the daughter of the rubbery-faced Welshman and the drab Yorkshirewoman he had married when well into his thirties. For the first thing you noticed about Glynis was her look of breeding. She had lovely white teeth, small ears and hands and feet, and level grey eyes. She could have been an earl's daughter from the look of her. There was no give-away trace of the working-class girl in her appearance and she helped along the illusion by the tasteful, though not extravagant, way she dressed. She carried clothes well on her tall slim figure and a worn tweed coat on her looked, he always thought, worth ten times the painful finery of the village girls.

It was this that had first drawn him to her. Her very

uniqueness had infatuated him before he ever spoke to her and his subsequent discovery of her simple, uncomplicated view of life and her commonplace interests would not seriously have damaged their relationship had there been other qualities to catch and sustain his interest. He had felt it right that he should court her because she was, simply, in his view, the most eligible girl in the small society of the village. But she was cool, cool, and this he couldn't bear.

She had never kissed him in passion, nor let him so much as rest his hand on her breast for longer than the moment it took her gently to remove it. Physical contact with him beyond a light holding of hands seemed of no interest to her. Yet she was content to be with him, happy in his company whenever he wished, and in the eyes of many they were as good as bespoken. They had discussed their differences tentatively and she had argued in her calm, quiet way of stating what was to her indisputable fact that physical intimacy was something reserved for man and wife. She was, in fact, altogether too calm and reasonable about a subject in which reason and calm had their limits. Not that he'd ever, from the start, nursed plans for seduction; yet there was no sign on her part that she found it temptation to be resisted; no indication on those now rare occasions when he strained her to him in the darkness of the entry outside her house that yielding might be pleasant and she could wish for circumstances which would allow her to do so with a clear conscience and a carefree heart. And it seemed to Wilf that it was expecting altogether too much of a marriage ceremony to ask it to change her nature. Glynis was kindhearted and honourable, a dutiful daughter who would become a dutiful wife, acquiescing to any reasonable demands. But acquiescence had no place in Wilf's view of marriage. The body's flare should react to the heart's, passion match passion. Sweet reason was no substitute for fire and yearning.

In twenty minutes of unhurried strolling they had climbed out of the village and were descending the path to Coppley Pond. There was a full moon. Two miles away, across the fields, the coke ovens at Ashfield lit the sky with a dull glow. Wilf had deliberately kept the conversation on the plane of trivialities, feeding Glynis with enough remarks to sustain her talk of her day's work.

'She never came back,' Glynis said; 'and I got ticked off by the manageress for putting the blouse on one side without a deposit on it. So I shan't do that again. I shall say "Sorry, madam, but it's against the rules; and if I break the rules I shall lose my job!" '

He smiled at her simplicity. How straight and true and guileless she was!

'Did you hear the broadcast last night?'

'Oh, yes. Didn't me dad say?'

'Yes, but I wondered what you thought of it.'

'I thought it was lovely. But so sad. I hardly like to tell you – you'll think I'm silly – but I cried.'

'No, I don't think you're silly. I'm glad it moved you. It was meant to do.'

'And when they said your name, I was so proud. Weren't you proud?'

'Well, not proud. But I had a kind of cold feeling down my spine.'

The moonlight glinted on the almost stagnant water of the pond. The dead white branch of a tree protruded from the water's edge like a limb bone of some drowned creature of impossible size. Someone had left a petrol can and a red oil-drum. The grassy hollows shielded by hawthorn and elder bushes were empty and Wilf and Glynis were alone.

It was here, one evening in summer, that, exasperated beyond reason by her cool closed lips and his inability to awake in her any response, he had pressed himself upon her with an ardency which made her struggle free and avert her hot flushed face. He asked her if he'd offended her and she said no, she knew that men saw that kind of thing differently from women.

'I won't be tolerated, Glynis,' he told her. 'When you marry you'll tolerate your husband gladly; but I won't have it.'

'Isn't that the way it should be?' she asked. 'Isn't that what every good wife does?'

He made no answer and in a moment she said, 'Anyway, all girls don't think like me so if that's what you want you should be able to find it.'

A few nights later he had done just that. After a few drinks with a colleague who lived in Calderford he found himself riding home on the last bus with a couple of the village girls, one of whom had cocked a bright, alert eye at him whenever they had run into each other during the past few months. He found her attractive in a brash, over-confident way and with the beer happily muffling the over-critical side of his mind he had no trouble in matching their bantering talk. When they alighted on the main road and began to walk along the lane in the dusk, Joan – he wasn't sure her name was Joan but it would serve for identification – contrived to be next to him and after a little way they were linking arms.

The other girl left them at the edge of the village, turning off with a saucy 'See you tomorrer, then. An' don't stop out all night!'

'Do you have to go straight home?' Wilf asked.

'Not if I want to stop out.'

'And do you want to stop out?'

'It just depends.'

'On what?'

'Where you might be thinkin' of taking me.'

'Oh, well,' he said, 'there's the Palm Beach or the Coconut Grove or the Roxy Roof Gardens. You just name it.'

She laughed. 'And we'll go in your Rolls-Royce.'

'You'll have to make do with the Armstrong-Siddeley tonight. It's the chauffeur's night off and he's taken the Rolls.'

'In that case, then, I think we'll walk.'

Sometime later, when his hands were inside her blouse, cupping her astonishingly perfect little breasts, and her breath touched his cheek in small hot gusts, she said, 'Doesn't that Glynis Wardle like to do this?'

He said, 'Let's leave her out of this, shall we?' and covered her mouth with his . . .

'I don't like this place,' Glynis said. They were skirting the pond and moving towards rising ground again. 'Even in summer I don't like it and in winter, when it's dark, it gives me the creeps. Did you know a woman once drowned herself in there?'

'Yes, I knew.'

She shivered suddenly and slipped her arm through his. He was detached enough now to be amused by her action and the reason for it.

He said, 'I suppose if I told you that Dracula was lurking behind that tree over there you might even throw your arms round me?'

'Oh, stop it,' she said, pushing at him with her linked arm. 'Now you're trying to frighten me.'

'No, I'm just wondering if fright mightn't do the trick.'

'What trick?'

'Get you to put your arms round me.'

'Oh, that. You've got a one-track mind.'

'No, it's just the way you operate the points that makes it seem so.'

'Talk,' Glynis said. 'Talk, talk, talk. And it doesn't alter anything.'

They had to disengage to climb a bank. Wilf clambered up first and gave her his hand. He held her by the shoulders and looked at her.

'One day you'll meet a man and marry him and make him a good wife and give him children. And I hope he'll be a man who can show you what love can be. Not everyday caring and affection; not loyalty and sticking together through the best and the worst, because you'll never need to be shown that – but the simple natural coming together of two people with all the world shut out.'

She turned her face away. 'I don't like you to talk like that.'

'You're a dear sweet girl, Glynis, and I want you to be happy. And I know that even if you don't discover what I said you'll still be happy because you have the quality of happiness in you.'

'You sound,' she said, 'you sound as if you're saying good-bye.'

'I handed in my notice at work today,' Wilf said. 'I'm going away.'

He led the way along the path and on to the narrow road. 'Is it something to do with your writing?' she asked as their feet struck on the metalled surface. He had sensed before that, as with Harry, his writing was to her, while a possible source of pride, something vaguely to be mistrusted. It was what put him beyond the ordinary, outside the complete reach of her understanding, or the formation of an image which would substitute for understanding. There would always be a shadowy patch on the exposure, whose detail she could not make even a satisfactory pretence of filling in. And now, he supposed, she could blame it for taking him away from her. Though whether she regarded his leaving as a deprivation, whether it would be a loss to her because of the deeper relationship to which they might have progressed, he didn't know. They had spoken of marriage only in the abstract or as it affected people they knew. And whatever the notions in the minds of people who had seen them together, lacking the kind of physical contact which released emotional declarations – true or misguided – their relationship had remained one of fond and uncommitted friendship.

He said, 'You see, I know now that I'm not wasting my time. That I have a talent of some sort. I think there must come a time when every creative person finds that basic confidence without which he couldn't carry on. I've found it now and I know that sooner or later I shall make good. Sometime I shall have a name, however small. I'm not boasting and I know I'm not a world-beater, a Dickens or a Dostoevsky or a Hemingway. But sometime, somewhere, people will talk about contemporary writers and there'll be a good chance that my name will be mentioned. Even,' he added with a self-deprecatory grin, 'if it's only to say how bad I am.'

'And you've got to go away to do all this?'

'For a time anyway. If I'm to go on I've got to be free of present associations. I've got to be free of the grip of family life and friends and this place. This is the kind of life I want to write about because it's the only life I know; but I've got to get away from it first.'

'And where will you go? To London?'

He shook his head. 'No. I won't go to London a nobody. When I go to London it'll be as a somebody. They'll be waiting for me; they'll want to see me because what I've done has gone before me . . . No, I'm not sure where I'll go. To some city where I can be anonymous, but not far away.'

'But how will you live? You can't live on air. You'll have to find a job.'

'So I'll find a job. But nothing too tying. Nothing that smacks of a career. "Ideal position for young man with ability and ambition." That's the sort of thing I'll avoid.'

She walked along beside him, serious and quiet, her gloved hands held together.

'Shall I tell you something?' she said after a few minutes.

'Go on.'

Now she hesitated. 'You might have thought,' she said at length, 'because . . . because I don't like a lot of . . . well, kissing and that sort of thing, that it was because I didn't like you in that kind of way.'

She stopped and Wilf said again, 'Go on.'

'Well when you came round tonight unexpected and said you thought we could go for a walk and a talk, I knew you wanted to say something special. I knew from something about you.

'No,' she said as Wilf broke in on her. 'No, I've started now and I'm going to finish . . . I didn't know what it was but I thought I knew what it might be. And if it had been that I was . . . I was going to say yes.'

He didn't know what to say. He took her hand and held it as they walked along. 'Oh, Glynis. Glynis, love.'

In the entry by her house he put his arms about her and drew her gently to him, her cool cheek next to his.

'Suppose I said now I'd changed my mind and decided to stay?'

'I'd say no now, because it's not what you really want to do and you'd regret it for the rest of your life.'

She gave him a sudden quick light kiss on the mouth and freed herself.

'Write and let me know how you're getting on,' she said.

'Yes,' he said. 'Yes. Be happy, love.'

5

The girl on the train had put aside her magazines again and was gazing through the window of the second-class compartment. In the heightened emotional state in which she had started the journey, culminating in ten minutes of agonising indecision in the station restaurant, during which she had almost turned back into the stone wilderness of London, then dashed for the train with seconds to spare, she had avoided the racks of books, both paperback and bound – anything which might require concentration – and chosen the lightest, most diverting of reading. But the articles irritated her with their triviality and the contrived situations and happy endings of the stories were bitterly ironic in the light of her own circumstances.

It was a mid-week afternoon train and she had been alone since Grantham, where the last of the three or four people who had taken seats in the compartment at Kings Cross had got off. He had been a neatly dressed, prematurely grey and distinguished-looking man with a fat briefcase who had read first the *Daily Telegraph* and then the *Financial Times*, darting glances from behind both at her knees, which her fashionably short skirt made no attempt to conceal, glances that you could consider furtive or discreet, depending upon how charitable you were feeling. Since she was not feeling charitable so far as men's little ways were concerned she labelled the glances furtive and accepted them with silent disdain until accidentally meeting the man's gaze head-on, she held it for a cold, hard moment till he looked away with small signs of confusion.

Now, with the brief diversion of afternoon tea behind her, there was nothing left to do but look out at the dreary South Yorkshire mining landscape with the shaggy fields of yellow grass and rose-bay willow herb, the enormous slag-heaps, the winding-gear of pits and the drab, featureless towns of plum-coloured brick and grey section-built council houses. Nothing left to do but look, hardly seeing, and think.

Because there were other things she didn't want to think about she concentrated deliberately on her recent companion. Oh, she hadn't minded his looking; not really. She couldn't mind to be fair. For if uplift brassières could be defended on the grounds of both comfort and bodily preservation, tight sweaters worn over them, and skirts which barely reached the knees were, when you put aside all the cant and humbug, simply invitations to admiration. And what was admiration from a stranger but an impersonal biological preening of male feathers one step from wondering what you were like in bed? Adultery was committed in the heart a billion times a day by people who mostly, she'd say, would shy from the act itself. The whole set-up was geared for casual lust and what girl could object to harmless glances at knees she chose by her adherence to fashion to reveal? He had looked nice enough, going about his business, with half an hour alone in a railway compartment with a strange girl unlikely to make the tiniest real impression on a mind pre-occupied with its own life – the mortgage paid off next year, promotion when what's-his-name retired at Christmas, would John make it to university and why didn't Barbara show interest in something other than pop singers, boy friends and new clothes? On the other hand, what bulged the briefcase could have been saucy studies of girls in their underwear acquired in the anonymity of London which her presence in the compartment had robbed him of the pleasure of perusing. And with, say, another hour's journey to a common destination, the sidelong glances could have been the prelude to a carefully casual series of remarks about nothing in particular, leading to a discreetly worded suggestion that, since they were both to be in the same town, they might meet again. Still, she wished now she hadn't snubbed him. It was so easy really for a girl with anything at all about her both to excite men and humiliate them. Until one came to mean more to you than the others, and then how uncertain the powers became. Nevertheless, despite her experience, she hadn't yet reached the stage of thinking all men beastly; though she could readily sympathise with the state of mind of any woman driven to utter that particular *cri de coeur*. How she could!

If her watch was right she had been on the train for a little under three and a half hours and it was precisely half past five. On any normal weekday she would have been caught up in the bustle of going home: covering her typewriter, calling good night to those girls not going in her direction, and descending into the teeming crowds of Kingsway to make her way, with what seemed like the entire rest of the civilised world, to Holborn Underground Station and a train for Earls Court. She had done that yesterday, knowing that after the decision she'd fought to reach all week-end she would never do it again. The break had had to be that way: quick, disruptive. She could have given notice and hoped that her will would hold over the necessary period; but the working of notice would have involved questions about her plans, and staying in London she could hardly have avoided seeing Floyd. So she had put into the post on her way to the station a letter which told her employers the white lie that she'd been called out of London to see an aunt who was gravely ill. That would cover the abruptness of her departure and a later message, saying that circumstances prevented her from returning, would terminate the connection. Unable to put a false face of emergency on what was a final good-bye, she had walked out of the office with no more leave-taking than the usual cry of good night. Though she had wished for the chance of a quiet farewell word with one or two of the girls, there was no one in the office with whom she was intimate. To Evelyn, her one real friend in London, she would write tonight, explaining herself as much as she could and begging her to seal her lips to any enquiry that might lead Floyd after her.

About six-thirty Floyd would 'phone and the conversation between him and Mrs Mulvaney would probably be something like:

'Gone? What d'you mean "gone"?'

'She packed her bag and left this morning. Said something about visiting a sick aunt and it looked like being a long drawn out business.'

'But she couldn't just leave like that without a word to anybody.'

'She was a month's rent in advance so as I see it she could go when she liked.'

'Did she leave any messages or letters?'

'No, not a thing.'

'What about a forwarding address?'

'No. She may have made arrangements with the post office. I don't know anything.'

'Well where did she say this aunt lived?'

'She didn't say. Somewhere out of London. In the country.'

(Anywhere out of London was the country to Mrs Mulvaney and it was doubtful if she would have remembered the name of a town had one been mentioned.)

At this point Floyd would probably start to lose his temper.

'You know, lady, you're not being very helpful, are you?'

And Mrs Mulvaney, the quick blood of her Irish ancestors flowing in her, would give as good as she got:

'I'm just the caretaker here, Mister, not her keeper. If she wants to go away without telling you about it that's her business.'

And she would ring off.

Floyd . . . If anyone had prophesied while she was at Amhurst that she would one day meet an American called Floyd, let alone fall in love with him, she would probably have gone off into a fit of the giggles. Amhurst Towers was for the fee-paying daughters of local solicitors, doctors, bank managers, farmers, tradesmen and business executives. Some of them were there because they had failed to pass the eleven-plus for a free place at the Girls' High School; others because there would always be people ready to believe that what you paid for was bound to be better and more satisfyingly exclusive than what the State offered you free. The girls were taught English Literature and French Language because this was culture; hockey and netball to develop healthy bodies; elocution, etiquette, deportment and household management to carry them safely in society and help them catch a man; and proficiency in shorthand and typing to keep them occupied between leaving school and the biggest day in a girl's life. The overall plan was to turn out young ladies of the English middle class and to such young women, steeped in the traditions of Royalty, Conservative government, the Church of England, even of Empire, and the values of gentility, restraint and understatement, the more brash and vulgar manifestations of American life as typified by most Hollywood films were hardly to be taken seriously. So characters called Floyd *were* no more than characters: the third gangster from the left, the mixed-up juvenile delinquent, the boxer's best friend, the private eye who spoke out of the corner of his mouth, kept an automatic under his arm, a bottle of whisky in every drawer and a blonde (tall and naked) in every bed. In short, a fiction.

But her Floyd was far from being a fiction. *Her* Floyd!

She had about half an hour before the train got in and

if she was going to think about it all, as she inevitably was, she might as well do it with some degree of coherence instead of letting her thoughts run round in circles. She took down her case and got out a writing-pad. She found a ball-point pen in her bag and began a letter:

'Dear Evelyn, I'm writing this on a train and as I don't know where I shall be staying in the immediate future I can't put on an address for you to reply to. It's no good your writing to the flat because I settled up there this morning and I shan't be going back. I've also thrown up my job with the Bureau – just walked out without giving notice or even saying a word. I couldn't see you because I knew you were away and my decision to run was something I had to catch hold of and act on before other influences could get to work on me.

'If I didn't intend to tell you why I'm running away I shouldn't be writing this at all, so you may as well know without any more beating about the bush. I'm running away from Floyd.

'Though you only met him twice you knew I'd been seeing Floyd for six or seven months and you surely knew I was in love with him though I've never discussed it with you. What you didn't know, though you might well have guessed, being the perceptive person you are, was that about three months ago our relationship developed into a very intimate affair – and anything you like to read into that phrase will be correct.

'I went into it wholeheartedly, happily with, as I thought, my eyes wide open. It was just as though loving Floyd was something I'd been waiting to do all my life. I haven't loved many people in my life. I learned at an early age the kind of tricks life can play on you and I've never trusted in much since. (And if all this sounds like self-pity, well I'm afraid that's very much the mood I'm in at the moment.) You are one of those people, but what passes between a man and a woman is a different thing altogether. I suppose it's the woman who usually tries to bring some sort of permanency into these things, but I deliberately avoided any such attempt with Floyd and me. I suppose I was, in a way, scared of bringing some kind of bad luck on it all, and so I left things to work themselves out. I knew he wouldn't stay in England for ever. His job over here wasn't on a permanent basis and one day (one hazy, distant day) he would have to go home. By that time we might have worked something out. I wasn't promising myself a future with him, you see. But what I didn't know was that it was already decided, had been from the beginning, that there could be no future for us. It's that now that I can't stand. That and the deceit that hid it from me.

'What happened was really quite simple. Floyd was going away on business and he gave me a key to his flat so that I could borrow some of his records. I'd been in before, but never alone. I wandered round from room to room in a kind of orgy of imagining his life there – his own personal private life – and feeling him stamped on everything, his clothes, his books, even the few kitchen implements and a spare toothbrush. I was in such a state of loving him that I wanted to *be* him and was trying to imagine this through contact with his things.

'There was a letter behind an ornament on the mantelshelf. It was careless of him to leave it there – I know that now. But when you're deceiving you've got to work at it every minute of the day if you're not to be found out. It had an American stamp on it and I knew it wasn't a business letter because it was addressed in someone's handwriting. I should never have touched it. No girl from Amhurst Towers should have done what I did. But there I was, consumed with this urge to climb into his skin, with every inanimate object feeding my intense awareness of him, and here was a letter, probably personal, from a friend. The temptation was too much and Miss Mackenzie's teaching went out of the window.

'Well I opened the letter and out of it fell a snapshot of a woman and two young boys. It was from Floyd's wife and the photograph was of her and his two sons. It was a happy letter from a quietly happy woman. They were all thinking of Floyd. They'd missed him since his last trip home four months before and were looking forward to his next visit and to the day when his assignment in England was through and he'd be home for good.

'I won't try to describe what I felt; I could never put all that into words and it's all too recent for me to make the attempt. I walked miles and miles last weekend, trying to think what to do. And what it came to was that I had to get away, and quickly. I couldn't stay in London without seeing Floyd, or him finding me, and I just can't face him again. I can't face him and his look of a man found out. I can't watch his attempts at explanations, his excuses, his apologies. I can't have the old Floyd, who existed only in my image of him, and I couldn't bear the new one.

'Tonight, when the train gets in, I'll have a room in the best hotel in town and damn the expense. And tomorrow I'll try to find a permanent bedsitter or something, and think about getting a job.

' "But why there?" you'll be thinking when you see the postmark. "Why there of all places?"

'Well, it's the only other place I know except Amhurst and I couldn't face that again so soon. Though I've been away from here a long time and will probably find it strange, it *is* where I started and somehow I've got an urge to be where I began, a feeling that if I can make my peace here it may work out pretty well in the end. It's such a vague, unformulated feeling I can't explain it and even to try distorts it somehow.

'We can't be far off my station now so I may have to finish this later. I'll write to Mrs Mulvaney and tell her you'll be taking away what things I've left behind there. Will you go for them? There's my record-player and some records and a few books. Not much, but anything I've left I mean you to have . . .'

The parallel tracks ran out into a spread-out network of sidings. A signal box bearing the name of her station drew level and slid by until it was a little nearer London than she was. She put away the almost finished letter and, taking out a compact, mended her make-up. She stood and settled her skirt, pulled down the hem of her jumper and slipped into her short green suède jacket.

Four minutes later she stepped from the train on to the platform. Her present journey was over and she was back where, twenty-two years before, she had set out on the journey of life.

6

About eleven o'clock the next morning she was walking with her suitcase along a quiet residential street in the Cross Park district of the city, looking for a house whose address was written on a slip of paper in her pocket. For all she knew of this district she might have been in a completely strange town. She had only ever, as a child, made infrequent bus journeys along the main road which led out of the city on this side and carried the daily traffic of Bentleys, Jaguars, Armstrong-Siddeleys, Humbers and Rovers, bearing the company directors and senior executives to and from their homes in Harrogate, Skipton, Ilkley and the villages in between. It was the predecessors of those directors and executives, the manufacturers and industrialists of sixty and seventy years ago, who, before the motor car swept them away into the outlying country towns and spas, had built the houses among which she was walking now, and it needed little imagination to picture carriages at their doors, see lights blazing in the lofty drawing-rooms, shining on heavy mahogany furniture, glinting on glassware and cutlery, gleaming on napery and the shirt-fronts of dour prosperous men; and to hear, falling on the quiet of long-ago nights, the strains of piano, violin and 'cello with, perhaps, a soprano voice lifted in song . . . 'Mid pleasures and palaces though we may roam. Be it ever so humble, there's no place like home . . .' And there, yes, she could just see them, a young girl with bare shoulders and an artificial rose in the neck of her frock and a young man in evening dress, standing shyly, happily hand in hand while the glasses were raised in a toast to a long life, wealth and happiness. And now . . . now? Dead, under the sod, gone for ever; like her mother, like Peter and Angela and Uncle Edward. And who to mourn them, who to care if they'd been happy, good and kind, bad or cruel, rich or poor? God? But she had stopped believing in God on a day thirteen years ago on the other side of this city.

Why had she come here, to a place filled with ghosts, that touched you in daylight and filled you with their own desolation?

She turned into a gateway. Untidy pink rhododendrons flanked the short drive. It had been raining earlier and the shrubbery was soaked and dripping in the dank air. She rang the bell beside a door with coloured glass in its upper half. A thin slatternly woman with metal curlers in her hair answered and the girl looked past her with dismay at the peeling dark-brown paint and the grubby wallpaper in the hall. An unpleasant odour caught at her nostrils and revulsion made her step a few paces back.

'The room? Oh, it's taken. Taken on Saturday, love. Yes. What a pity. Still, you can let rooms ten times over these days. 'Specially if you're not too particular, like. These darkies in particular, never off your step. Mind, I never open the door if I see who they are first. Live an' let live's my motto, but that doesn't mean you have to have 'em in your house. Have you come a long way, then? From London? All that way. What a pity. Still, that's life, in't it? That's what I allus say. Plenty more disappointments without brooding over this one. Still, you'll find a place, I daresay, a nice clean-looking girl like yerself.'

The girl turned away and walked towards the gate. Then the woman called out, 'Just a minute,' and came after her, slippers flapping on her bare feet. She took her by the arm and leaned close to point as though instructing a child or someone simple in the head.

'It's just come to me. Mrs Swallow across the road might have a room. One of her people left the other day. It might be taken now, mind, I can't promise. But it won't cost you nothing to enquire. Number seventeen on the other side. Just across the road.'

The girl said thank you and left her and crossed the road. The house she was directed to was smaller than the other one, but still big by present-day standards. The other house was detached but this was one of a pair. There seemed to be attic bedrooms and the windows at the front of the house, on the two main floors, were large square bays. A big ornamental flower-urn full of packed-down soil but no flowers stood to one side of the square step. There was a bell but it didn't seem to be working so she knocked, her knuckles making only a feeble sound on the heavy door. When she had knocked a second time and there was still no answer she stepped down on to the path and walked along under the ground-floor window. She caught an impression of someone moving inside the room and, thinking she might have been seen, went back and knocked on the door again. A moment later it was opened and a young man in his early twenties stood there.

'Good afternoon,' he said.

At least, she thought, this was more promising than her first call. He, who ever he was, was quietly polite and there was no smell.

'Is Mrs Swallow at home?' she asked. 'I believe she's got a vacant room.'

He said, 'Oh, the room. Will you come in?'

He stood aside to let her pass and closed the door behind her. She glanced quickly about the shadowy hallway. You couldn't call it smart but though it had obviously seen better days it looked reasonably clean and the tiled floor must have been washed lately.

The young man hovered about uncertainly as though not knowing what to do with her next. There seemed to be no other sign of life in the house.

'Actually,' he said, 'Mrs Swallow's out. But she won't be long. She's popped up the road to the shops.'

'Well, if you wouldn't mind me waiting . . .'

'Oh, no, not at all. She should only be a few minutes.'

He looked round, one hand to his short black hair. Then he turned and pushed open the door behind him. 'You can wait in here, if you like.'

She followed him into the big front room. She supposed it had once been the drawing-room. It had a high moulded ceiling and a picture-rail on the walls. There was a divan bed with a blue day-cover over it in a corner and a couple of shabby easy-chairs – one a rather splendid wing upholstered in wine-coloured velvet, worn along the arms – near the fireplace in which an electric fire was fitted with the surrounding aperture boarded up. What drew her quick eyes and gave the room a touch of individuality were the books and magazines stuffed haphazardly into painted shelves in one of the chimney-piece alcoves and the portable typewriter surrounded by a litter of papers on a large square table under the window.

He tugged at the smaller of the two armchairs, moving it a foot out of place. 'This is my room, actually; but if you don't mind waiting here . . . Please sit down.'

She moved towards the chair, at the same time gesturing to the signs of activity at the table.

'I hope I'm not disturbing you . . .'

'Oh no, that's all right.' A smile came briefly to his lean, high-cheekboned face. 'Glad of an excuse to break off, really. I feel a bit guilty about it, to tell the truth,' he said after a pause. 'I've just had a bout of 'flu and I feel that if I can do this I could be doing my work at the office. But the doctor said I mustn't go back this week so I suppose that salves my conscience a bit.'

'I don't think it pays to go back too quickly,' she said. 'Though you'd perhaps be better outside getting some fresh air.'

'That's what Poppy says – Mrs Swallow. But it's poor

weather. I might catch a chill, and then where would I be?' He smiled, as though the weather and the doctor were conspirators bent on allowing him time to work on whatever he was doing at the table.

He sat on a straight-backed chair, one arm curled over the back, and glanced at her from time to time.

'I'm afraid I don't smoke,' he said presently, 'so I can't offer you a cigarette.'

She opened her bag. 'That's all right. I have some here.'

He went to the mantelshelf and brought her a match, then returned to his chair. She drew on the cigarette. It was the first she'd had since sitting after breakfast in the hotel dining-room and wondering what deterioration in her circumstances she would be experiencing by tomorrow morning. She found herself hoping that the room was still free and that she would like it when she saw it, and the terms. What she had seen of the house was pleasant enough and the young man seemed civilised. She stopped herself from looking round the room to augment her first quick survey when his back was turned. She was about to ask him how long he'd lived here when she noticed him looking intently at her cigarette and sniffing at the smoke coming from it. He lifted his eyes and they twinkled at her.

'That smells marvellous,' he said.

She started to open her bag again. 'Do have one. I thought you said you didn't.'

'I don't,' he said, 'as of ten days ago; but I can still eat one if anybody lights up nearby.'

'Well, I don't want to tempt you but if you'd like one you're welcome to one of these.'

He held up his hand. 'No, thanks. I've survived for ten days and I can stick it out now until the urge finally leaves me.'

'What made you give it up, health or expense?'

'Both, though the health part of it's really a bonus. I thought I was beginning to smoke so much that it wasn't a pleasure any longer so much as a nervous habit. When the last few coppers of tax were put on I decided it was as good a time as any to make the break.'

'I don't smoke very much,' she told him, 'so it doesn't bother me. If you've stuck it out for ten days I'd say you're over the worst part. What's the secret?'

'Keep away from cigarettes,' he said with a grin. 'No, what you must do is hang on like grim death until you break the habit part of it, till you no longer automatically think of smoking at certain times of the day. Then you're pretty well out of the wood. All you've got to do then is get through the next phase, which is an overwhelming desire to bite off the hand of anybody smoking close by.'

'I'll put it out,' she offered, 'if it's really bothering you.'

'No, of course not. You carry on. It'll give my willpower a little more practice.'

'Have you lived here long?' she asked him.

'About six months.'

'You must be fairly settled.'

'I suppose I am.'

There was a silence during which he looked at his watch.

'Are you living in town or have you come from away?'

'I've come up from London. Yesterday.'

'London? I've only been there a couple of times in my life. I'm a local boy myself.'

'I guessed you were,' she said gravely and he laughed outright, showing her a glimpse of strong, slightly discoloured teeth.

'No,' he said, 'I don't belong to this place but I come from not very far away.'

'Then I have the advantage of you. I was born here.'

'Were you really? You probably know it better than I do, then.'

'Oh, I doubt that. We moved away when I was quite small and I've never been back since.'

'It seems funny for someone to come back up here after living in London. It's usually the other way round.'

'Oh, different people have different reasons.'

'Yes, I suppose they do.'

She wondered how long they were going to have to make polite conversation. She didn't mind talking to him but she couldn't help noticing his hand over the back of the chair moving idly among the papers on the table.

She said, 'I do wish you'd go on with that, if you want to. You needn't make small talk with me. I can sit here quite happily till Mrs Swallow comes back.'

'No, no,' he said. 'No, I couldn't.'

'What are you doing, anyway?' she said. 'If it isn't frightfully secret. Are you writing a play?'

'A novel, actually.'

'How interesting! Should I have heard of you?'

'It's extremely unlikely,' he said amiably. 'The name's Wilf Cotton.'

'Mine's Marguerite Fisher. No, I'm afraid I haven't.'

'But you will one day,' he said. He spoke calmly but there was a hint of arrogance in his voice.

'And then I'll be able to say I once lived in the same house as the celebrated Wilf Cotton. If I get the room, that is.'

'Yes, something like that.'

'Is this your first novel?'

'Well, to all intents and purposes, yes.'

'So I really can be excused for not having heard of you?'

'Lord, yes. Don't let that bother you. I have had the odd short story broadcast and there was a piece of mine in the last number of *Etude*; but you don't make a name on that sort of thing.'

Marguerite was a little impressed. At least, then, he wasn't just a poor misguided scribbler who thought that knocking off a novel in his spare time was a quick way to fame and fortune.

'*Etude*. I don't think I've seen that.'

'Oh, it's one of these little magazines. Run on a shoe-string. Half a dozen issues and then they die the death. They offer you a fiver for a contribution and then go out of business and send you a paperback copy of *Little Women* as a consolation prize. Not that it's happened to this one yet, but it's only a matter of time.'

He got up to poke about on the bookshelves and fish out a thin blue-backed magazine printed on coarse paper. He passed it to her and she opened it and found his piece – a short sketch of miners coming off shift – and read the biographical note.

'A miner's son, are you? Perhaps another budding D.H. Lawrence?'

'There are resemblances but I think they're probably all superficial. Have you read any of him?'

'A little. I started with the abridged edition of *Lady Chatterley* when it was passed surreptitiously round the school as hot stuff. Very disappointing. Then I read the Penguin when it came out.'

'Oh, yes, a lot of people have heard of Lawrence now who didn't know he existed before Penguin published *Lady Chatterley*.'

She was a little nettled. She said, 'Would you like me to deliver a disquisition on the relative merits of *The Rainbow* and *Women in Love*?'

'Point taken.' He inclined his head towards her, smiling.

She was disarmed. She said, 'I don't think I could, mind; but I'll try if you like.'

'Anyway,' he said, 'what did you think of "Lady C." after your earlier disappointment?'

She glanced at him. This could be a genuine question, a piece of idle conversation or, not for the first time, a sexual gambit. How did men expect you to answer such a question?

'Not being able to recapture my youthful innocence, I found it hard to make a comparison. I enjoyed the book, though, and thought there was a great deal of truth in it. Rather naïve in parts, perhaps.'

She had the feeling that she was shocking him slightly and wondered if this was the effect she'd intended. But she went on.

'The four-letter words don't offend me providing they're not used in my presence by someone who hasn't enough respect for me to curb his language.'

That should settle him, she thought.

Before he could speak they heard the front door open and Wilf Cotton got up and hurried out of the room, pulling the door shut behind him. When he came back he was with a rather handsome, well-made woman in her middle forties, with dark hair and a fresh complexion. She said good afternoon to Marguerite with a pronounced West Riding accent.

'Come about the room, have you?'

'Yes. The woman at twenty-two – Mrs Randall – told me about it. I went there first but her room was taken.'

Marguerite stood up under the woman's appraising glance.

'Miss Fisher came up from London yesterday,' Wilf Cotton said.

'Did she now? All that way . . . Come up to a new job, have you?'

'Well, not exactly. I intend to look for a job. Some kind of secretarial work. I shouldn't have any trouble after the work I was doing in London.'

'Miss Fisher was telling me she was born here,' Wilf Cotton put in.

'Oh? I expect you intend to stop awhile now you're back?'

'That will depend mainly on whether I like living here,' Marguerite said coolly. 'If I might look at the room . . .'

'Aye, the room. Well, happen you're lucky Mrs Randall was full up,' the woman said dryly. 'I flatter meself 'at this room's a cut or two above owt she's got to offer.'

'Oh, I shouldn't have taken it,' Marguerite said. 'One

look through the front door was enough for me.'

Mrs Swallow gave a deep throaty laugh. 'Aye, it would be.'

Marguerite took a couple of expectant steps towards her and Wilf Cotton, who was still standing near her by the door.

'Reason I ask if you're likely to be stopping is because I like my people to give me time to get to know 'em. Not poking me nose into their business, mind. But you can get some rum characters on your doorstep an' I don't like people that stop a week an' then move on. I like to get on well with my tenants an' them to get on with me. Like Wilf here . . .' She threw one arm round Wilf Cotton's waist and squeezed him to her. 'We get on like a house on fire, don't we lad?'

Wilf Cotton struggled free. 'Get your hands off o' me, Poppy,' he said, his accent broadening. 'Yer'll break me flippin' ribs.'

Mrs Swallow laughed again. 'That wouldn't take much doing! I've been trying to fatten him up since the day he walked into this house and it hasn't made a ha'porth o' difference. Anyway, you get on with what you're doin' while I show this young lady upstairs.'

It was a quite spacious room overlooking the wet and neglected garden at the back of the house. Marguerite saw at once that it was big enough to become a sitting-room where she could stay without feeling crowded in, though it might not be too warm in winter with that high ceiling. The yellow wallpaper wasn't what she would have chosen, but it was bearable. The fireplace opening was boarded up and there was a free-standing electric fire on the hearth with a shilling meter on the wall.

'The back of the house gets all the sun first thing,' Mrs Swallow said, standing by the window. 'You've got plenty of space for your things with that wardrobe and them drawers. You can shift it about as you fancy so long as you don't do any damage, and you can bring your own stuff in to make it like home. I like my people to think of the house as home. I never have catered for a floating population and I don't intend to start. And I don't make a lot of rules and regulations, either. I like to rely on common sense and consideration all around. And I'm not slow to open me mouth when I don't think I'm getting it.'

They spoke for a little while longer, discussing the customs and habits of the house. Mrs Swallow was a widow and there were two other tenants besides Wilf Cotton: a woman briefly referred to as Sylvia, who occupied the attic room, and a man called Mr Mostyn. Presently they got to terms. Marguerite was relieved to find these a little lower than she had expected and this brought her to a quick decision.

'All right, I'll take it.'

'Good. I hope you'll be comfortable and happy with us.'

'A month in advance?'

'Please, love.'

Marguerite took her wallet from her bag and counted out the notes. 'There we are. Now all I have to do is get my case and I'm in residence.'

'I'll send Wilf up with it.'

'Oh, please, don't bother him again.'

'Oh, the exercise'll do him good. He spends altogether too much time crouching over that typing machine. He'll ruin his health if he doesn't watch out. Cooped up all day in an office and then at it at night as well.'

'You know,' Marguerite said, 'it's just possible that he has a great deal of talent.'

'Aye, an' a lot o' good that'll do him when they're putting him into a box.'

Mrs Swallow gave the impression that she would like to talk at some length about the young man downstairs, whom she obviously outrageously mothered and spoiled, but she seemed to have second thoughts about discussing an established favourite with an untried newcomer.

'What're you doing about your dinner today?' she asked, switching subjects.

'I've no plans.'

'Well, I don't usually make lunches during the week but I'm having to feed Wilf so you might as well join us.'

Marguerite thanked her.

'I'll send your case up and give you a shout when the dinner's ready, then. I shall be having to get on with it. I'm all behind-hand this morning. Bathroom's across the landing,' she said over her shoulder as she went out. 'You can't miss it. The name's on the door.'

Marguerite stood in the middle of the room and looked about her. Yes, yes, it had possibilities. She already saw ways of transforming it, of putting her stamp on it, making it hers. But before she spent any more money she must find a job and see what kind of salaries they paid up here. Lower than in London, no doubt. But then the room was cheaper than her last place and the cost of living should be a little less all round. She refused to think about the future. She would concern herself with living from day to day, with establishing a new pattern of living, but one which would not be hard to break when the time came for her to move elsewhere.

There was a knock at the half-open door and Wilf Cotton's voice called, 'Can I come in?'

'Yes, come in.'

He entered and put her case in the middle of the floor.

'I don't know how you managed with that,' he said. He was out of breath from hurrying up the stairs with the heavy case. 'It nearly dragged me back down. I'm glad to hear you're staying.'

'Thank you.'

He pushed his hands into his trousers pockets.

'Not a bad room, is it?'

'No, quite pleasant. What was the previous tenant like?'

'He was a West Indian called Appleyard Dearborn. Worked on the Corporation buses and studied engineering in his spare time. He's gone to Birmingham to join some relatives. Didn't Poppy say anything about him?'

'No, she didn't.'

'Probably never thought to mention it. Anyway, she's changed the sheets since then.'

Marguerite felt herself flushing. 'I think we can take it, Mr Cotton, that my views on the colour question are at least as enlightened as yours.'

He looked away for a moment. 'Sorry. Only Poppy wasn't too popular with some of the people in the street for taking Appleyard in. They said it lowered the tone of the neighbourhood, though God knows whatever tone it had it must have lost round about the First World War. In fact, Sylvia – she's upstairs – she was always making snide remarks about him and cutting him dead on the stairs. Poppy reckoned it was because he never made a pass at her. Still,' he smiled, 'I mustn't pre-influence your opinion of our tenants with my gossip.'

'I don't think you'll do that,' Marguerite said. 'I usually take people as I find them.'

'Yes, it's the best way.'

'Thank you for bringing up the case.'

'Don't mention it. Just shout if you want anything else.' He turned to go, then stopped. 'If you need any other bits of furniture or knick-knacks to make the room more comfortable there's a rather good saleroom in town. You can pick up some decent bargains there. You noticed that wing-chair of mine – got that for fifty bob there.'

'Thank you. I'll remember.'

'Okay. See you at lunch, then.'

'Yes, all right.'

He went out and she took off her jacket and opened her case. She unpacked her clothes and put them into the wardrobe and the chest of drawers. This done, she blew her nose thoroughly and looked at herself in the mirror on the wall over the fireplace. 'Well, here you are, then,' she said out loud to the girl in the glass. She turned away and lit a cigarette which she didn't really want and sat down in the armchair and rested her head back. She closed her eyes and then the loneliness and everything else hit her with such overwhelming force that she began to cry.

7

On the morning Wilf went back to the office there was one of his stamped and addressed manilla envelopes behind the front door along with a letter for Marguerite Fisher and a gas bill for Poppy. The envelope was bulky with the manuscript inside it and in the time it took him to tear it open he wondered which it was of the three stories he'd sent out ten days ago. It turned out to be the one he liked best, and here it had come first to roost, and without even a covering letter to indicate that the editor had found it in any way exceptional among the stacks of unsolicited contributions which must reach her desk (or at least, those of her underlings) to be rapidly scanned and turned round for the return journey. He glanced at the rejection slip which contained the usual regretful message. Nothing personal, of course. Nothing personal even in the way the regrets were conveyed. 'Order up another 50,000 rejection slips, will you, Daisy dear. These budding authors will never learn.' And wouldn't these editors ever learn that their very livelihoods depended upon authors who, budding once, *had* never learned to take rejection as the final verdict on their talent?

So it wasn't possible to write a letter to every misguided idiot who plonked words down on paper and sent it off in a spirit of hope that was more amazing than the piece itself. Agreed. But when something civilised came along, a piece that first of all *looked* workmanlike and in its reading showed the author to have *some* feeling for language and more than a little grasp of short-story form – when such a piece couldn't be accepted because of certain reasons, was it asking too much to expect a few specially written words saying why?

'Editors and publishers go to great lengths to discover and encourage new writers,' he had read somewhere. Whoever had written that was, as far as Wilf was concerned, lying in his teeth. The truth was that it was an overcrowded profession and while a publisher might regret failing to encourage a writer who took a later bestseller elsewhere, magazine editors were working with smaller stakes and could afford to be distant because there would always be the material to fill their pages.

'Oh, but I'm renouncing this caper,' he said out loud. 'And that's a fact.'

'What caper is that?' asked Marguerite Fisher. She had come quietly down the stairs and was crossing the hall towards him.

'Casting my literary pearls before editorial swine,' Wilf said, turning. 'There's a letter for you.'

'Thank you.' She took it but made no move to open it. 'I take it this is a morning of disappointments?'

'You take it correctly,' Wilf said. 'Not only don't they want my efforts, they time their return with sadistic glee so that they land on the mat first thing Monday morning.'

'Is that a rejection slip? I've never seen one.'

He handed it to her. 'You must come in and look at my collection some time. Actually that one's a bit more expansive than most. Somebody must have composed it in a maudlin moment.'

'*Fair Girl*,' she said, looking at the slip. 'I've seen the magazine, of course.' She read, ' "*Fair Girl* is interested in stories of literary merit which deal with everyday life in terse dialogue, strong characterisation and dramatic plots with which our readers can identify themselves." Hmm.'

'Explains everything, doesn't it?' Wilf said. 'Now I

know that there'll be no keeping me out.' He took back the slip and gazed at it. 'Marvellous. Bloody marvellous.'

She was looking at her watch. 'I shall have to be going. I don't want to be late on my first morning.'

'Hang on a minute and I'll join you.'

He opened the door of his room and sailed the envelope in the direction of the table, then went down the hall to the kitchen.

'Greetings from the North Eastern Gas Board,' he said to Poppy, who was about to start washing up the breakfast pots. He put the bill down on a cupboard top and leaned over to kiss her squarely on the mouth. 'So long, ducky. See you tonight.'

Poppy pulled back her head. 'That's enough o' that. There's a time and place for everything, an' it's time I was doing the washin'-up and you were on your way to work. Get off now; you're keeping that young woman waiting.'

Apparently absorbed in her work, she hadn't failed to be aware of them talking by the door.

'You don't miss much, do you?' he said.

'I don't miss anything.'

'How can you be so warm at night and yet so cold in the morning?' he asked her, only half banteringly.

'It's something that happens to your blood when you get old,' she said. 'Now off you go. Stop yer yattering and get out from under me feet.'

He left her. The front door stood open and Marguerite had gone out. He caught up with her in the drive. She was walking very slowly, her head bent over her letter. She looked up as he reached her and thrust the letter into her handbag.

'Carry on,' he told her. 'Don't mind me.'

'No, you can't read a letter properly when you're in a hurry.'

He gathered from her heightened colour and her silence as they walked along the street that something in the letter had disturbed her; so he kept quiet himself, allowing her to dictate the mood and quantity of their conversation. He thought about Poppy's sourness. It was one of her endearing qualities that she was always amiable, if a little tart at times. But very tart this morning; and that crack about being old . . . almost as if . . . He glanced sideways at Marguerite's profile. Could she, seeing them together, have suffered a sudden attack of jealousy – jealousy not so much of the girl herself but of what she represented: youth? He felt a rush of warm feeling for Poppy. He wanted to run back to the house and take her in his arms and fondle her and reassure her. But of what?

'Why do you send your work to women's magazines?' Marguerite asked.

'Easy. Three reasons. One, apart from them there's hardly any market for the short story in this country. Two, very occasionally they print good stories by writers who aren't the kind to make compromises; and three, they pay well, so I understand.'

'You can't be giving them what they want,' she said.

'A conclusion I came to some little time ago.'

'So if you want to get in you will have to give them what they want.'

'The trouble is, I don't seem to write what they want.'

'You'll have to learn to.'

'I'm not a baker taking orders for a dozen buns of a certain size, shape and flavour,' Wilf said. 'I'm a writer, of sorts, with a personality, again of sorts. I write what I want to write and then look round for a market.'

'You seem intent on doing it the hard way.'

'Look,' Wilf said, 'there are two kinds of writers, broadly speaking: the caterers and the creators, and they can be found at all levels except the very top where you just find creators. The caterers work to satisfy a ready-made market and hope the requirements of the market won't be subject to too much variation; in other words, that they won't be called upon to learn too many fresh tricks. The creators work to make their own market. Some of them have a harder time at the beginning and a lot of them never make much money all their lives. But at least the people who know them and read them can trust them to give them a square deal. You wouldn't trust a politician who lied to you to get your vote, so how can you trust a writer who lies to you to get your money?'

'I suppose most ordinary people never think about it,' Marguerite said. 'They just know the kind of books they like and never give the matter another thought. Anyway, there are people in the world who prefer lies to the truth.'

'Don't we all at times,' Wilf said. 'Well, fair enough. You pays your money and you takes your pick. And I'm not saying there aren't creators who are very dull dogs and caterers who are entertaining. With some writers I suppose the question never arises. They find they have the happy knack of writing what a large public wants and it's just plain sailing. With others, like me, it comes up as soon as they begin to put pen to paper.'

'But you're not really going to give it up, are you? That sketch of yours in *Etude* was really very good. As I see it, what you're trying to do is put down on paper a kind of life that hasn't had its fair due in fiction. Lawrence started out by doing the same thing, but he was writing about his time and you're writing about yours.'

'That's exactly what I'm trying to do,' Wilf exclaimed appreciatively. Oh, but she had her head screwed on the right way, this girl. He must talk to her again when they had the time. 'No, I haven't come this far to pack it in now. What I meant was that I shan't carry on sending manuscripts out to come bouncing back. I'll give the short story a rest and concentrate on my novel. There's more opportunity in that field.'

'Well, I can't do anything except wish you the best of luck.'

'You're a good listener,' Wilf said with a smile, 'and that always helps.'

They stood together at the bus stop and watched the morning traffic roll by down the long road to the city.

'It's sometimes,' Wilf said presently, 'like sitting in the waiting-room of a club and hearing people talking on the other side of the door. You can't wait to get in among them and become one of them, but somehow every time you try to speak the password you jumble it all up and receive a shake of the head.'

'And it's particularly hard for you because you're making up your own password.'

He laughed. 'Oh, well, just say I'm the awkward type.'

8

The letter was from Evelyn. She had visited Mrs Mulvaney and collected Marguerite's things and was insisting on boxing them up and sending them to her. She had given Mrs Mulvaney her own address in case there were any letters to be forwarded and through doing this she'd had a phone call from Floyd who had apparently called personally once and found her out.

'I must say he's very keen and quick off the mark,' Evelyn wrote. 'He must have gone round to your old address just after I did and wheedled my address out of Mrs Mulvaney. (I couldn't tell her to give it to everybody but Floyd because she was already grumbling about the sudden and mysterious way you'd done a bunk, though she had no real complaint because you'd paid your rent and if she lets the room within the next three weeks she'll be getting double money for it.)

'Anyway, I gather he came hot-foot to my place, found me out, then phoned the same evening (Saturday) i.e. last night. He'd only had the pleasure of meeting me once, he said (he hasn't got a very good memory because I've met him twice, as you know) but he knew I was a very close friend of yours and he was appealing to me in the hope that I could give him some idea of your whereabouts. He'd been worried stiff ever since ringing you with no other thought than that you'd be at home, and talking to this "Mrs Mulvaney character" who said you'd just packed up and walked out without a word to say where you were going.

‘ “I’ve got the awful feeling she may be sick herself, or something,” he said, “for her to go off like this without a word to me.” And every morning he’d watched for the mail he said, expecting, *knowing* there’d be a letter explaining everything.

‘Well, Marguerite my love, liar or not, deceiver or not, the man *is* fond of you. It would take a good actor to put that kind of concern into his voice if it wasn’t genuine.

‘What could I say? I should have thought you’d at least have written to tell him you’d found out the awful truth, but apparently you hadn’t. You put me in a bit of a spot, my girl, and I can’t say I liked it. All I was glad of was that I was on the phone and not talking to him face to face. I can tell a man what I think of him as well as the next girl, but doing it for a friend, at a moment’s notice, so to speak, is another matter.

‘Anyway, I rose to the occasion and put on my best Duchess’s voice.

‘ “I really don’t think there’s any point in your trying to find Marguerite,” I told him, “because you’re the last person she wants to see just now.”

‘So he said, “Look, will you tell me where she is and what’s wrong with her and please stop talking in riddles?”

‘ “No, I won’t tell you where she is,” I said, “but if you think hard enough it might dawn on you why she should go away.”

‘ “You tell me.”

‘ “All right, then,” I said. “She’s gone away to get over the shock of finding out about you. The little unimportant bits you didn’t bother to tell her about yourself.”

‘Well this set him back, I can tell you. He was quiet for so long I thought we’d been cut off, and I was just going to say “Hallo, are you still there” when he said in a very low voice, “So she knows.”

‘ “Yes,” I said, “she knows.” And I said, “Marguerite’s a dear sweet girl (I hope I’m not making you blush) and she went overboard pretty badly for you. She might or might not have had an affair with you if she'd known you were married but she'll never forgive you for deceiving her all the time she was giving herself to you."

' "She's taken it pretty badly, has she?"

' "Pretty damn' badly, my friend."

' "But look, if only I could see her, talk to her."

' "I wouldn't even try if I were you. In the words of the poet, chum, You've had it!"

'You'll notice that by this time I was warming to the job and the dialogue was coming off my tongue as if Noel Coward or somebody was standing there prompting me. Well he made another appeal for your address and I said nothing doing. So he said he must find you somehow, that this wasn't fair as he was being judged and condemned without a chance to tell his side of the story. So I said he should have told you his story before he dragged you into a game where all the cards were stacked against you before you started. And there the conversation ended.

'I don't know if he'll contact me again or make any serious attempt to find you. You know him better than I do so you can make up your own mind about that. What I *do* know is – and I never realised it till I spoke to him over the phone – that with that Yankee twang of his he could charm the birds out of the trees and if he does get to you, what with the way you feel about him (or did) you might find yourself accepting him at his face value again.

'So don't relent, my dear. If you do write to him, send the letter to me for posting. And don't worry – he'll have to use the Iron Maiden to get your address out of me. You'll get over him, and the quickest way is to remember that you've a lot of years to live and his are already mortgaged to someone else . . .'

She read the letter properly in the first few minutes she could find to spend alone in the cloakroom. Tears were pricking her eyes when she had finished but she held them from spilling over and carried out a skilful repair job on her make-up before going back to her office. If anyone said anything, she thought, she could always pass it off as being the wrong time in the month for a girl either to look or feel her best.

The job she had taken was with a fair-sized firm of provision merchants in the city. She had accepted the situation not because of the wage, which wasn't very good even for the provinces, nor because of the job itself which she felt sure would bore her to distraction within a fortnight, but because it seemed the best of those immediately available and in it she would be earning money while she looked for something else. She had been put to work in a room with two other typists, a woman of approaching thirty, unmarried, plain, humourless, and a rather hopeless girl of eighteen with a loose mouth, ungainly hands and feet and dark hair that was lank from lack of regular washing. The work was routine of the most uninteresting kind which nevertheless demanded an exacting standard of accuracy: accounts, invoices, orders, advice notes, bills of lading. Correspondence, such as there was, seemed to come to the woman, Brenda, because of her seniority. Audrey, the girl, pottered about with filing, making tea and running errands to and from the warehouse.

On her way back to the office Marguerite met in the narrow corridor a fair curly-haired young chap of about her own age wearing a carelessly unbuttoned khaki overall over a good-quality check sports shirt and a tweed tie. He smiled at Marguerite and looked her up and down in rapid appraisal.

'Hello. Are you the new typist?'

Marguerite said, 'Good morning. Yes, I am.'

'Well I must say you're an improvement on the last one. In looks, I mean; I don't know about your work. We used to call them the Three Witches. We shall have to think of something else now.' He leaned nonchalantly against the wall as he spoke, and his words were drawled and condescending enough to rub her the wrong way.

'I shouldn't let it occupy your mind too much,' she said. 'I should imagine your work strains it as much as is good for it.'

His eyebrows lifted slowly. Marguerite put this down as another affectation like the drawl and the casual stance.

'My, my,' he said, still in the same infuriatingly silly voice, 'what spirit! I think we'll let the description stand after all. Here,' he straightened up and held out the sheaf of papers he was carrying, 'give these to Brenda, will you. Save me walking the last few yards.'

She took the papers from him. 'Anything else?'

His glance fell insolently, then lifted again. 'I could think of a number of things. But later will do. Tell Brenda I love her, will you?'

'All right.'

He moved away from her, pretending to raise his hat in the manner of an old-time gallant. 'Until we meet again, sweet mademoiselle.'

'A lifetime hence would be too soon, monsieur,' Marguerite answered.

He laughed. 'What spirit,' he said again as he left her. 'My, my my!'

Brenda stopped typing as Marguerite dropped the papers into her tray. 'Who gave you these?'

'A very self-assured and rather silly young man in the corridor.' Marguerite sat down behind her own desk, facing Brenda. 'He said to tell you he loves you.'

Brenda turned faintly pink and her eyes glinted behind her glasses. 'Silly devil.'

'Who is he, anyway?'

'What did he look like?'

Marguerite had already noticed that there was some peculiar quirk in Brenda's nature that stopped her from giving a straight answer to a simple question.

'How many men in the place send messages saying they love you?'

There was an adenoidal giggle from Audrey, who was setting out the cups for their mid-morning tea. 'It's Mister Stephen,' she said, and giggled again.

'He walks about as if he owned the place.'

'He will when his father dies,' Brenda said.

'What is he doing in an overall – learning the business?'

'Yes, from the bottom up. He hasn't been here very long. He went straight into the army to do his National Service when he left university.'

'Which university did he go to?'

'Leeds.'

'Oh.'

'It's a very good university.'

'No doubt.'

'In fact, we have a lot of first-class universities up here in the North: Manchester, Sheffield, Hull.'

'Yes, I know.'

'I sometimes think they must be more progressive than these older places like Oxford and Cambridge.'

'You don't have to convince me. After all, there's Mister Stephen as living proof.'

Brenda glanced sharply at Marguerite but the sarcasm was mild in her voice and the look was not met.

'Did he say anything to you?'

'Nothing important apart from the message. Why?'

'You came in looking a bit nettled and now you sound sarcastic.'

'Oh, he made some arrogant comment about my looks, so I answered him back in kind.'

'Did you offend him?'

'Hardly, I think. But he was on the verge of offending me so I thought I'd better let him see what he was up against from the beginning.'

'Talking about him being arrogant, but you're a bit that way yourself, aren't you?'

'It's surprising what a little sweetness brings out, though,' Marguerite said.

'He's a devil, Mister Stephen is,' said Audrey, pursuing some line of thought of her own. She poured milk into all three cups then said, 'Ooh, I never asked if you take milk.'

'That's all right,' Marguerite said.

'What d'you mean he's a devil?' Brenda said.

'Well, the first morning I was here he come up to me behind some packing cases and leaned with his arms on both sides of me so's I couldn't get away. "An' who's little girl are you?" he says. "Not yours," I says. "Would a kiss make you mine?" he says.'

'You've never told me about all this before,' Brenda said. 'Are you sure you're not making it up?'

'Cross my heart and hope to die,' Audrey said. 'I didn't like to say anything about it after.'

'What happened then?'

'Well I said, "Try it an' see." '

'You never did!' Brenda exclaimed. 'You mean you invited him to kiss you?'

'No, I was kinda threatenin' him not to, if you see what I mean. But anyway, he did.'

'He kissed you?'

'Yeh.'

Brenda was watching Audrey with a mixture of fascination and revulsion in her eyes. She licked her lips in a quick flicking movement of her tongue.

'Did he . . . did he put his arms round you?'

'Oh no, he didn't try to maul me. He kept his arms where they was – were. But he kissed me, all right.'

'You mean a kind of peck.'

'Naw, a long one. Dead centre, no messing. It must have lasted half a minute. It seemed like half an hour to me at the time. I was on eggs thinkin' somebody'd walk round behind an' see us.'

'What happened then?'

'He just laughed and chucked me under the chin and walked away.'

'You know if you're making it up you can get into trouble for telling stories like that.'

'I'm not making it up,' Audrey said indignantly. 'It's true. Every word of it.'

'I believe her,' Marguerite said, and Brenda switched her gaze to her from Audrey for a moment. 'You would,' her look seemed to say, and Marguerite, looking from the clumsy, ungainly girl who had been kissed behind the packing cases to the prim, immaculately dowdy Brenda, who had probably never been kissed anywhere, knew she was looking at jealousy, but jealousy its owner would probably not admit even to herself.

A cloud of steam rose up behind Audrey's desk and Brenda said peevishly, 'Well, hurry up and make the tea. And I'll have a couple of codeine with mine. I don't know where to put myself this morning.'

'Do you have a lot of trouble?' Marguerite asked.

'Do I? It's fit to cut me in two sometimes. And don't ask me if I've been to the doctor because I have, and all he can say is perhaps I'll find it less troublesome when I get married. Damn' fine reason for getting married, I must say.'

'Why don't you try a night out with Mister Stephen?' Marguerite said. 'That would be a bit less drastic than marriage.'

'Well that's a rotten thing to say!' Brenda cried. She had flushed deeply, her throat and cheeks darkening.

'Now what's wrong?' said Marguerite, astonished at the other's reaction. 'I only made a joke.'

'Only a joke. And not a very nice joke. What you're trying to say is that I'd let Mister Stephen take me out and make love to me if he wanted to.'

'Look, all I meant was—'

'I know what you meant. You've been skittish and sarcastic with your London ways ever since you came in at nine o'clock this morning. You come up here and start throwing your insinuations about as if we all carry on in the loose way they do down there. Well let me tell you—'

'No,' Marguerite cut in, 'let me tell you. If you're nursing a secret passion for this Mister Stephen, that's your affair, but when people can't mention his name without you pricking up your ears and acting as though you've got some proprietary rights in him, then it becomes theirs as well. I only made the kind of joke anyone might make and if you'd a scrap of humour in you you'd have laughed and answered me back with another. But no, you've got to blow up an innocent remark and turn it into some kind of evidence for your astonishingly provincial and old-maidish conception of London. You seem to think that every hardworking girl there spends her spare time sleeping around with one man after another and this goes on everywhere until we reach the Trent and past there all the girls become suddenly virtuous and untouchable. Well you want to walk about with your eyes open and read a couple of newspapers and you'll see that people up here sleep out as well, and get divorced and have babies out of wedlock.' God, she thought, you're overdoing it. Pull up before it's too late. But the weight of spoken words seemed to pull those unsaid after them. 'Just because you've never been farther south than Sheffield yourself you don't have to start this North and South business with me because I've lived in them both. For your information I was born right here in this city and I lived here for the first nine years of my life. And I could tell you things about one Northcountry childhood that would make your hair curl.'

Audrey goggled as the door closed behind Brenda.

'Crikey, that was worth a three-and-sixpenny seat in the stalls, that was.'

'If you repeat a word of it outside this room I'll break your neck,' Marguerite said.

'Oh, don't worry. I can carry corn.'

Marguerite rubbed her hands over her face. They were trembling and her heartbeats were fast. She thought, What a start!

'Pour the tea, Audrey,' she said in a moment. 'I'm gasping.'

'I should think so, after that little speech.' Audrey poured tea into two of the cups. 'How much sugar?'

'One, please.'

Audrey passed her a cup. 'Brenda's going to miss hers. I wonder if I ought to take her a cup. It'll probably be cold by the time she comes back.'

'Where will she be?'

'Cloakroom, I expect. There's nowhere else much she can go.'

'I should leave her alone. She won't thank you for barging in on her now. Bad enough you being in here when I let fly. It might have been forgivable if there weren't a witness but I've probably cooked my goose with a vengeance now.'

'Oh, I don't know. People get over rows.'

'Not with a stranger, so easily.'

'Well, she did ask for it. And she is bossy, y'know. If she can get people under her thumb she will do. You've just shown her she can't do that with you.'

Marguerite put her cup down on the corner of her desk and pulled her typewriter towards her. 'Anyway, we'll stop discussing her behind her back, shall we, and get on with some work.'

It was half an hour before Brenda reappeared. She walked in and sat down without looking at anybody. She had been crying and her efforts at covering the traces of it with powder were not so successful as Marguerite's earlier attempts on herself. She began straightaway to type, her fingers at first tentative, almost uncertain, until gathering strength with the return of her spirit they were moving with swift expertise.

Marguerite glanced at her a number of times over a period of several minutes but Brenda's eyes were fixed on her work. At length she said:

'Brenda.'

'Yes?'

'I'd like to say something.'

'Don't you think you've said enough?'

'I'd like to say something else. Will you stop typing for a minute and listen to me?'

Brenda lifted her hands to the top of her machine and leaned on her elbows. She didn't look at Marguerite but watched the small movements of her own fingers. She had rather pretty hands with long fingers and well-shaped nails.

Audrey made a move as if to go out. 'I'll just pop downstairs with these flimsies.'

'No, don't go for a minute, Audrey. You heard the other things so you ought to hear this.' She looked across at Brenda. 'I want to apologise for the way I carried on just now, Brenda. There was really no justification at all for the way I went for you. I hope you'll accept the excuse that I've had some personal trouble recently which upset me very much, and I'm apt to try to put people in their place before they can get near to me, either one way or the other. I'm sorry I said what I did say. I came here to work and get on with everybody, not to make enemies. I'd like to be friends with you, if you'll let me.'

Brenda looked at her hands. There was a silence. Audrey coughed noisily. 'All right,' Brenda said.

Marguerite said thank you and nodded at Audrey to tell her she could go now. She thought that in similar circumstances at school in Amhurst, since when she had never quarrelled with anyone like this, there would have been a muttered 'shake' and a clasping of hands. Such an action rounded off a speech like she had just made and was, while mannish in the way some schoolgirl habits are, more satisfactory than just sitting in an embarrassed silence. Brenda hadn't moved since Audrey went out. She said now:

'Can I ask you something?'

'If you like.'

'Was it – this trouble you just mentioned – to do with a man?'

'Yes, it was.'

She gave a little nod of her head. 'I thought so.'

'It happens to people all the time, you know,' Marguerite said. 'The main thing is to get over it and not let it do anything permanent to you.'

'But it's forced to affect the way you look at men and let them treat you.'

'I suppose it is. Just at the moment I can't imagine letting myself become fond of a man in that way ever again. But all men aren't alike, and circumstances change.' She smiled wryly. 'I daresay I'll come round in time.'

Brenda nodded again. She still hadn't looked directly at Marguerite. 'It's right what you said, you know.'

'What was that?'

'About me and Mister Stephen . . . I am sweet on him.'

Marguerite wondered how long Brenda had wanted to confess this to someone.

She said, 'I'm sorry.'

Brenda's lips moved in a rueful little smile. 'Yes, it is something to be sorry about, isn't it?'

'I think we've all got to face it sometime that certain people just aren't right for us,' Marguerite said. 'You'll get over this and meet somebody else; someone your own age, a bit more responsible.'

'Perhaps so.'

Marguerite toyed with the paperclip she was holding as she waited for Brenda to say something more if she wished. But after several moments of silence the other girl sat up and straightened her shoulders, becoming business-like as her hands poised themselves on the keyboard of the typewriter.

'Well, in the meantime there's some work to do and this kind of talk won't buy the baby a new bonnet.'

9

This district on the south-west side of the city had always been predominantly working-class, the terraced houses and weavers' cottages clinging, dourly grim, to the steep hillside that fell abruptly from the lip of an escarpment overlooking the river and the mills on its banks. Starting with cottages in the millyards themselves, the owner had populated the area round their premises at a time when lack of public transport meant that a man lived near his work or walked to and from it, often over considerable distances, at the beginning and end of a twelve- or fourteen-hour working day. Now, at the end of the first day's work in the first job she had ever had in her native town, Marguerite was swung up there on a Corporation bus in ten minutes from the city centre.

She had avoided the crowded rush-hour transport by sitting for thirty minutes over a sandwich and a cup of coffee in an espresso bar a few minutes from the office. Two swarthy youngish men whom she took to be Greek Cypriots were working behind the counter. Their dark jaws were smooth shaven and they wore short white coats and expensive-looking gold wrist-watches on gold straps. Talking to each other in their own language, they served the customers without looking at them, their only apparent recognition of their presence the silent passing across the counter of whatever was asked for. This in itself Marguerite recognised as a minor revolution in English provincial life. A far cry, this bland, hygienic efficiency behind the barrier of another language, a foreign culture, from the warm, steamy atmosphere of the little cafés in the covered market she had known as a child, where pork pies and peas were served with hot sweet tea on bare wooden tables by someone as homely as the woman next door. She wondered if those cafés were still there. She must go and look sometime. But this was the first change you noticed about the industrial provinces – the new cosmopolitanism: the Greek Cypriots in the coffee bars, the Chinese in the restaurants, the Pakistanis and West Indians in the streets. And she liked it, if for no more reason than the opportunity of eating exotic dishes as a change from roast beef and Yorkshire pudding, and the privilege of sitting in surroundings as pleasant as these while one killed time over a cup of coffee. A considerable amount of money had been spent in fitting the place out. There were venetian blinds at the windows. A wrought-iron rail guided the customers' hands as they descended the short flight of steps from street level and on three of the walls was an expensive red flock wallpaper above a dado of imitation black marble. The coffee was dear at a shilling a cup but she recognised that the décor had to be paid for and there couldn't be an enormous profit to be made from the teenagers who would crowd the bar after nightfall, using it as a rendezvous where they could meet their friends and linger all evening for the price of one or two cups.

She knew no one in the room, which wasn't surprising since she'd been in the town less than a week. Nor did it give her any particularly acute feeling of being alone in a strange place. For not since Amhurst had she lived in any community small enough to make it virtually certain that at any moment of the day she would see faces, if not of people she actually knew, which she had seen before. On one level of personality she had become accustomed to the anonymity and independence of city living. On a deeper level there was a loneliness which reached back as far as she could remember and this had little real connection with whether she lived in a village or a great metropolis. It was simply that in a small town or in the community of a school the true, the inner self lay behind a surface gregariousness that probably misled many people into mistaking an ability to mix for a confidence and self-sufficiency she had in fact never possessed. She knew very well both the cure for this and its dangers. The episode with Floyd had brought her happiness such as she'd only dreamed of and at the end a pain and disillusionment which seemed to rule out all hope, and all hope of hope. What she had said to Brenda was a defence against possible pity, words with which to flank her pride. They weren't untrue in themselves – there were other men and other circumstances. But these were academic facts; she felt that they had no bearing on her life. She couldn't see how she could ever love another man as she had loved Floyd.

She had not expected the drastic changes to the city centre where streets had been widened, squares enlarged, and new glass and concrete cubes raised up on the sites of mid-Victorian buildings no longer sufficient for the town's commercial needs. But here . . . no change at all, or none apart from the gentle mouldering of time . . . Her mind's-eye view of grass-covered foundations was erased as she turned the corner into the lane by the sight of the roofless shells of seven cottages, and the sudden actuality of them after thirteen years brought her heart into her throat and she had to pause for a moment before going on. Each one had been partially demolished as the rehoused inhabitants moved out, to prevent occupation by squatters. One by one the families had gone and Marguerite had missed them: the Phillipses at the end, whose small son was killed by a lorry the summer before; the Lawrences who had a pretty daughter, Elspeth, who married a policeman; and the O'Connors. Mr O'Connor, an Irishman with an

Irishman's temper, had chased his wife all along the row with a belt one time because, he said, she'd been carrying on with the ginger-haired man who collected the rents. They sent a new rent man after that and Mrs O'Connor went all mean and moody and there wasn't a civil word passed between her and her husband from morning till night. Most of all she had missed plump Mrs Wilson from next door, who had nursed Marguerite's mother when she was ill and loved Marguerite like one of her own children. It was Mrs Wilson who had told Marguerite later that she must be brave because her mother had been very poorly and only by going to Jesus in heaven could she be made better again. She had been able to talk to Mrs Wilson and keep her mother's memory alive. When Mrs Wilson went, there was no one to talk to, because her father never mentioned her mother and it was only in her heart that she could remember her and when, at times, she had difficulty in bringing her face clearly to mind she was frightened and disturbed. She felt that when she could no longer see her mother in her mind's eye she would have lost her for ever; for to her, her memory of her was the last slender thread holding her mother to life on earth. Then all the families were gone and they were the last people left along the row. The other houses, partly demolished already, were sad and empty. Rubble littered the flag-stone floors and big pieces of plaster had fallen from the walls, leaving what remained in strange shapes like huge continents on a map of an unknown world. And the demolition men's work on the last house was done for them by a small boy with a lighted match and a paraffin stove.

Her father and Laura had gone early to the club that night, leaving her to give the two young 'uns their supper and get them off to bed. It was nothing new to her but on the long summer evenings the children delayed as long as possible the end of the day. There was a quarrel over the strawberry jam which ended in her clouting Peter, who had provoked it, and his turning on her. He struggled for words to express his outrage and burst out, 'I'll pee on you if you hit me again.' With Angela in her arms, being comforted, she couldn't reach him to give him a second smack and he ran out of the house unhindered.

A little while later she went to the door. It was a warm evening with a light breeze which carried the acrid odour of smouldering rubbish in a dustbin somewhere in one of the lower terraces. The town was bathed in a low-slanting sunlight that the still-lingering haze of the working day turned to a dusky gold. Dust lay thick on the unsurfaced lane which ran past the cottages, leading nowhere now, but petering out at a small abandoned colliery, its shaft bricked over, the surface buildings in ruins. Feathery grass had taken stubborn root on the dark metallic-grey slag-heap and big-leafed dock and rosebay willow herb grew profusely on its lower slopes. The boy was leaning over the low wall tossing stones into the gardens of the houses in the terrace below, whose slate roofs were on a level with the lane, so steep was the hillside on which they were built.

She called to him: 'Peter, come on. It's time for bed.' He ignored her and went on throwing stones over the sheer drop. She ran towards him, her shoes scuffing up the thick dust, and grabbed him as he made a last-minute attempt to elude her. He giggled with excitement as she laid hands on him.

'Haven't you been told about throwing stones down there? If you break a winder or hit somebody wes'll all get into bother.'

He went on struggling, giggling and writhing in her grasp. She took a firm hold of him by the back of his ragged jumper and led him back to the cottage. 'It's time you were in bed, an' if you cause any more bother tonight I'll give you a proper good hiding.'

'I'll tell me dad if you do.'

'You tell him. He'll give you another hiding then for not doing as you're told.'

The boy relapsed into silence and stopped struggling, allowing himself to be led quietly into the house. He knew that he had no appeal against his sister. He and Angela were often left in Marguerite's care while his father and Laura went out drinking or to the pictures and any rebellion against her authority only brought further retribution if reported.

'Will you tell us a story, Margy?' he asked.

'I will if you're good; but there'll be no stories if there's any more alecking about.'

'I'll be good, Margy. Will you tell us that one about the giant what gobbled everybody up till Jack climbed up the beanstalk and killed him with a chopper and pinched all his gold money?'

'Don't you want another one? You know that one backwards.'

'I like that one, Margy. Will you tell us it?'

'If you're good.'

Her heart could always warm to him when he was in a winning mood. It was Angela, plump and golden-haired, who drew attention wherever they went and though Marguerite loved her too it was Peter who was her favourite. He was thin, whey-faced and always looked undernourished; and he could be a devil, driving her to the limit of her patience when the mischief was on him. But when well behaved and repentant he had a charm that captured her heart.

She undressed both children and got them into their night-clothes. In Angela's case it was a washed and shrunken flannelette nightgown which, at this stage in her growth, reached only to her knees. It was adequate in summer but when autumn came and the nights turned chilly she would need something more substantial to keep her warm. They all needed new clothes. Peter's jumper was full of holes and his trousers had been patched and mended till there seemed to be hardly any of the original material left. She herself had a hole in the sole of one of her shoes and her cotton frock was ready to rub through at the next washing, which would probably be when she did it herself. Laura didn't like washing, or housework at all for that matter. In this, as in almost every way, she was different from Marguerite's mother. There had never been a lot of money (and now there was even less with Laura powdering and lipsticking herself and flashing her ear-rings in the looking-glass prior to taking Marguerite's father into town nearly every night); but there had, it seemed to her, been a kind of sparse cosiness, a warmth, and a willingness to clean and mend so different from Laura's constant peevish plaint of 'cleanin' an' workin' an' washin' from mornin' till night for a pack o' mucky kids'. Marguerite resented being called a mucky kid since she did a good deal of the troublesome washing and cleaning herself when she was at home from school. She wasn't very good at mending but she had no doubt that much of that would be passed on to her as her proficiency grew. And wasn't it her reliability in looking after Peter and Angela that allowed them so many nights out together when other women with young children stayed at home and the man went out alone?

She gave the children's hands and faces a cat-lick rub with the moist flannel then settled down with them in her father's chair for the story.

'About the giant, Margy,' Peter said. 'About the giant. You promised.'

'All right, then,' Marguerite said, 'I'll tell you about the giant.'

'Tell us how Jack fun' him asleep with all his gold money an' killed him with a chopper.'

'We'll get to that bit in time. You're a bloodthirsty little tyke.'

Peter snuggled down between Marguerite and the upholstered arm of the chair. 'That's the bit I like.'

'Well then,' Marguerite began. 'Once upon a time there was a boy called Jack who lived with his grandma in the middle of a big forest. He was a woodcutter and he chopped trees down an' made them into firewood so's he could get money for him an' his grandma to live on. And Jack had a big garden that he liked to grow things in—'

'An' one day,' babbled Peter, 'he went into the village an' a man gave him some special seeds an' he planted 'em an' when he wakes up next morning there was a great big beanstalk growin' right up into the clouds . . . I know all that part. Let's get to the bit where he goes to the castle an' finds the giant.'

'Impatient, impatient,' Marguerite said. 'You've got to tell all of a story or it isn't exciting.'

'The exciting bit's where he meets the giant,' Peter said.

'Well I'm gunna tell it properly or not at all. Look' – the other child's fair head was heavy against her shoulder – 'Angela's asleep so you'd better listen quiet.'

'I'm listenin'.'

'Well, when he'd climbed up the beanstalk, right up into the sky where he couldn't see the earth any more, he found a long road. He walked on this road for hours an' hours an' he didn't see a single soul. He was very, very tired and ever so hungry and he was beginning to wish he was sitting having his supper with his grandma in their cottage. And then all at once he saw this great big castle standing on a hill. It was the biggest castle he'd ever seen and he thought he'd knock at the door and ask the king or whoever it was lived there if he could stay for the night.

'But he didn't know that it wasn't a king what lived there but a horrible wicked giant.'

'No, he didn't,' Peter said with horrified glee. He shivered with delight and snuggled down further into the chair. 'Go on, Margy.'

Marguerite told how the giant at first captured Jack, and then how Jack escaped and killed the giant and took his gold to share among the people on the earth. 'And then they all lived happily ever after.'

'Who lived happily ever after, Margy?'

'Jack and his grandma and all the other people in the country.'

'Because the wicked giant was dead?'

'That's right. An' now it's time you were in bed.'

'Weren't there any more wicked giants, Margy?'

'No, just that one. Once Jack killed that one there wasn't anything else for them to worry about.'

'Why did Jack live with his grandma? Why didn't he live with his mam an' dad like everybody else?'

'Because the wicked giant had gobbled them up a long time ago, an' there was only his grandma left for him to live with.'

'We've got our mam an' dad to live with, though, haven't we, Margy?'

'Laura isn't your mam,' Marguerite said.

'What is she, then?'

'Nothin'. She's just Laura.'

'Well, what's she doin' here if she isn't our mam?'

'She lives here with us, that's all.'

Their father liked them to address Laura as their mother and though the habit came easily to the young ones Marguerite clung too fiercely to the memory of her own mother ever to let the thin, gauntly pretty woman their father had brought into the house to live with them eighteen months ago take her place.

'Where is our mam, then, Margy?'

'Our real mam's dead.'

'Dead?'

'She went away to Jesus a long time since. But you can remember her, Peter, can't you? You can remember what it was like when our real mam lived with us?'

The boy was confused. 'I don't know.' He was really not very bright and the effort of trying to remember was too much for him. Marguerite herself had little real conception of the finality of death and sometimes thought that Jesus might eventually tire of her mother's company and let her come back to them. But it seemed to her that

He would never do this if once they allowed anyone else to take her place. So she refused to forget and never relinquished her hold on the fact that whatever Laura might be she was not their real mother.

'If our real mam's dead an' gone away, why can't Laura be our mam?' Peter asked, and Marguerite said, 'If you have a real mam when you're born and she dies or goes away nobody else can ever be your real mam again.'

She stirred in the chair. 'Stand up,' she said to Peter. 'I want to get Angela upstairs before she wakes up.'

Peter got up out of the chair and began to stalk about the room, saying in a deep voice, 'Fee, fi, fo, fum, I smell the blood of an Englishman.'

The child murmured in Marguerite's arms and she hissed at the boy. 'Will you be *quiet*!' She moved across the room and opened the door to the stairs. 'I'll be down for you in a minute.'

When she came down again she found Peter crouching in front of the paraffin stove in the hearth with a lighted match in his hand. She leaped at him and sent him sprawling. 'How many times have I told you not to meddle with matches?' She pulled him to his feet. 'An' leave that stove alone, will you. You're forever meddling with things 'at don't concern you. Look, you've spilled some paraffin on the rug now. You'll have the house afire one o' these days.'

'It's cold,' Peter said. 'I was lighting it for you.'

'I'll light it when it wants lighting. You're going to bed. You'll be warm enough there. An' you leave them matches alone.'

'Give us a piggy-back, then.'

'All right, then; if you'll promise to be quiet an' go straight off to sleep.'

'I don't want to go to bed, Margy. I'm not tired. I want to stop up a bit an' be with you.'

'I'm busy, an' it's past your bedtime. C'mon, hop up.'

He scrambled into the chair and she stood so that he

could clamber on to her back. With his arms wound round her neck in a stranglehold and his legs hugging her waist she carried him into the big bedroom where the thin curtains were drawn to dim the evening sunlight. It was the only upstairs room in the cottage and it contained besides the curtained alcove that served as a wardrobe, and a shabby chest of drawers, Angela's barred cot, the double bed where her father and Laura slept and the smaller bed she shared with Peter. She dumped him, giggling, on to their bed and began to tuck him in.

'Now no noise; an' go straight to sleep.'

He looked up at her from the pillow. 'Come on in with me, our Margy, an' let's cuddle up.'

'Later on,' she said. 'It's not my bedtime yet. I've a lot of things to do.'

'I'm cold.'

'What a tale! It's as warm as anything in here.'

Angela's mattress creaked as she turned in her sleep.

'We're gunna wake our Angela up if we're not careful,' Marguerite said. 'Now you snuggle down and go to sleep.' She kissed him on the forehead and left the room, looking back through the stair-rail to give a last whispered warning. 'No noise, remember!'

Which were the last words she ever spoke to him . . .

It was decided at the inquest that Peter had got out of bed and gone downstairs to light the stove after slipping the latch on the door to make sure she wouldn't surprise him in the act. No blame at all was attached to her but her father was censured for his gross negligence in leaving her in charge of the children at her age. And they sent him to prison for three months for his subsequent violent attack on her person.

She carried the marks of his assault for some time afterwards along with the inner scars of her self-imposed blame. And her sense of guilt lingered when the visible scars had disappeared. The dead children haunted her nights and she would start out of a restless sleep calling for them and beating at the invisible door which stood between them and the fire, and herself.

If only she hadn't been tempted by the warmth of the evening outside . . . If only she hadn't lingered with Mavis O'Rourke . . .

She looked down now over the low wall at the house where the O'Rourkes had lived. Possibly still lived, for not all the O'Rourke children would have grown up and gone away. One was born in the early morning of the day after the fire.

The houses in the terraces were better than the cottages. They had gardens, and doors at both back and front, and more than one bedroom. The O'Rourkes didn't make much of their garden because nobody in the family was interested in cultivating it. So it was just a rough grass plot for the children to play on.

'Me mam's in bed,' Mavis O'Rourke told Marguerite when she had descended the high bank into the garden. 'They've sent for the midwife.' She was bouncing a ball with a broken-stringed tennis racquet. Mavis was small, like all the O'Rourke children, and dark, with her father's bright blue eyes. She was about a year older than Marguerite and despite Marguerite's heavier family responsibilities Mavis always assumed the lead in any project they undertook together.

'Wes'll have a new baby in the morning,' Mavis said.

Mrs O'Rourke was always having babies. This would be number seven to add to the four girls and two boys who already filled the house.

'What d'you want?' Marguerite asked her, 'a boy or a girl?'

'Me dad says a lad 'cos they can fend for themselves, an' me mam's not bothered.'

Mavis herself showed little excitement. A new baby was no novelty to her. It was from Mavis's superior knowledge and the coincidence of Mrs O'Rourke's thickening waistline with each new child that Marguerite had learned one of the facts of life. But though she knew that a woman carried a baby inside her till it was born she wasn't sure how it got there in the first place. She wasn't sure if Mavis herself knew this and somehow they had never discussed this aspect of the matter. Marguerite was sure it had something to do with men and women being built differently and that they slept together and sometimes made strange noises in the night to the rhythmical creaking of the bed. But to date Laura had shown no signs of having a baby to confirm the theory.

'They've sent us all out to play till bedtime,' Mavis said, bouncing the ball. 'I think I'm off down to the rec. Are you coming?'

Marguerite would have liked to go with Mavis to the recreation ground by the park and slide on the helter-skelter and play on the swings but her duties tied her to home.

'I can't. Me dad an' Laura's gone out an' I'm lookin' after our Peter an' Angela.'

'Me dad's gone to the pub out of the way,' said Mavis. 'Me Auntie Flo's put the nippers to bed an' she's stoppin' the night. Haven't you got any aunties to look after Peter an' Angela when your dad wants to go out?'

Marguerite shook her head. 'Me mam came from somewhere away an' me dad has no relations.'

'What about Laura?'

'I don't know where she comes from. Me dad just brought her home one time an' she's stopped here ever since.'

The ball bounced crookedly on the uneven garden-path and Mavis leaped after it. When she came back she said:

'Are your dad an' Laura married?'

'I don't know. I don't know if they can be.'

' 'Course they can. Your mam's dead, isn't she?'

'Well, mebbe they are, then.'

'I don't think they are,' Mavis said. 'I think they're livin' in sin.'

'What does that mean?'

'It's when a man an' a woman live together without

being married. The priest calls it livin' in sin and nobody who lives in sin can go to heaven when they die.'

'Where do they go, then?'

'They go to hell, silly thing. Where else can they go if they don't go to heaven?'

An awful shock of fear struck Marguerite's heart. 'Me mam an' dad weren't livin' in sin, were they?'

'*I* don't know,' Mavis said. 'Anyway, it doesn't matter if you're married or not, if you're not Catholics you're still livin' in sin because that's the only true religion.'

'Who says so?'

'The priest – Father Barlow.'

She was all at once near to tears. Her heart thumped sickeningly in her thin breast. 'What does a silly old priest know about my mam an' dad?' she cried.

'Priests know everything,' Mavis said, 'because the Pope tells them an' he gets it all from God.'

'My mam's gone to Jesus,' Marguerite said. 'Mrs Wilson told me. He'd taken her away to make her better and let her live with Him.'

'How can Mrs Wilson know better than a priest?'

'Well she knows that anyway, because she told me.'

'I don't think Mrs Wilson goes to church at all. Not to any church. I think she's an . . . an atheist.'

'She isn't at all!'

'*I* think she is.'

'Well she isn't, so there! What d'you want to call people names for?'

'I'll bet you don't know what an atheist is.'

'Yes I do.'

'Well what is one, then? Go on, tell me what an atheist is.'

'Well, it's . . . it's . . .' Marguerite floundered because she really didn't know what an atheist was, unless it was someone who didn't go to church, and she could see nothing very wicked in that. She herself no longer went to Sunday School very often since her mother's death, partly because she had no nice clothes to wear and partly because nobody bothered about her going so long as she made herself scarce in some other way after doing any chores that fell to her on Sunday afternoon. But now she was actually fighting back tears because Mavis O'Rourke was being horrible about the people Marguerite loved.

'There, I knew you didn't know,' Mavis said. 'Well an atheist is somebody who doesn't believe in God. An' they're worse than anybody in the world.'

'Well Mrs Wilson's not an atheist, else how could she tell me me mam had gone to heaven?'

Mavis tossed the racquet away and began to bounce the ball off the wall of the brick-built lavatory.

'Grown-ups say all sorts of things they don't mean just to get rid of kids.'

'You're a horrible thing, Mavis O'Rourke,' Marguerite said through a throat thick with tears, 'saying Mrs Wilson's an atheist an' me mam hasn't gone to heaven.'

Mavis stopped bouncing the ball and turned an innocent gaze on Marguerite. 'Well what's wrong now? What yer roarin' about?'

'What you said. I don't know how you can say things like that. I thought we were friends.'

'Well we are.' Seeing the havoc she had wrought, she said, 'Don't be daft, Marguerite. I was on'y kiddin'. I didn't mean it.'

'Yes, you did. You're allus sayin' rotten things an' then reck'nin' you didn't mean 'em. Well I've had enough of it. We're not friends any more.'

'Oh, come on. 'Course yer mam's gone to heaven. They on'y send bad people to hell an' yer mam wasn't bad, was she?'

Marguerite had no handkerchief and she lifted the tears off her cheeks with her fingers, finally raising the hem of her frock to dry her eyes.

'No, she wasn't. She was the best mam in all the world. She was better than your mam, anyway. She didn't swear an' shout an' fight with the neighbours.'

'No, she was too stuck up,' Mavis retaliated. 'She thought she was Somebody. Me mam says she thought she was too good for anybody round here.'

Marguerite clenched her fists and sobbed with frustration at her inability to make Mavis see what a wonderful woman her mother had been; and with anger because now she wanted to hurt her friend. She was on the point of hurling herself at Mavis to relieve her feelings by scratching and biting and kicking when Mavis's Aunt Flo appeared in the doorway and called out.

'Mavis. Mavis, come here a minute.'

A woman came out of the house and crossed the garden to empty a bucket into the dustbin. She replaced the dustbin lid and looked at Marguerite standing by the wall.

'Were you looking for somebody?'

Marguerite had no desire to see any of the O'Rourkes but the logical answer framed itself.

'I was wondering if a family called O'Rourke still lived in that house.'

'O'Rourke? No, there's nobody with that name here now. Some people called Robertshaw lived here before us. We've been here a good twelve months.'

Marguerite called out thank you and turned away.

She began to walk back along the lane by the low wall where they had laid out the bodies of the two suffocated children and tried in vain to snatch back the life that was already gone. She could remember a woman covering her face with her apron and wailing in the shock of the tragedy. There was so much that she could remember of that time, so much she would never forget. But it was sad that for a long time now she had not been able to recall the faces of her brother and sister.

10

He waited until Poppy's arms were raised to pull the slip up over her head then reached out from behind and, running his hands up under her breasts, nuzzled his mouth into the firm flesh of her back between her shoulder blades. She laid the slip across a chair and stood still as he took the weight of her breasts in his hands. They were full but still taut: of a childless woman, they had never fulfilled their primary function, nor even suffered the damaging preliminaries, but retained late their subsidiary power to excite men. Not for the first time, Wilf wondered how many men had found them exciting and, more to the point, what number of those men had held them as he did now. He was faintly ashamed of the thought but accepted it as the paradoxical working of a mind which was, in this respect, like many men's. You looked for uninhibited sexuality and suspected it when you found it of being mere licence.

Poppy moved her shoulders. 'Have you finished?'

'I'm only just starting.'

'If you'll let me go I'll get something on. I can't stand here all night while you mess about.'

Her voice held no particular shade of expression but the words themselves cut through to the core of diffidence in him. He tried to carry it off.

'If you tell me you don't like it I won't believe you.' He brushed his hands lightly over her nipples before drawing away from her. 'I know the signs.'

'It happens when you're cold an' all,' she said. 'And

I'm cold.' She reached for her nightdress and slipped it on. He looked at it with some dismay: winceyette, ankle-length, high-necked, fully concealing.

'What brings that old passion-killer out?'

'My others are in the wash.'

'What, both of them? I don't believe you, Poppy. You're suffering from an attack of the old non-conformist guilt.'

'Oh, you an' your fancy talk. Save it for your book.' She tied the narrow scarlet ribbon at her throat.

'The chapel childhood, Poppy: it goes deeper than you think. Sex a monthly ritual in darkened rooms with a suffocating weight of bedclothes and heavy breathing. I thought we'd agreed that it could be something superbly enjoyable between two grown people, with no strings attached. I thought you'd taught me that.'

'I've taught you nothing,' she said, emotion colouring her voice for the first time. 'Don't you say what I've taught you. You knew all you needed to know when you came here.' She put on her pale-green quilted dressing-gown and walked over to switch on the second bar of the electric fire. The curtains were drawn against the pale darkness and the big-shaded lamp on the bedside cabinet threw a fan of soft light on to the wallpaper behind it. Wilf sat down on the upholstered blanket-chest at the foot of the bed with his hands between his legs. Dismay grew in him. It was over: he knew it surely. It might go on for a time but it would never be the same as before. Already it was spoilt.

'Two grown people,' Poppy said. 'Aye, one of 'em a lad with all his life in front of him and the other a woman with her best years gone. I'm old enough to be your mother, lad. Is what you're talking about the kind of thing your mother 'ud teach you?'

'The world's full of women twenty years older than me who aren't my mother.'

'How many of 'em do you go to bed with? How many of 'em teach you things?' She sat down on a stool facing her dressing-table and picked up a hairbrush, but made no further move to attend to her hair.

'Look, Poppy,' Wilf said, 'we're two people. The twenty years are just . . . just an accident of birth. Nothing.'

'All right, then, if it's nothing why don't we make a right do of it and get married? Eh?' She looked at him through the dressing-table mirror. 'That makes you think, doesn't it? You know that's just plain damn' silly, just like I do.'

'I don't know what's come over you, Poppy. Does liking somebody, being fond of a person and wanting to make love, mean nothing else but marriage? That's surface morality, Poppy. I believe in warm, honest relationships between people.'

'That's a man talking, if ever I heard one,' Poppy said. 'And a young one at that.'

'Oh, sure, bring the battle of the sexes into it and we'll never finish.' He was exasperated. 'What are we looking for, Poppy? Someone to throw the blame on? Are we trying to unload some kind of guilt? Nobody's betrayed anybody. We both knew what was happening, what we were doing.'

'It was my fault,' she said. 'I could have stopped it if I'd wanted to.'

'But you didn't want to, and I'm glad. I'll be eternally grateful that you didn't. Don't you see what it's meant to me, Poppy, all this? Don't you know?' He looked at her through the mirror and his face, despite the lurking exasperation, was tender and fond.

'I could have stopped it before it started,' Poppy said. 'That night you changed the bulb on the landing.'

'You were holding the stepladder because you're always expecting people to fall down. Heights make you dizzy. When I came down you thought I was missing a step and you reached out in the dark and took hold of my arm. Remember how we stood close together for a minute and then I kissed you? What did you say?'

'Something about it being dangerous to kiss widows in the dark.'

'Yes. And I said, "A widow needn't live like a nun. Do you want to live like one?"

' "No," you said, "only I'm particular and that makes a difference." '

'You've got a good memory.'

'It was only four months ago, Poppy. I can remember conversations further back than that. Important conversations. This one was important. I could smell sex and it was exciting. You're a handsome woman; you've looked after yourself. I thought you were giving me an opening and I'm like most young men – I don't look a gift-horse in the mouth. Not an attractive gift-horse like you.'

'All laid on, was it? Only not a gift-horse but an apple. A bit over-ripe but still good for plucking.'

'I can't defend myself, Poppy. There was nothing high-flown about my thoughts. Oh, I liked you as a person the minute I set eyes on you; but this was an unexpected development. I was flattered.'

'It took you long enough to do anything about it.'

'Well, I say I was flattered, but I wasn't sure. I've said you're an attractive woman with a strong personality. I'd have hated to be slapped down. So I waited for the signs and when they came I knew it was all right.'

Through ten days or so he'd waited for the signs, recognising them when they came – the sidelong glance, the unnecessary contact of hands – with a mounting excitement that grew out of the only interpretation he could put on them. In a young girl they could have been the symptoms of infatuation or true love of the virginal romantic kind that took no account of intimacy outside marriage. In a woman of Poppy's age they were the unmistakable evidence of desire. He had put it to the test when she came into his room on some errand and, with thudding heart, he took her in his arms behind the door.

'No,' she said, holding his hands after the kiss; 'not now.'

'Later?'

'Yes, all right.'

'When, tonight?'

'If you like.'

'Yes, yes; I do like.'

Her eyes closed as he kissed her again and her breast rose and fell with her heavy breathing.

'Come up when all the others are in. Don't make any noise. I'll leave the door open.'

Wilf smiled in recollection. 'I thought I was on to a good thing, Poppy. Quite simply, that's how I expressed it to myself. She's dying for it, I thought, and it's all laid on for little me. I don't even have to go out in the rain to collect.'

'I didn't know you could be such a nasty little bugger when you want to be.'

'I can't help the way my body reacts, Poppy. I'm talking about biology.'

'I don't know why you have to talk to me about it. D'you think all this . . . this randy talk makes me feel any better?'

'I'm telling you this so that I can tell you the rest. You see, it wasn't the way you think, the way you make it out to be, at all.'

He shuffled a couple of inches along the chest. He couldn't see Poppy's reflection now. He squeezed his hands, palms together, between his knees, glancing up now and then at Poppy's motionless back.

'Afterwards, after that first time, I found myself full of a tender regard for you. You weren't just someone I'd used and was done with till the next time. I'd always liked you and now I was fond of you. I wished I could do something for you. I wanted . . . I wanted to pluck happiness out of the air and give it to you in gratitude for what you'd given me. These times with you, Poppy, they've been I think the most wonderful thing that ever happened to me. Don't be sorry for them, love.'

It took him a moment to see that she was crying. He

went and stood behind her with his hands on her shoulders.

'What brought all this on, love?'

'There's always strings,' Poppy said. 'You can't get away from 'em. We're not just animals rutting in a ditch, and there's always strings.'

'All strings have to be broken sometime, Poppy. But don't say it hasn't been worth having, because it has.'

'There's just summat not right about it, that's all.'

'It's that girl, isn't it – Marguerite? You've been edgy with me ever since she came.'

Poppy raised her head and dabbed at her eyes with a handkerchief. 'I look at her and I see myself, twenty years ago, full of hope, all my life before me; and I see you standing there with her, the same generation. Seeing you together like that I feel like a mother watching her boy with his girl . . . And when you touch me like you did just now it's like . . . like . . .'

'God, Poppy, you must be mad! I've got a mother, who can give you seven or eight years. One look at her and you'd know how silly all this queer thinking is. And Marguerite, she's nothing to me. Just somebody who lives in the same house. I like her; she's intelligent and attractive. But I don't have to prove anything by trying to make love to her.' He was walking about the room now and he stopped to appeal to her. 'Come on, love, snap out of it. I don't like to see you upset like this.'

Poppy pulled loose strands of hair out of the brush. 'Me flamin' hair's coming out now. I shall have to do summat about it . . . And we shall have to have no more of these debates with her in the next room.' She looked at him standing by the door. 'Where are you going?'

'I reckon I'd better get back downstairs.'

'Don't you want to stay?'

'I haven't been asked.'

'Have you ever needed asking?'

'I do tonight, Poppy. And anyway, I didn't think you were in the mood.'

'I'm not, but I don't want you to leave me on my own. We don't have to do anything every time, do we? Can't you just stay with me?'

'It's asking a lot, Poppy, but I will if you want me to.'

'No, don't laugh. I don't want you to go.'

'All right.'

She looked at him for a long moment of silence, her gaze moving over his face. He wondered what she was thinking. As she finally dropped her glance and got up from the dressing-table he began to undress, scattering his clothes carelessly, and followed her into bed. She switched off the light and lay slightly curled up with her back to him. He fitted his body into the curve of hers and rested his hand, the fingers slightly spread, on her thigh. After a time she took his hand, squeezing it with gentle pressure, and pulled his arm around her. 'Just like an old married couple,' she murmured, and she smiled in the darkness. It was a long time to morning.

Marguerite had lain awake for some time listening to the voices in the next room. She knew only that two people were talking, not what they were saying. She thought that one of them was a man and Wilf Cotton came readily into her mind along with the image, invested with new significance, of Mrs Swallow throwing her arm round him and saying, 'We get on like a house on fire . . .' She would have tried to put an innocent construction on this midnight conversation, but she had heard voices on other nights, not talking at such length, but definitely there. They had stopped now but she'd heard no one leave the room.

So Mrs Swallow was Wilf Cotton's mistress. She accepted the thought without blaming either of them. Poppy was a decent, kindly, straightforward person with a reserve of sympathy and common sense that Marguerite hadn't yet drawn upon, but which she felt instinctively would be hers whenever she chose to ask for it. And she was healthy, presumably with appetites that couldn't simply be damped down when the means of satisfying them were abruptly withdrawn. Why shouldn't they have an affair? There were no loyalties involved on Wilf's side so far as she knew. Poppy was taking nothing that belonged to anybody else. There was buried in the make-up of most Englishwomen the instinct to regard sex as something not quite nice. In some it was deep, in others barely below the surface, a kind of defence mechanism built in through centuries of the development of a society in which the family was the basic unit of stability; and the roots of that unit were grounded in marriage, ideally in the eyes of the church an inviolable, indissoluble union. The passing years could dull appetites and when the ardour of youth was no more than a faded memory the instinct could emerge in the form of intolerance. But when age and experience were combined with circumstances which sharpened natural desires in a woman who was handsome and of good figure, then maturity was in itself a draw because the instinctive in women was instinctively understood by young men. And so two people like Poppy and Wilf came together. They probably made love very satisfactorily, Wilf with a fervour which Poppy would moderate to the gentle lingering enjoyment of pleasure for pleasure's sake where there was no need for the hurried appeasement of hunger.

Suddenly her eyes were smarting. She should never have gone back there tonight. She hadn't realised that her memories were quite so vivid. Seen from their correct distance of years, free from present associations, they had become something sad in her past. Now it was as though everything was telescoped into an unhappy yesterday: the fire, her father, Uncle Edward and Aunt Martha, the loneliness of London, Floyd, everything. It bore down on her in an accumulated weight of grief that was almost insupportable. She let the tears come. She had never thought of herself as the crying kind. But what did it matter? Who was there to see? She turned to the wall and hid her face from the dark.

Wilf woke about five. He was glad, because Poppy was an early riser. He reached out to her through the cocoon of warmth. It was a wonderful peaceful time. Her nightdress had ridden up in her sleep and he put his hand on the heat of her skin and caressed the curve of her hip. She came drowsily awake, conscious of his presence, and murmured a request for the time. 'Five o'clock,' he said, his lips against her ear. 'Loving time.' He shifted his hand and she turned slightly towards him, moving her legs.

'You devil. You think you can get me while I'm half asleep, don't you?'

'I can get you any time. I know what you like.'

'You clever devil. How d'you know?'

'You showed me, love.'

'Yes, I did.'

'That's what you like, isn't it?'

'Mmm.' She took his hand.

'I'd forgotten, though,' he said. 'We said we wouldn't.'

'Give up.'

'You said you didn't want to.'

'I'll push you out if you don't stop plaguing me.'

'Perhaps I'd better go before it's too late.'

'That's a rotten trick to play on an old woman.'

'Who's an old woman?'

'Me. I am.'

'A lovely, lovely old woman.'

'Get on! How am I lovely?'

'You want me to tell you?'

'Yes, tell me.'

'Sure I won't make you blush?'

'I don't care.'

'Well first of all I love the way your glass eye changes colour when you're annoyed, and your wooden leg sends me into raptures every time I see it . . .'

'Can't you be serious?'

'If I get serious we might do something you'd regret.'

'You'd better go, then, if that's the way you feel.'

'Okay.'

'Go on, then. You can't catch me now. I'm awake.'

'I couldn't catch you anyway when you've got that blasted bell tent on.'

'You're not doing so bad.'

He put his head down on her shoulder and moved his hand to her waist to hold her tight.

'Ah, Poppy, no more daft talk, no more soul-searching.'

'You do love me a little bit, don't you?'

'You know I do, Poppy. You know I do.'

She turned fully towards him and took hold of him, drawing him to her. Then there were no more words. She sighed as he came to her. He strained against the pressure of her hands on his back, exulting in the greed with which she took from him. That was what she did for him. He felt that he could do anything.

11

He had struck a bad patch with the novel. For four or five weeks now it had been doing well, the sheaf of type-written sheets thickening in the folder; and now he'd reached this stage where he was rewriting and destroying the same few pages time after time. It wouldn't go forward.

He didn't connect it at all with the change in Poppy's attitude since Marguerite came into the house; but it was, all the same, part of his debt to Poppy, a part he hadn't touched on in his explanation to her, that their relationship in eliminating the nag of unsatisfied sex, had given him a basis of emotional calm which could only be beneficial to the peaceful progress of his work. Well, not exactly peaceful, for the rub of creative desire could be appeased only by words on paper and they sometimes came very slowly. Fast or slow they were too often, to a greater or lesser degree, an inadequate manifestation of his high hopes and ideas. The occasional rewards came when the reading back showed something well done within the limits of his ability and, more important, revealed signs of that ability's potential for expansion with time and application.

Time and application . . . All the time he wanted to spend outside that claimed by the job he couldn't afford to discard. And application commensurate with the intensity of his determination to prove himself as a writer. In what she gave him Poppy was better than any wife and he doubted if any wife would have tolerated his self-imposed routine. He didn't need a wife with all the emotional entanglements of marriage and, worse, the possible demands of a family. He'd left home to free himself from the strain of living with other people and he wasn't hankering after a condition still more binding. Basically, he wanted someone to feed him, to clean his room, to send his shirts to the laundry. An opportunity for regular lovemaking he hadn't expected. But Poppy gave him this and looked to his other needs too, yet left him free to pursue his own routine. There were no demands on either side. Their relationship was, to him, ideal and would hardly have been possible had the gap between their ages not been so great as virtually to rule out all thought of any more permanent arrangement. 'You know it's plain damn' silly,' she'd said and he'd heard it with some relief, glad that she'd said it and not he. But, as she also said, there were always strings: you couldn't go to bed regularly with someone without some kind of emotional situation growing beside the physical one. He was selfish enough to hope that Poppy's apparent pre-occupation with their different ages, or whatever it was that was bothering her lately, would be just a passing thing. He liked things as they were. He liked them very much. He was lucky and he knew it. And he knew that it would be senseless to get any more deeply involved than they already were. After all, they'd both had a great deal from the affair as it was. Poppy as well as himself. Perhaps the trouble was that they both knew it would have to end one day and each of them viewed it from opposite ends of twenty years of life. It was easy for him to visualise a general picture of a future without Poppy; but what kind of future did she see? It seemed to him now that she saw a bleak prospect and this was something he couldn't altogether understand. He wondered why she didn't set out seriously to find a husband, why she hadn't done it long ago.

His other present needs satisfied, it was intellectual

stimulus that he missed, especially now, when the work was giving trouble. Not that he wanted to discuss immediate problems with anybody else – a book was, to him, a kind of inner vision carried about by the writer and the place for it to come out was on paper, not in conversation – but there was a level of general conversation, a contact with like-minded people, that would to some extent have relieved the feeling he often had of working in complete isolation. Among the people he mixed with every day there was no one who had any more interest in books than a liking for the occasional good read. There was certainly nobody with any idea of a writer's problems. Outside the office, apart from the occasional evening's drinking with colleagues, he spent long hours in writing or walking the streets of the city alone, not consciously looking for copy but thinking, observing, storing up impressions. He was fond of the cinema and earlier in their relationship he'd given an evening a week to taking Poppy to the local flea-pit. But with steadily diminishing audiences the management had looked for a more lucrative attraction to offer the public, and found it in bingo. Somehow they never thought of going into the city together. He supposed there must be some kind of intellectual society in the town – other writers, painters, musicians, plus the people who existed at the fringe of all creative activity, those who talked about everything but did nothing, and were useful because of this – but he'd never looked for it and it had certainly never looked for him. The members of the real, the active, literary world, who displayed their wares in the Sunday papers and the weekly reviews, those people who, according to the authors of numerous articles and books on publishing and agency, went to any lengths to seek out and encourage new talent – they treated him with a disregard so sublime it could only be accounted for as simple uncaring ignorance of his very existence. The literary world's response to his two broadcast stories and the sketch in

Etude had been nil. No letters from editors asking for short stories, no approach from publishers suggesting that he try a novel and let *them* see it first. Nothing, except a note, forwarded by the BBC, from an expatriate Yorkshirewoman living in Bournemouth who had been moved to nostalgic tears by the background of one of his stories. He was learning that the often praised freedom and independence of the writer was a two-edged sword. He was learning also that failure could breed its own peculiar arrogance. When you had work to show it spoke for itself; when you had nothing, or little, there was only your own conviction of ultimate success to protect you from the indifference of others. To the score of fiction editors who had returned his work he said now with silent defiance, 'All right, then; but one day you'll come to me.' And the cry, backed by nothing but his own confidence in his talent, made the wilderness an easier place to bear. It put a limit, though undefined, on the length of time he would have to live there.

This confidence was basic, the only thing that had kept him going for so long. The other kind of confidence, the superficial day-to-day kind, ebbed and flowed according to the state of the work. When it was on the ebb, as now, he wondered if he would ever see the end of the novel, even if he was a novelist at all. He loved the effect of the written word, as opposed to the drama, and in that medium the short story form with its paring away of inessentials, its evocation of mood or atmosphere made with a few sharp strokes, and its illumination of character at some crucial stage in its development. But he recognised that the challenge to him as a writer lay in the extended narrative and the character development demanded by the novel. It was an awe-inspiring experience, he thought, to sit at the wrong end of 80,000 or 100,000 words and wonder if you had a novel at all. You wondered how much you ought to know before you began, how much should be planned and how much left to grow out of itself. And you had little experience to guide you. The main thing you knew was to beware of plot. You knew from early experiments with the short story that to the inexperienced writer plot could be very much a mixed blessing. The anecdote that could be told in a hundred words was, quite simply, best told in that hundred words, and complete in itself. The deception of plot was that it left nothing to be developed on paper. It sprang fully fledged into the mind at night and you couldn't wait for a chance to write it down. When you'd finished the pieces of the jigsaw fitted together but the people remained pictures pasted flat on cardboard. It was the failing of so many detective stories: the puzzle was all. But it should be the people. The people were everything.

While he knew the barren feeling with which he sometimes sat down to work only to find it fructifying as words generated words, one sentence leading to two, the sentence becoming a paragraph, the paragraphs growing into pages, he recognised too the futility of chasing the words when they had remained persistently absent for two hours, and he pushed away the typewriter, gathered his papers together, and stood up. Tomorrow would be better. He opened the folder and fingered the reassuring wad of typescript. As in other experiences in life you thought you were alone; yet literary commentary was full of the troubles of writers – better writers than he would ever be – who had got stuck and had to struggle to work a piece out of the morass. He reassured himself as he put away his things by thinking of examples. There was Dostoyevsky with all those abortive story plans for *The Idiot* and Flaubert in his endless search for *le mot juste*. And many a professional writer found a thousand words in a morning adequate. A thousand words – four pages of typescript – and here he was in the dumps if he didn't fill six or seven sheets in every evening session of three hours.

He opened the door of his room with the intention of going across the hall to watch television in Poppy's kitchen; but saw Marguerite coming down the stairs.

She said hello. 'Has the muse departed for tonight?'

'It struck me about seven and I struck it back. I haven't seen it since.'

She laughed. She was wearing that green suède jacket with a silk scarf tied round her neck.

'Going out?'

'Just to post a letter.'

He stood there indecisively. 'I was going to gawp at the telly but I suppose I could do with some air. D'you mind if I walk along with you?' He dived back into his room and pulled on a heavy long-sleeved sweater and joined her at the front door.

'How's life in the jam trade?'

'I beg your pardon.'

'The job; how's it going?'

'I would ask you, sir, to refrain from adopting that condescending attitude towards the commodities whose sale provides me with my livelihood.'

'Blimey!'

'And I'd have you know that not only do we fill the family's jam-pot, we also put the sugar in their tea, the butter on their bread and the currants and raisins in their spotted dog. Moreover, apart from these everyday necessities we handle nuts, dates, figs—'

'And all the spices of the Orient,' Wilf chipped in.

'Oh, very romantic, it is. You've no idea. I droop over my invoices and dream of faraway places—'

'Of Wazirs and Viziers, Sultans and Sheikhs, Maharajahs and Grand Panjandrums.' He clapped his hands. 'Bring on the dancing girls and fetch me my aftershave lotion.'

'Now don't get carried away or you'll have the police on to us.'

'How can you be such a killjoy? There I was, being transported from my daily round of totting up wages for totties who make shirts and you bring me back to earth with talk of the police.'

'You must have had a good session.'

'On the contrary, I've had a very bad one. I haven't written an acceptable word since about ten minutes past seven. You'd know if it had gone well because I'd be all moody and irritable.'

'Oh, I see.'

'You know you don't at all really.'

'Well now you mention it, no I don't.'

'Well that's all right, then. I thought for a minute you were one up on me.'

'You know you're not always as exhausting as this to talk to. What's the matter?'

'Oh, I'm flushed with failure, that's all. Anyway, you don't have to knock yourself out. Once you get me going you can just sit back and listen.'

'Thank you.'

'Especially when I've had a couple of pints.'

'Oh?'

'Yes. Which leads me to suggest that we might stroll on after posting your letter and have one together.'

'A pint?'

'If you like pints, yes. If not I'm sure they can cater to your tastes.'

'Is there a decent pub near here?'

'The Tower up on the main road isn't bad. Some Beaton of the brewery trade had been tarting it up a bit lately but it's still possible to sit in there without too much discomfort. The main thing is they keep good beer.'

'Let's do that, then.'

He leaned with his arm on top of the pillar-box as she slipped the letter through the slot.

'There, that's on its way.'

'All for the price of the threepenny stamp. Marvellous institution, the postal service.'

'You don't have to go into raptures about it; it's been in operation a long time.'

'That's the point: we tend to take these things for granted.'

She patted his hand. 'Well you just write to the Postmaster General and tell him how much you appreciate his efforts. It'll make his day after all the complaints he must get.'

'From the kind of person who wraps jelly in brown paper and wonders why it doesn't get there . . . Anyway, I have a thing about the post.'

'Really?'

'No, seriously, I mean. You see, I know that when success arrives it'll be the postman who'll bring it.'

'You mean one of these days there'll be an ordinary everyday rattle of the letter-box and an ordinary everyday-looking envelope on the mat; but when you open it – bingo! life will be changed?'

'Something like that.'

'Well I hope it comes true for you.'

'Oh, it will,' he said. 'It will.'

The big asphalted parking ground along two sides of the pub had a lot of cars in it.

'It looks as though it might be crowded,' Marguerite said.

'Oh, a lot of those cars will have brought just one or two people. It is popular, though. Since they renovated it it's become rather fashionable with the people who like to drive out for a drink.'

The main road was carrying a heavy stream of evening traffic and they paused on the kerb till the lights changed. Halfway across Wilf slapped his trousers pockets.

'Now that's very stupid of me.'

'What is?'

'I've invited you for a drink and I don't think I've any money . . . Hang on; yes, half a crown. That won't take us far.'

'I have some loose change. Here – two and eleven, three and tuppence, three and eight. You take this before we go in.'

'No, I can't do that.'

'Why not?'

'Well, I invited you.'

'And now you can't pay. But I still want the drink.'

'All right. I'll give it you back later.'

The pub was doing a healthy trade but the lounge was not crowded to the stage of discomfort it almost always reached on weekend evenings and they had no trouble in finding seats at the far end of the thickly carpeted room from the bar, under whose canopy the bright lights blazed and were reflected in the mirrored wall behind the glass shelves of liqueur and spirits bottles. A white-jacketed waiter with straight straw-coloured hair and a cyst on his nose came and took their order.

'A pint of bitter and . . .' Wilf looked at Marguerite.

'Oh . . . a lime and lager, please.'

The waiter went away and Marguerite said, 'I'd have had a gin and bitter lemon but we're economising aren't we?' She smiled at him.

Her teeth, he noticed, were good. He'd never really been so close to her before with nothing to do but think how attractive she was. He wondered if she'd ever gone all the way with a man and thought that he wouldn't push her out of *his* bed anyway. Intelligent, too. Very. The kind of woman you could talk to happily for more than five minutes was rarer than the kind you could imagine yourself making love to. And the combination of the two was rarer still. Well *he* hadn't met it. Something of a mystery girl as well. No background. Had a job in London then decided to come back here where she'd never been since childhood. Now why?

'I haven't any cigarettes,' she said.

'Would you like me to get you some out of your money?'

'No, it doesn't matter. I'm not frantic.'

She rested her elbows on the little table and folded her hands under her chin. Her gaze swept briefly round the room then came back to him.

'How is it going really?'
'What, the novel?'
'Uh, uh.'
'Oh, basically pretty well, I think. Give me another three months and I'll tell you better.'
'Tell me, do you dash it all off, then go back to revise, or do you revise as you go along?'
'I don't think dashing it off is a very accurate description of my methods of composition, but apart from that, I use the first method.'
'It's one of the things I've wondered when reading novels.'
'Oh, don't take me as a criterion. There must be almost as many methods as there are writers. The thing with me is that I'm a learner.'
'I wouldn't say that. That sketch of yours in *Etude* was very professional. Very good, I thought.'
'You said so before.'
'Did I? Well it is.'
'There's a big difference between that sort of thing and a novel, and the biggest and most obvious difference is in the length.'
'I've noticed that.'
'Yes, well. The first thing that strikes you when you start a novel is that you don't really know if you have a novel. You don't know if what you're saying will work out to novel length. You can test the value of a short story in a night or two, but with a novel this process might take a year.'
'I see.'
She sat back so that the waiter could put down their drinks, then leaned forward again, one hand fingering her glass.
'So the big thing is to get it down as quickly as possible and make sure the novel is really there. To reassure yourself, as it were. Am I boring you? You ask what seems like a simple question and come in for all this.'
'No, go on, please.'

'Well, secondly, without previous experience of writing about characters at length it's not easy to think those characters out too deeply before you start. So you find yourself learning about them as you write. This means that since you presumably know more about them at the end than you did at the beginning you must go back and revise in the light of that increased knowledge.'

'Yes, but this seems to suggest that you don't know a great deal about the plot before you begin.'

'Please, don't use that word.'

'Which word?'

'Plot. I hate it. I'm a lousy hand at plots and the more I write the more I feel that it isn't at all a bad handicap to have.'

'Well, story, then.'

'All right, story. How much story? You may have heard of novelists to whom a novel unreeled itself like a film before they put a word on paper. I think this is rare and if it happened to me, which isn't likely, I'd distrust it. You see, what happens to people in real life can often seem completely arbitrary, the unpredictable workings of fate, as it were. The field of accident and coincidence. Life is always open to the effects of accident and coincidence but in fiction it must be used sparingly or you rob the story of any credibility and significance in terms of human action. You know Thomas Hardy? You know the feeling you sometimes get in Hardy that the people don't stand a chance whatever they do because there's a malicious providence hovering nearby all the time to wreck their plans? Well, apart from this element what happens to people is largely dependent upon what kind of people they are. This is the interesting thing about people. Anybody can get knocked down in the street and be crippled for life. But the interesting thing is what they make of it and this is dependent upon character and personality.'

'What you're saying is that the story comes out of the people and not the reverse.'

'Yes. How can you know the story if you don't know the people? You have to be a peculiar type of writer, better than I am at present, to invent real people who will fit into a preconceived plot. I'm talking now, of course, about plots of a fairly complex type.'

'So how much do you start with?'

'It depends what kind of book you're writing. You could write a story about a man who was convicted of murder, but was innocent. That would be full of the field of accident and interesting because of it. Or you could want to write a story about the business world and start by assembling a group of characters whose personalities and ambitions were likely to bring them into conflict with one another and start from there. In that case you might start with people who were mere types, flat characters recognisable by one significant character trait, but you'd hope that in writing about them you'd be able to bring them to life.'

Marguerite sipped her drink and Wilf took the opportunity of gulping at his beer. The glass was half-empty when he set it down.

'Mmm, I was ready for that.'

'I'm not altogether with you yet,' she said. 'My life, for instance, would make a very poor novel from your point of view because it's been full of incidents over which I'd no control.'

'The interesting part is your reactions. What you did after the incident took place.'

'In one case I had no choice. I was a child and I did as I was told.'

'No physical choice, you mean. But what about your mental reactions? Surely they were a result of both the incident and the course of action imposed upon you afterwards? And I should imagine, if you're referring to a major incident, that both factors could be partly responsible for the kind of person you are now. But only partly. There's always the freedom of choice. We can resist the influence of events. Not totally, but to some extent.'

She nodded without answering. He knew he was talking too much but she didn't appear to mind. In fact, she seemed genuinely interested. It was a change to be able to get it all into words.

'For instance,' he said, 'suppose we were the characters in a novel . . . Now our sitting here together is a result of pure accident, the accident of our both choosing the same house to live in. We can accept this providing we also accept other conditions. What I mean is that we can't dismiss the accident business altogether. It's an accident when two brothers have the kind of temperaments that generate conflict. It's an accident when a board of directors is composed of people who can't see eye to eye. But it's the conflict that interests, so we must accept the initial accident of the characters coming together. Here we are, then. Where do we go from here?'

'You're the writer. You tell me.'

'Well, let me see. Obviously if we're the main characters it's what happens after we meet that matters. But why we're here is perhaps important as well because it may help to show what kind of people we are. That we're both here together is accidental; that each of us is here is because of his own reasons. All right, let's start with me. I come from a mining village in South Yorkshire. I was a wages clerk at a pit. But I wanted to become a writer and I felt inhibited by family and village life. I wanted the anonymity that living in a larger town can give and the freedom to live my own life. So one day I packed my bag and here I am. In your case there seems to be a stronger link because you were a child here. Why are you here?'

The sudden direct question brought a little half smile to her face as she lifted her glass. 'It's a long story.'

He smiled himself. 'There you are.'

'You've proved your point.'

'Well I certainly made it at length.'

'The audience was entertained.'

He inclined his head. 'Thank you.' Another long drink and his glass was empty. He spread coins on the table. 'Will the exchequer run to another round? Yes, I think so. Same again for you?'

'Please.'

He signalled to the waiter and gave the order.

'I notice,' he said, 'that you very skilfully evaded the question and my long lead-up went for nothing.'

'You didn't go to all that trouble just to get me to talk about myself.'

'No, but it was a little unsatisfactory when you didn't follow through.'

'Sorry.'

He waited. 'There, you've done it again.'

'Have I?'

'Yes, you know you have.'

Three young fellows in casually worn good clothes came through the door, talking and laughing together, and approached the bar. Wilf saw Marguerite's eyes focus on them and when one of them turned and, seeing her, raised his eyebrows and lifted his hand she acknowledged him with a nod of her head and a little smile.

'Friends of yours?'

'No. The one I nodded to is Stephen Hollis. His father owns the concern I work for.'

'Not the Grand Panjandrum himself, but the Crown Prince.'

'That's right.'

He watched as the trio were served at the bar and carried their own glasses of whisky and bottles of Schweppes' dry ginger to a nearby table. He thought that Hollis was interested in Marguerite and he found a small feeling of pleasure in the advantage of already being in her company.

'How well do you know him?'

'Mister Stephen? I've spoken to him three or four times. I have very little contact with him.'

'Mister Stephen, eh?'

'Everybody refers to him in that way. He's working his way through the firm.'

Wilf said, 'It reminds me of the American industrialist who called one of his men to his office one day. "My boy," he said, "you came into this firm on the shop floor. In three months you were foreman of your department; in six months you were manager of a whole section; in another three months you were production manager and three months after that you were made a vice-president. There hasn't been a success story like yours in the entire history of the concern and now there's a vacant seat on the board and we're going to give it to you. Now whad'ya say to that?" "Gee, thanks, Dad." '

'Don't look now,' Marguerite said, 'but your prejudices are showing.'

'They often do. It's like I was saying to Poppy the other night—' He stopped, momentarily confused, on the verge of indiscretion.

'What?'

'Oh, just that a person's upbringing leaves a deeper impression than one thinks. I don't think you can ever quite emancipate yourself from the first twenty years of your life.'

'Or the first nine, for that matter.'

He looked at her quickly. 'The first nine in your case?'

She nodded.

'That was the time you spent here as a child?'

'Yes.'

'I always think the formative years extend well beyond nine.'

'In any case, though, the life I led after nine was very different from that before.'

He waited for her to go on and when she didn't, said, 'I see.' He didn't but he was too polite to press her to talk if she didn't want to.

12

Their glasses were empty. It wasn't yet closing time but they hadn't enough money to buy anything else.

'I suppose we'd better go,' Marguerite said.

'I suppose so.'

They stood up and he followed her out of the room. Hollis looked up from his conversation with his cronies and waved good night to Marguerite. Wilf gazed with admiration at her legs as he walked behind her. He couldn't blame Hollis for being interested. No man who wasn't altogether past it could fail to appreciate how attractive she was. He felt a curious spasm of something like jealousy at the thought of her and Hollis becoming more friendly. He dismissed it as a natural male reaction. She was nothing to him: just an attractive, likeable, intelligent girl. Nothing more. Let men like Hollis use their cars and money in the campaign of conquest; he had Poppy to keep him happy. Poppy with the warm firm flesh into which he could sink and lose the cares of the world outside. Beer heightened his sensuality and he thought with happiness of Poppy moving about her room, complimenting him with her very nakedness, the shadows cast by the bedside lamp sculpting deep the curves of breasts and thighs.

They crossed the road again, in the dusk, and walked down the avenue.

'Don't you find a provincial city hopelessly dull after living in London?' he asked Marguerite.

'Oh, I don't know so much. There is more distraction in

London but a great deal of it costs money. You can't go to theatres and concerts every night on a typist's wages.'

'No, but the people.'

'There are people anywhere. You can be more lonely in London than anywhere else in England. You've got to find the people there just as you have in other places. That takes time. You might think of London being full of writers and artists and the like, but I never met any writers while I was there.' She turned her head and smiled at him. 'I had to come back to the provinces to do that.'

'But that's not why you came back.'

'No.' After a moment she said, 'I don't really know why I did come back. I had a definite reason for leaving London – a personal one – but why I chose to come here is something I can only vaguely explain to myself. I was free to go anywhere in the country and heaven knows there are more obviously attractive places to live ... Why did you come here? I thought London was the mecca for writers and artists.'

'It is; but the life up here is what I want to write about and I don't see any point in leaving it yet.'

'Do you live in the future?'

'Yes, I'm afraid I do, quite a lot. Not too far ahead, though I have milestones and the first is completion and acceptance of my novel.'

'And after that?'

'Publication and critical success combined with nice fat sales.'

'Oh, oh! you want the bun *and* the penny. You don't scorn the filthy lucre, then?'

'Who does? Money to me means independence. But if I'd written primarily to make money I'd have given it up long ago. It's a funny thing, though, this business of living in the future – wishing your time away, my mother calls it – because as soon as you reach one milestone you find yourself looking at the next one.'

'And merrily to the grave.'

'Yes. And particularly foolish today because what's to say somebody won't send off a few rockets and wipe all the milestones out?'

'Do you feel strongly about it – the bomb and all that?'

'I think it's an abomination, but I live like most people, keeping it out of my mind as much as possible. I'm not given to sitting down in Trafalgar Square and advocating national suicide, so there's not much else I can do. I sometimes think the entire world is steadily going round the twist. The only hope I have is that we can all walk the tightrope until the people in charge come to their senses.'

'You haven't much of a policy, have you?'

'Who has, or one that makes sense? The quicker the Russians realise that the Western position is basically one of goodwill and negotiate seriously before the hot-heads who want a war now and get it over with are given a free hand, the better.'

'There is quite a lot to be said for the Russian point of view.'

'Yes, there is. And when you've said it you're still left with a bunch of cynical power-seeking bastards who'll tell you black is white if it suits their purpose. I don't like totalitarianism of either the right or the left.'

'So we all walk the tightrope and wait for it to come right?'

'Yes, we do, the ordinary people. We only vote the so-and-so's in; we can't do their job for them.'

'And suppose it doesn't come right?'

'I know. I see newsreel pictures of some crowd of mad sods acting the goat on the East-West border in Berlin and my blood runs cold. But underneath all that I think it'll come out right. It has to or there's no point in anything.'

'Does there have to be a point? You sound as though you believe in God.'

'Do I?'

'Do you believe?'

He hesitated. It was all very well to turn it over in your mind and form private conclusions which could be modified to suit changing events and emotions with no reference to anyone else. But to lay it out flat and emphatic to someone virtually a stranger was a different matter.

'No,' he said, 'I don't.'

She was silent for a moment in turn. Then she said, 'I gather that it's not so much not believing as not accepting.'

He looked sideways at her. 'Smart, aren't you?'

'Oh, not so smart.'

'What about you? Do you believe?'

She gave a short laugh, shying from the question as she had shied from others this evening. 'Ask me tomorrow.'

'And what does that mean?'

'Oh, it's a catchphrase of mine. I lived with an aunt who became increasingly neurotic as she grew older. There came a time when she could hardly reach a decision about anything. "Ask me tomorrow," she'd say. "Ask me tomorrow." '

'And when tomorrow came, the same answer?'

'Yes, I'm afraid so. Until, in the end, she had to be taken away to a place where all the decisions were made for her.'

There was a light on in the hall but the front door was on the latch as it always was in the evening.

'Have you got your key?' Wilf asked Marguerite.

He opened the door and handed the key back to her.

'I wonder if Poppy's got any cocoa going,' he said. 'Let's go and see, shall we?'

They went along and past the stairs and opened the kitchen door. Poppy was sitting by the fire with a mug in her hands.

'Nothing interesting on television, Poppy?'

'I don't want to look at it. I've got a splitting head. You two been out, have you?'

'Just up to the Tower.'

'I thought you'd be working.'

'I was but I gave it up.'

'Something more interesting to do, I suppose.'

Marguerite was beginning to look uncomfortable.

He said mildly, 'Drop the cross-examination, will you, Poppy? I'm not a child and you're not my mother.'

She flashed a look at him. 'No, so you say.'

'I think I'll be going up,' Marguerite said, but Wilf lifted his hand to keep her.

'No, don't go, Marguerite. We haven't had our cocoa. We were wondering if there was any cocoa in the offing, Poppy.'

Poppy set aside her mug and got up out of her chair. She swayed slightly on her feet and closed her eyes for several seconds.

'You don't look well,' Marguerite said. 'Are you all right?'

'I feel as if I've a bout of 'flu coming on,' Poppy said. She stood with one hand on the mantelshelf. 'You'll have to see to your own cocoa: I'm going up to bed.'

'Shall I come with you and see that you're all right?' Marguerite moved towards Poppy round the big square table.

'I can manage. You stop and get your cocoa.'

'I'll see to that,' Wilf said. 'You go up with her, Marguerite, and tuck her in.'

'Oh, don't talk so daft,' Poppy said in sudden low-pitched fury. 'Have you had too much to drink, or summat?'

Wilf raised his eyebrows, but said nothing.

Marguerite opened the door. 'Come along. I'll just go up with you. It's no trouble.'

'Have a good night's sleep, Poppy love,' Wilf said. 'You'll perhaps feel better in the morning.'

'I'd better,' Poppy said, 'or you'll all go out without breakfast.'

Marguerite said, 'You make the cocoa, Wilf. I won't be long.'

'I'll see she hurries back,' Poppy said.

He was sitting in Poppy's armchair with two mugs of

steaming cocoa on the table behind him when Marguerite came back.

'I didn't sugar yours because I don't know how much you take,' he said. 'Is she all right?'

'I think so.' Marguerite put sugar into the cocoa and stirred it, then sat down in the other chair. 'She probably does far too much work.'

Wilf jerked his thumb over the back of the chair. 'She's been ironing tonight while we were out. There's a couple of my shirts that she wouldn't let me send to the laundry. She goes into my room while I'm out at work and the next thing I know my stuff's washed and ironed.'

'We should have taken her with us to the pub and given her a change.'

'Yes. I didn't think of going for a drink, though, till we'd got along the road . . . She's a duck, Poppy is. One of the best.' The beer, consumed half an hour ago, was now taking its full effect and adding to the sentimentality of his feeling for Poppy. On six or seven pints he could probably have wept over her goodness.

'I like her,' Marguerite said.

'Is she in bed now?'

'Yes, all tucked in. I filled a hot-water bottle for her in the bathroom.'

'She'll probably be all right in the morning.'

'Yes.'

'She'll get up anyway, if I know her.'

They sipped the hot cocoa.

'This is good,' Marguerite said. 'You must have a knack.'

'Just one of my minor accomplishments. Would you like a biscuit? There should be a tin about somewhere.'

Marguerite said no. 'I was a bit taken aback when I saw her bedroom,' she said. 'It's beautifully furnished, isn't it?'

'Yes. Yes, it is.'

'The carpet, and that lovely white candlewick bedspread.'

'Yes, they are nice.' He wondered if he should invent and deliver some casual explanation of how he came to be familiar with the inside of Poppy's room, but contented himself with adding, 'Poppy likes nice things.'

'Her underwear as well.'

'Oh?' Here he had to feign ignorance.

'Well, perhaps I shouldn't have mentioned it. I shouldn't want to embarrass her . . .'

'She's not listening.'

'No. Still, I won't go into details.'

He looked up and their eyes met for an instant. He wondered then if she could possibly be ever so gently taking the mickey. Did she know that his relationship with Poppy was more intimate than it appeared to be on the surface? But her eyes left his and he thought perhaps not. He didn't know.

'Sure you don't want anything to eat?'

'I don't think so.' She looked into the low fire. 'It's nice and cosy here, isn't it? Just like home.'

'Yes, it is.' He got up. 'I'm a bit peckish. I think there should be a basin of pork dripping somewhere.' He went into the scullery and presently returned with a plate of bread spread with the dripping. He held it out to her. 'Here, try some of this. I dug down to the bottom for the brown bits.'

She took a half-slice and bit into it. 'Mmm, it's delicious. Mucky fat. It's years and years since I've had any.'

He was grinning.

'What's wrong?'

'I'm smiling at the way you use north-country expressions in your refined voice.'

'Oh dear, is my voice refined?'

'Not affected. I didn't mean that. It's accentless, though.'

'It wasn't always, I can tell you. There was a time when I talked as broad as anybody; and I could swear as well. I was an embarrassment for a long time to my aunt and uncle.'

'Where did they live?'

'In Amhurst, a rather snooty country town in Gloucestershire.'

'You went to live with them when you left here, at – what was it – nine?'

'Yes.' She reached out to the plate. 'May I have some more?'

'Sure.' He pushed the plate towards her. 'I cut enough for two. I thought you might be tempted.'

'Sly thing.'

He watched her slender fingers fold the bread and carry it to her mouth. Her tongue flicked out across her lips and took a stray crumb.

He said, 'Were you an orphan?'

'Not exactly. My mother died when I was nearly six, but my father's alive today for all I know.'

'You mean you've no idea where he is?'

'None at all. Perhaps here somewhere, but I don't know.'

'Is there no way you can trace him?'

'I haven't tried. I haven't seen him since I first left here as a child. I probably wouldn't know him and I doubt if he'd recognise me.'

'This aunt and uncle: they'd be your mother's relatives?'

'Yes. My aunt Martha was my mother's eldest sister. There was another one in between them but she was drowned in a troopship disaster during the war. She was a nursing sister. My mother's people were well-to-do tradespeople in Aldershot. My father was a regular soldier before the war and the family were scandalised when she married beneath her. No, don't grunt like that. She really did marry beneath her. She was worth ten of him. He was kindly enough in a rough, offhand sort of way, but he could be a brute when the mood was on him. I don't think he ever beat my mother but he did me – only once really badly, I'll say that for him, and he was in a highly emotional state at the time – and he got three months in prison for it.'

'And the authorities took you out of his custody?'

'In a way, yes. I don't think he cared. Anyway, he never made any attempt to see me again as far as I know.'

'You have no brothers or sisters?'

'No.'

They heard the front door open with a crash, then the high-pitched squeak of a woman's voice in the hall.

Wilf said, 'It sounds as if Sylvia's home early tonight.' He got up and went to the door and opened it a couple of inches. There was a man with her. He couldn't make out what the man was saying but he could imagine from the snatches of Sylvia's voice which reached him.

'. . . too late. You'll have the house up . . . never did promise. It's against the rules . . . get me thrown out . . . home to your wife . . . I can't help that, can I? You men, you're all alike . . . yes, tomorrow, if you behave . . . that's enough o' that . . .' There was a short silence, then, 'That's enough . . .'

He closed the door and returned to his chair. 'Struggling for her honour on the doorstep. I've seen the day when she'd have had him quietly inside and upstairs. Only Poppy laid the law down.'

'Straitlaced is she, Poppy?'

He looked at her but the eyes which met his were bland.

'She's no spoilsport, but with Sylvia it's a different one every week. As far as I can make out she's next door to being on the game and Poppy can't afford to let the house get a reputation.'

'What does Sylvia do for a living?'

'Oh, she seems to drift from job to job. Waitress, barmaid, millhand; work in factories. She's done practically everything a woman can do without any particular training. She's nearly always behind with the rent. Poppy's threatened to get rid of her many a time; but every now and then she'll be in funds and pay some of it off. And Poppy's as soft as a brush really. She thinks if she chucks Sylvia out it'll help her along the downward path . . .'

He cocked his ear at the door. 'It sounds as if she's coming in here.'

The door was flung open and Sylvia stood in the opening. She blinked in the light, turning her sharp thin face from one to the other of them. Her dark blonde hair was dishevelled. She pushed a lock of it back from her cheek. She was dressed up tonight, in a dark-blue out-of-fashion costume which, rather grotesque though it was, Wilf thought a pleasant change from the matted and shrunken jumpers she usually wore round the house. He thought it unfortunate for her in her life that she started from the disadvantage of being unattractive. Not that it seemed to stop her finding men friends, of a sort.

'You two havin' a nice cosy little supper by the fire, are you? Where's Poppy?'

'In bed,' Wilf said. 'She wasn't feeling too good.'

'That's all right, then. I thought she might have heard that performance at the door.'

'What performance was that?'

'Don't tell me you didn't hear anything. I was near to shoutin' me head off at the end. Bloody men.' She moved, a trifle unsteadily, towards the table, propped herself against it with one hand and reached down with the other to remove her left shoe and rub her foot. 'Buy you a couple o' shorts and they think they own you.' She glared at Marguerite as though she had caught her out in some appalling indiscretion. 'Best piece of advice I can give you is keep your knees together and don't let 'em get you on your own in a car. I wouldn't ha' got out o' that one when I did if he hadn't thought he was goin' straight upstairs to bed.'

'I think I can take care of myself,' Marguerite said.

'Aye, don't we all. Married, that one. Worse than the single 'uns. Allus after a bit o' novelty. Oh, don't start thinkin' I'm a prude or owt like that. I like a bit o' fun meself and I've had a bit in me time – after all, life's short, in't it; we're here today an' God knows where tomorrow. But I am a bit particular an' it's comin' to a pretty pass when you can't exchange a friendly word with a chap wi'out him expectin' you to strip off for him. I hope I'm not embarrassin' you, love, talkin' like this in front of Wilf here . . .'

'Don't mind me,' Wilf said.

'. . . but a bit o' plain speakin's very useful now an' again, I allus think; an' it's a job if a lass can't take a bit o' good advice from an older woman.' She sniggered suddenly. 'Hark at me! Older woman. I wouldn't talk like that in front of everybody.' She patted her hair. 'Anyway, how old would you say I was, love?'

'It's hard to say,' Marguerite said. 'Appearances are deceptive.'

'Oh, I know they are. I know they are. That's why I wanted you to guess.'

'Don't worry, Sylvia,' Wilf said; 'nobody in his right mind would put you at more than forty-six.'

'Forty-six!' Sylvia shrieked. 'I'll have you know I've yet to see thirty.'

'Yes, the second time round, I agree.'

'What d'you mean the second time round? You're in a bloody clever mood tonight, aren't you? What's up, haven't you been gettin' any co-operation, either?'

He was on his feet. 'Cut that out, Sylvia. I was only pulling your leg.'

'Well try somebody else's leg. You've no need to come the high and mighty sarcasm in front of her, because you're no bloody angel, and neither is—'

'I said stop it!' The authority in his voice and the blaze of anger in his eyes cut her off abruptly. 'You want to remember who your friends are,' he went on in an even tone. 'That kind of talk'll get you nowhere except out in the street with your bag in your hand.'

For a moment Sylvia's face was held in its lines of peevish defiance, then it relaxed and maudlin tears came into her eyes.

'I know, I know. You don't have to tell me what sort of a bloody future I've got.' She opened her handbag, sniffling, and took out a handkerchief which she dabbed at her nose. 'It's you bloody men 'at get the best out o' life. Take what you want an' go marching on to the next stop.'

'You know too many of the wrong kind.'

'Is there a wrong kind? Aye, some of 'em might look different, and talk different, but there's not much difference when you dig down a bit. I could tell you some tales.'

'But not tonight, though, Sylvia, eh?' Wilf said.

'No, I'm off to bed. Get an early night for a change.'

'You'll be losing your brooch . . .' Marguerite pointed.

Sylvia looked down at the cheap cameo brooch hanging by its pin from the lapel of her coat. She fastened it in place.

'Lucky it's not broken. That feller again. As many hands as a bloody octopus. All over you, they are . . .' Her glance fell on the plate on the table. 'Is that drippin'?'

'Yes,' Wilf said. 'Want some?'

'If it's goin' beggin' I don't mind. All I've had since me tea's a bag o' crisps an' a couple o' cheese straws.' She took two half-slices of the bread and put them together in a sandwich. She bit into it as she went to the door, turning there to say with her mouth full, 'The bathroom will be occupied for the next twenty minutes. I'll leave the door unlocked in case you feel like comin' up to scrub me back.'

'I'll think about it,' Wilf said.

Sylvia chuckled. 'Aye, you would an' all, you young sod. You've got the same ideas as all the rest of 'em.' She opened the door. 'Don't leave it too late or the water 'ull go cold.'

'Good night, Sylvia,' Wilf said.

To Marguerite he said, 'Don't mind her. She has to issue these random invitations to keep her spirits up. It doesn't matter much who the man is. I don't know what she'd do if I did go up and offer to scrub her back.'

'Perhaps pull you into the tub with her.'

He pulled a face. 'That could be interesting. But not with Sylvia. Anyway, I'm not her type.'

'She could fancy an intellectual for a change.'

'If the intellectual fancied her, which he doesn't. And if he was an intellectual, which he isn't.'

'You amuse yourself by putting words on paper. That makes you an intellectual in Sylvia's book.'

'I suppose so.' Wilf yawned hugely. 'Ugh . . . First beer makes me feel amorous, then it puts me to sleep.'

Marguerite said, 'That's a useful thing for a girl to know.'

He blinked vaguely. 'Hmm?'

'It could help her to plan her tactics.'

He was in an instant clear-headed and alert and they were man and woman facing each other across the eternal topic.

He said, 'Defence or attack?'

She shook her head. 'Military secret.'

He watched her stand up. He thought she was perhaps not so composed as she would have him believe.

'You shouldn't have done it,' he said.

'What?'

'Fallen for the temptation of picking up my remark about the beer. I was just talking.'

'So was I.'

He looked up at her from the depths of his chair. 'Well I'll tell you: if ever I do make a pass at you – and if I don't it won't be because I don't think you're a very attractive girl – I'll do you the honour of being stone-cold sober at the time.'

'Exit attractive girl in confusion,' Marguerite said, 'leaving pompous young male in command of the stage and his self-esteem.'

'You'd better go to bed,' Wilf said.

'And wedge a chair under the door handle?'

He stood up. 'If it'll make you feel any happier.' He yawned again and stretched. 'Gosh, when I go, I go all at once.'

'Anyway, thank you for this evening. I've enjoyed it.'

'It certainly seems to have broken the ice a bit.'

'Ice?'

'Well, you know . . .'

'Yes, I suppose it has.'

'We must have a real evening out together sometime. Go to a theatre or something.'

'That would be nice. You'd better be getting on top of that novel, though.'

'I suppose so. All play and no work makes no jack . . . or something like that.'

He switched off the kitchen light and followed her into the hall, which was now in darkness.

'I'll turn the light on.'

'No, don't bother. I can find my way up.'

She stopped at the foot of the stairs and he almost bumped into her. Her perfume was heady when you got close to her.

He felt for her hand but at first contact she squeezed his and started up the stairs.

'I'll probably see you in the morning, then.'

'Yes. Good night.'

He stood, feeling a little foolish now, and watched her dim figure move upward and out of sight. 'You silly sod,' he said to himself; 'you nearly made a pass after all.' He felt that he'd had the initiative and given it back to her without any gain. He had handed her back her superiority and she would be hugging it to her this minute as she hurried to her room. The darkness on the landing lifted for a moment as she opened the door of her room and switched on the light.

13

A few days later Stephen Hollis asked Marguerite if she would go out with him one evening. He approached her with what she thought a characteristic lack of diffidence, stopping her in the corridor by her office. She was glad that where they were standing they couldn't be seen from inside the room. It was Brenda whom Marguerite was thinking about. Her confession about Mister Stephen had cast Marguerite in the unwilling role of confidante and inhibited her own attitude towards him. Not that she had any particular feeling for him, one way or the other, but she was conscious that, observed by Brenda, she could not adopt any attitude that wasn't affected by knowledge of Brenda's infatuation, because any tiny step outside the most impersonal business relationship would be seized on by Brenda as in some way reflecting on her. Brenda's passion, unreturned as it was, gave her no proprietary rights over Stephen Hollis but it charged even the most casual mention of his name in the office with a particular significance. And she really didn't want to fall out with Brenda again. They now worked together in a harmony that the older girl, to give her her due, had helped to foster in various small ways, including, one day, a suggestion that they might share an evening at the cinema. Marguerite, recognising the gesture and the inference Brenda would read into any attempt to put her off, went with her to see *The Nun's Story*. For Brenda the evening seemed a success. She cried during the film and chattered with acid volubility about people she knew before and after it. Marguerite found the picture enjoyable and Brenda impossibly dull.

Now Marguerite found she couldn't refuse Stephen outright to his face. There was something rather boyish and appealing, something even, in a way, defenceless behind the air of assurance.

'I don't know,' she said. 'What had you in mind?'

'You name it, I've got it.'

'There aren't any good films on this week.'

'Oh, the pictures is for old married couples. I was thinking we could run out of town somewhere for a drink. Have you ever been to the Crossed Keys?'

Marguerite said no.

'They have dinner-dances there three nights in the week. There's one tonight, as a matter of fact.'

The door of the office opened and Brenda came out. She gave them a quick look then made to walk between them. As Stephen Hollis straightened up to let her pass he took the sheaf of papers from under his arm and handed them to Brenda without looking at her. 'Look after those, will you, ducky?' The dismissive tone of his voice and his offhand action brought a flush to Brenda's cheeks. She was obviously on her way to the cloakroom and now she had the choice of carrying the papers with her and finding somewhere to lay them down or turning back. She hurried back into the office. Marguerite didn't think she would come out again while she and Stephen were standing there, and decided to end the conversation quickly.

Why not say yes? She liked to dance and dine in pleasant surroundings and she would probably enjoy the evening. She could hold her own with Stephen Hollis any time, and there could always be more to him than casual conversation showed.

'Tonight's a bit short notice,' she said, her mind now on practical considerations such as her hair and clothes.

'It doesn't have to be tonight, though it might as well be if you've nothing else on.'

Her hair was all right. She'd washed it the night before last. And there was the little black frock she'd brought with her from London. She'd only worn it twice. It suited her. Floyd had liked her in it. Oh, God! Yes, she'd wear that and go out with Stephen Hollis and laugh and dance and drink his wine. She'd sweep him off his callow feet and let him kiss her and slap his face when he tried to go too far.

She sent him on his way whistling with her address written on a leaf from her shorthand notebook.

Brenda was alone in the office, typing furiously, and she didn't look up when Marguerite went in. She ripped the papers out of the machine with a peremptory tug as Marguerite sat down and applied her mind to work.

'Clever devil,' she said, her mouth hard.

'Who?' Marguerite couldn't resist asking.

'That stuck-up lord of the earth you've just been talking to outside.' She shuffled the sheets together and secured them with a paper-clip. 'Just because he's the boss's son it doesn't mean he can treat you like the dirt under his feet.'

Marguerite said, 'I thought he was a bit casual myself.'

'Oh, you did notice it, then? He put those bills of lading into my hand as if I was a piece of furniture. Thinks if he calls you ducky or love or darling he can walk right over you. I'd like to know what he was talking about that was so important.'

'Oh, would you?' Marguerite said sweetly. She recognised a fair amount of the bitch in herself and people like Brenda unfailingly supplied occasions for it to come out. How short-lived was sympathy for a plain girl who carried her heart on her sleeve; especially one like Brenda who was so unremittingly plain right through. Her nostrils were red and swollen with a head cold just now and this made her nature even less sweet and her appearance more apparently plain. With girls like Brenda sympathy soon gave way to exasperation. She was so hopelessly not with it. So she hadn't been blessed with a pretty face (she and millions of other girls). Too bad. But what aroused Marguerite's impatience was the conceit that prevented her from recognising the many ways in which she could make herself more attractive, to Stephen Hollis or any man. A little more skilfully applied make-up. A different hairstyle. New spectacle frames. A determined consigning to the ragbag of those horribly clashing cardigans and jumpers – handknitted with such misguided patience and care – along with the shapeless skirts whose hemlines remained persistently two or three inches below the knees. But no, she wasn't a girl you could talk to about such things. She was a plain girl who would be plain all her life. Perhaps one day a plain man would be lonely enough to find in her the love and companionship he needed, and give her something to live for in return. In the meantime Stephen Hollis's casually contemptuous ways stabbed her to the heart; and there was nothing anyone could do about that except leave it to time to heal.

At this point, Marguerite thought, as a loud sniff from Brenda followed her provocative 'Oh, would you?' a real bitch, a practised and merciless wielder of the knife, would follow with the *coup de grâce*: 'As a matter of fact we were arranging to go to a dinner-dance tonight.' But she hadn't the malice for that and kept her mouth shut as Brenda, balled hanky dabbing at her nose, got up without speaking again and went out, presumably to resume the errand that Stephen had interrupted.

He called for her at eight, as arranged. He was, in fact, a few minutes early. Since there was nowhere suitable for him to sit down and wait except in his car and no one to announce him when he arrived she had set herself to be ready on time and planned to chat with Poppy in the kitchen if he was late. As it was, she was just brushing off the shoulders of the black dress before slipping on her mac when someone tapped on her door. Wilf was outside on the landing.

'There's the Crown Prince downstairs asking for you.' She asked him in and he followed her into the room. She was smiling as she reached for her coat. He came forward and helped her into it. 'If I were you I'd leave this off and give him the full effect from the stairs.'

She turned to face him. 'Perhaps I want to lead up to it gradually. Anyway, thanks for the compliment.'

She knew she was looking her best but it was nice to be told so. She picked up her bag and her white cotton gloves.

'Right.'

'Are you going straight down? I thought it was standard practice to let your escort twiddle his thumbs for twenty minutes?'

'I'm an honest open-hearted girl,' Marguerite said. 'I don't play tricks like that. Where is he, anyway?'

'Looking at the family oil paintings in the hall.' Wilf perched himself on the arm of the easy-chair. 'You told me the other night you hardly knew him.'

'Well don't look so reproachful about it. It's true. I've never been out with him before; and in case you think I was holding out on you, he only asked me this morning.'

'Not that it's any of my business,' Wilf said.

'You said it, not me.' She looked at him amiably. 'Any other little points we ought to clear up?'

He shrugged and stood up. 'Are you going anywhere nice?'

'To a dinner-dance at the Crossed Keys, wherever that might be.'

'Somewhere in the industrialists' belt. When you go out with me it'll be a half-crown seat in the stalls and a fish and four-penn'orth of chips from Wilson's Deep Sea Fisheries.'

'And I'll wear my best haircurlers,' Marguerite said.

She opened the door and he went out before her. As Marguerite stepped out Sylvia, on dangerously high heels, came down the upper stairs from her room, resplendent in white imitation leather raincoat and yellow knitted beret. She said 'Hello, you two' as she passed by and went on down to the hall where Stephen Hollis was waiting.

'Oh, lord!' Marguerite held Wilf's arm. 'Just let her get clear. I must say he's getting a good look at the inmates.'

'Thank you,' Wilf murmured. 'I'm the nigger in the woodpile. He's wondering where I fit in. You should have seen the look he gave me when I answered the doorbell.'

They went to the landing-rail as they heard Sylvia's voice below. Stephen Hollis was holding the flame of his lighter to the end of her cigarette.

'Thank you very much. Is it still raining out?'

'No, it seems to be clearing.'

'I won't get wet, then, will I?'

'Not outside, anyway,' Wilf murmured. 'God, she just can't resist them, can she?'

Marguerite moved away from the rail. 'Sorry if your work was interrupted.'

'It's one of the hazards of the trade. Have a good time and—' He stifled a snort of laughter.

'What's wrong?'

He was grinning. 'I was nearly indelicate enough to repeat Sylvia's advice.'

She knew what he meant, and also that he didn't mean to be offensive. She said, 'Don't be indecent,' and went down the stairs.

Wilf stayed behind on the landing as she went down. She said hello to Stephen Hollis as she neared the foot of the stairs and he smiled and took a pace towards her.

'I'm sorry if I've kept you waiting.'

'Only a minute.' He pulled his mac up to settle it more comfortably on his shoulders as the front door opened and Sylvia stepped back inside.

'I hope you won't mind me asking, but is that your car outside by any chance?'

'Yes, it is.'

'You wouldn't by any chance be going through the city centre would you?' Sylvia's face was contorted into a smile of ferocious charm.

'No, the opposite way.'

'Oh, well, never mind. I just thought I might be able to save me legs a bit.'

'Some other time, perhaps.'

Sylvia twitched her eyebrows. 'I'll look forward to that. Bye bye, then.'

They followed her out. The dark grey Jaguar parked by the gate surprised Marguerite. She had expected the scarlet Mini-Minor in which Stephen ran to and from work.

'I thought we'd have a bit of extra comfort tonight,' he said in explanation.

'Is it your father's?' Marguerite asked.

'No, mother's.'

'I thought women went in for something a bit more docile.'

'Not mummy. She's the best driver in the family. Likes rallying and all that.'

He opened the door for her, waiting until she was settled in the low leather seat before going round to get in at the other side.

'She's gone off to a meeting in the Mini,' Stephen said, as he slid the ignition key home. 'I had to convince her it was a special occasion before she'd swap.' He looked sideways at her and smiled as he switched on and she smiled in answer to the compliment. Two compliments in ten minutes, from two different men! She was beginning to feel in demand.

When Stephen twisted in his seat to check his door the resultant faint stirring of air inside the car brought to her nostrils, over the smell of the upholstery that wasn't really a smell at all but more a kind of *atmosphere* which you got in good cars, a whiff of something discreetly perfumed. Soap, perhaps. Not hair-dressing. Stephen's dark fair hair lay neatly close to his head. A comb through it in the morning and it would be settled for the day. Probably aftershave lotion, or pre-electric . . .

'Do you use an electric razor?' she asked as the car moved quietly away from the kerb.

'Always,' he said. 'Why, do I look as if I need it now?'

'Oh no, it just occurred to me to wonder.'

The shaver and the lotion, whatever it was, went with the rest of him: the car, the gold watch and strap on his strong wrist, the slim, square-ended tie and the plain-fronted slightly pointed-toed black shoes which deferred to current male fashion without extravagance of style. She liked a man to be a man and be well-groomed. No sweat and tobacco breath for her. And she liked – yes she made no bones about it, as the car nosed up to the traffic lights at the main-road junction and she looked out at the huddle of macintoshes at the bus stop – she liked to be cossetted a little, looked after by a man who was easy with good things, composed over a wine list, unselfconscious with waiters. Floyd had had all these qualities in a relaxed American way different from that of class-plagued Englishmen. Floyd had had a lot of qualities, including those of a liar and a cheat . . .

'The young chap who answered the door just now,' Stephen said. 'Does he live in the house?'

'Wilf? Yes.'

'Isn't he the one you were in the Tower with the other night?'

'Yes, that's right.'

'He gave me rather a funny look when I asked for you. I thought for a minute that perhaps you and he were—'

'No. We just live in the same house.'

'He looked to me like one of these deep types. You know, say nothing for months on end, then suddenly take all the men out on strike. Is he a red, d'you know?'

'Not as far left as that, I think.'

'But definitely left, though?'

'Most people are these days, aren't they?'

'What?' He looked at her. 'The people I know aren't.'

She smiled. 'I shouldn't think they are. Somebody must have voted this government in.'

'Vote it in again, too. People know when they're well off.'

She felt a mild desire to bait him, but resisted the temptation. She'd had no real chance of gauging his sense of humour and she didn't want the evening to get off to a bad start. If she was any judge he wasn't one who would relish any suggestion of a girl's laughing at him. Come to that, was any man?

'Does he work, this Wilf?' Stephen said. 'Or does he just hang about in that sweater and flannels all day?'

His assumptions about Wilf stung Marguerite to the latter's defence.

'He does two jobs as it happens. He's a wages clerk during the day and a writer at night.'

'A writer, eh? One of these kitchen-sink types, I suppose.'

'If you mean he writes about what he knows and he's lived a lot nearer the kitchen sink all his life than you have, yes he is.'

He didn't react, his attention momentarily concentrated on taking the car through a glut of traffic at a busy roundabout. He swung out of the main stream and on to a well-surfaced minor road. As the no-limit signs came up he put his foot down and the Jaguar surged forward in a soft release of power which pressed her gently back into her seat.

'This isn't the shortest way,' he said, 'but it's pleasanter and there's less traffic.'

In a few minutes they were out through the northern residential suburbs of the city and among the green and gold of fields in a rolling landscape that lost itself in the blue-grey of distant fells. The sun was coming out to retrieve a day of grey skies and lashing rain. Stephen drove expertly, which she had expected, and a little flashily, which she took to be partly an effort to impress her and partly the natural exuberance of his youth and character in combination with the qualities of a fast car. He frightened her a couple of times until she realised that his judgement and his knowledge of the car's capabilities made him safer than the middle-aged driver of a family saloon pottering along at forty miles an hour. When the red nose of a farm tractor trundled placidly out of a concealed opening Stephen braked just as much as was necessary, throwing out his left arm to hold her in her seat. The tractor stopped, the Jaguar slid past and picked up speed again.

'All right?'

'Yes, thanks.'

'Are you hungry?'

'Yes, I am rather.'

'So am I. Won't be long now.'

'I don't mind; this is very pleasant country.'

'Yes, it is. My father once nearly bought a weekend farm out here. Decided against it, though, in the end. He's never been one to sit back and let other people run his affairs for him and the business claims all his attention. Have you had much contact with him?'

'No, Brenda does most of his work. From what I've seen of him I'd say he's very efficient.'

'Red hot. He acquired control of the business from an uncle who'd let it go till its only remaining asset was a reputation for quality. He built it up again by sheer guts and hard work. He trained new sales staff and went out on the road himself to establish personal contact and do some straight talking to customers who owed money. I don't know just what it's all worth now but I'm damn' glad I've got an interest in it.'

'Your father must be awfully pleased that you chose to follow him into the business.'

'Why not? I'd no particular inclination towards anything else. I think a lot of people kid themselves that they're interested in some particular product when what they really like is the world of business and trade attaching to it. And business is the same whether you're selling machine tools or canned meat.'

'Well, it makes a change to find somebody who's happy and settled with what he's doing.'

He turned his head to flash her a smile. 'But it's not everybody who's lucky enough to be the boss's son. Let's not forget that.'

It was one of the lines she could have imagined herself saying to him, and now he had beaten her to it, disarming her by taking the words out of her mouth. Oh yes, she'd underestimated him. He was a conformist; he shared the ideas and outlook of his class and his upbringing, but he was alert enough to see himself in a wider context and know that there were reasons why other people shouldn't share his views.

There was a fork in the road, the right arm of which took them back to the highway they had left at the roundabout. The Crossed Keys stood back across the main intersection, a long imitation-half-timbered building with metal-studded doors and latticed windows. The interior was in keeping: low ceilings with exposed beams, panelled walls with warming pans and horse brasses, stone-built fireplaces. She titivated herself in the cloak-room then joined Stephen in the cocktail bar. He was drinking whisky and dry ginger and nibbling at potato crisps from a glass dish on the bar counter. He pulled out a stool for her and she perched herself up beside him.

'What would you like to drink?'

She asked for a dry sherry and he ordered from the girl behind the bar.

'What do you think of the place?'

'Well, phoney – but pleasant.'

'Phoney? I suppose it is. I've never thought of it like that. If it's pleasant and the food and drink and service are good, that's all that matters.' His eyes moved discreetly over her, taking in the black frock, the multiple rope of imitation pearls, which, apart from matching ear-rings, was the only jewellery she was wearing, and rested for a second on her exposed knees. He took out a long silver case with his initials engraved on it and gave her a cigarette which he lit with his lighter.

'You look ravishing,' he said, narrowing his eyes against the back draught of smoke from his own cigarette. 'Was that dress awfully expensive?'

'A little extravagant. It cost me a couple of weeks' salary. My last salary,' she added, 'not what J. G. Hollis and Son pay me.'

'Are you getting less money now than you were before?'

'Yes, but I expected it.'

'I understand you were working in London.'

'Yes.'

'But you lived here before?'

'Uh, uh.'

'What made you come back?'

'Oh, I don't know. Roots tugging, perhaps.'

'Have you any family?'

'No.'

'I like London,' Stephen said after a moment. 'I like to go there as often as possible. But I prefer to live in the provinces. I find that they're . . . oh, I don't know, more manageable, if you see what I mean. Living here you get the feeling you know everybody who matters. Do you think you'll stay now?'

She gave him what she hoped was an inscrutable look. 'It depends on how good the prospects are.'

He looked directly back at her as he replied. 'I should say that for a girl like you they're practically unlimited.' He lifted his glass. The light picked out the pale clear gold glow of the whisky. A sudden bray of male laughter in the passage was as suddenly muffled by the closing of a door. A small dance-band struck up a quickstep in another part of the building. The cold finger of desolation touched momentarily her feeling of poise and well-being, and was gone.

'Here's to a happy return,' Stephen said.

As their eyes met again it struck Marguerite with the indisputable truth of a simple fact that if she played her cards right she could become his wife.

Wilf walked into the kitchen at half-past nine.

'Poppy, my love, you've got a genius in the house.'

'Well don't let 'em get to know at the town hall,' Poppy said, 'or they'll put the rates up.'

'In a hundred years they'll be putting a plaque by the front door saying "Wilf Cotton, author, lived here" and learned dons will be investigating this period in my life and trying to find out if the mysterious Mrs Poppy Swallow was any more more to the struggling young genius than the temporary provider of his board and lodging.'

'Never mind,' Poppy said. 'We shall all be past caring.'

He threw himself down into a chair and swung one leg over the arm. He was drunk with the success of the last two hours. He'd broken through. Now, after the uncertainties and disappointments of the past weeks, he had found his form and the way forward looked clear and bright. He'd stopped now, while he was writing well, so that he could sweep straight into tomorrow night's session. Was it Hemingway who had advised stopping when everything was going easily, carrying something over for next time?

'It'll take time, Poppy – time to get it all down – but I can see it now and it's good.'

'There's a couple of your shirts and some clean underwear. You'll manage for a bit longer now.'

'You know, you're a bloody marvel, Poppy. Only the other night you were dead on your feet and now you're working away as if nothing had happened.'

Poppy lifted another garment out of the basket and spread it out on the ironing board. 'If I stop, everything stops.'

'One of these days I'll put you in a book.'

'I'll wring your neck if you do.'

'Wouldn't you like to think that people might read about you years after you're dead?'

'When I'm dead I want to be dead, not hanging around in some dusty old book.'

'Well, suppose the novel's a big hit, Poppy, and they bring the television cameras to show the viewers where I live. Then you can tell them all how you've looked after me.'

'All of it?' Poppy said. 'That'd sound nice coming out of TV sets in all them nice respectable homes, wouldn't it?' The iron ran smoothly, competently over the board. The legs creaked under its pressure. 'No, if I go on television it'll be on one of these quiz shows where there's some money to be won. I'm sure I could do as well as some of 'em what do go on.'

'Well, why don't you, Poppy? Why don't you write up and see if you can get on?'

'Aw, it's one of these things you say an' never do owt about. What would I want to go on their damn' silly quiz shows for?'

'For the money, like you said.'

'What good is it? I manage to live, don't I? I couldn't win enough to retire on. Only enough to put me out of conceit with the way I live now. No, you're the one 'at ought to go on. Win yourself enough to chuck up your job till you finish your book.'

'Oh, going out to work does me good. It keeps me out of the ivory tower. In any case, I'm not the winning type. I've never even won a tanner raffle.' He swung his leg and watched Poppy, solid but shapely, a woman right through and attractive even in the faded overall she wore to do her chores in. He said, 'I was thinking it might be nice to have a walk up to the Tower and get cosily drunk. What d'you say?'

'And what, then, when we've got cosily drunk?'

'Well with some people it's an end in itself but with us it could lead to other things.' He grinned at her.

'That's what I thought,' Poppy said. 'Anyway, I don't feel like going out tonight.'

'Pity.'

'There should be a couple of bottles of beer in the scullery cupboard, though, if you want a drink here.'

'Poppy the great provider.' He leaped to his feet and went into the scullery.

'Bring one for me. I'm feeling a bit parched.'

'Where's the opener?'

'In the drawer among the knives and forks.'

'Found it.'

He came back carrying two tumblers as well as the bottles. 'Now you're going to sit down to drink this. Get the load off your feet.'

'Pour it out; I've nearly finished.'

He waited till she'd put the iron with a clatter onto its stand and switched off the power, then came round to sit in the other chair, before lifting his glass.

'Cheers, Poppy.'

'All the best, love.'

They drank.

'Who was that young feller that called for Marguerite tonight?'

'Stephen Hollis, her boss's son. "Mister Stephen" to the family retainers.'

'He looked a very presentable young chap.'

'He should with his backing.'

'You sound a bit sour. Has he put your nose out of joint?'

'Marguerite can go out with ex-King Farouk for all I care; but the casual arrogance of blokes like Stephen Hollis makes my back hair bristle.'

'I think you're just plain jealous.'

'Aw, knock it off, Poppy. We've had all this out before.'

'I don't say you know it yourself, but that's what I think it is.'

'You seem set on conjuring something up between Marguerite and me.'

'She's a lovely girl.'

'I'm not saying she isn't. But apart from her not being interested in me, lovely girls want wedding rings and homes and kids. They festoon a man with responsibilities and right now I want responsibilities like I want two broken legs. I've got things to do.'

'A woman can often help a man to make his way.'

'*You* help me, Poppy. You give me all I want from a woman.'

'And you think it'll be there till you don't need it anymore?'

'You're twisting it, Poppy. You know I've never demanded anything. I take what you give me and give what I can in return.'

'It's an arrangement,' she said.

'Well, an unspoken one, but yes, if you like, an arrangement. We respect each other's feelings but we have no contract.'

'The world's full of men who'd like an arrangement like that.'

'Of course it is. D'you think I don't know how lucky I am? It's not a question of measuring who's getting the best of the bargain. You don't seem to see, Poppy, that as soon as you start talking about it like this, analysing it, resentment creeps in and it's spoilt.'

'Oh, I see it, all right.'

He put down his glass and went and sat on the arm of her chair. He slid his arm behind her neck and fondled her cheek.

'Why couldn't it have stayed as it was, Poppy? Why let all this talk in to spoil it?'

'I've told you before,' Poppy said, passive under his caresses, 'we're human beings, not animals. We've got to talk. We don't just work by instinct. We've got to think things out and find reasons.'

'Our reason was that we got on well together and liked to make love.'

'Yes.'

'And now it's not good enough?'

She was silent. He got up and moved away from her and picked up his glass and drank from it.

'Why don't you get married again, Poppy?' he said in a moment.

'You know I can't have any family,' she said. 'That's why we've never had to worry about precautions.'

'But kids aren't everything to a man, Poppy. God knows you could find some steady-living widower with his own family grown up and give him a whole new lease of life.'

'Sexy Poppy, the old man's darling.'

'That's not what I mean. You should be thinking about it, though. You've got a lot of future left. You don't want to spend it on your own.'

'Happen I won't.'

'Would you marry me if I asked you?'

'No, I wouldn't. I wouldn't,' she went on, 'even if I could. And I can't. There's something I've never told you but you'll have to know now. I've got a husband already.'

He was looking at a fly scaling the smooth exterior of his glass and at the web of effervescence across the surface of his beer. He lifted his eyes to Poppy's face. She wasn't looking at him. He realised now that she'd been leading up to this ever since he walked into the room.

'Well, you kept that little bit of information quiet, didn't you?'

She stood up without answering and took an opened letter from behind the clock on the mantelshelf. She handed it to him in silence and he put aside his glass and took from the envelope a ruled sheet torn from a cheap writing pad. His hand was trembling slightly as he read.

'Dearest Poppy, You will be surprised to hear from yore old man after all this time. Perhaps you thought I was dead after all these years but no I am still alive and kicking though a lot less spritely than the last time you saw me. I got yore address from my brother Henry who says he saw you when he was up North 3 or 4 years ago. I hear yore taking in lodgers now and I'm sure yore well suited for this occupation because you were always first rate about the house and it's a pity I didn't appreciate yore good points a long time ago.

'I have done a lot of travelling about since we saw each other and I am sorry to say I have been a guest of the government at one of Her Majesty's institutions for the past 2 years. I got mixed up with a bad crowd in London and we did a warehouse job and somebody hit the night watchman. I got 3 years for robbery with vilence and what with time off for good behaviour I get out of here next month.

'Henry said in his letter he wouldn't blame you for not wanting to have anymore to do with me and hes surprised you haven't divorced me for desertion a long time ago. I wouldn't blame you either, Poppy, but I know yore a good girl and I remember all the good times we had earlier on. I am planning to come and see you when I get out. I have nowere else to go and I am tired of the life I've been leading. If you want to take me back and try to make a go of it when you've seen me that is all I can hope for and if you throw me out I shant blame you.

'Looking forward to seeing you after all this long time, I am, yore loving husband, Alfred Swallow.'

There was no address on the letter but the envelope carried a London postmark.

'Well?' Poppy said.

'He's either a truly repentant man or the best natural writer since—'

'Oh, he'll be repentant all right – now,' Poppy said. 'He probably cries himself to sleep every night thinking of all the wrong he's done me and imagining the grand reunion. Alf always had a sentimental streak a mile wide.'

Her eyes were shifty. He'd never known her to look shiftily at anything or anybody before.

She said in a moment, 'It hasn't upset you, has it?'

He said, 'Oh, bloody hell, Poppy.' His voice was tight in his throat.

'You said yourself it couldn't go on for ever. It'd have to end sometime.'

'I know.'

'You mean you wanted it to be you who'd end it. You'd be the one who'd walk out one day and not come back.'

Wilf looked at the letter again. 'He gives you no chance to write back and tell him to stay away.'

'No.'

He put the letter back into the envelope and pushed them back behind the clock.

'How did it all happen? Or don't you want to talk about it?'

'There's no harm in you knowing the rest of it. It was one of them quick wartime marriages. He was in the army and he went abroad soon after. It was hard to weigh a man up in those days. You put so much down to the war. When he came back we settled down for a while but then the restless side of him began to show through. Perhaps if we'd had a family it might have been better. But that's one thing I can't blame him for. He began to drift from job to job and he was drinking more than was good for him. He was waiting for my mother to die and leave her money, you see. He thought he wouldn't have to work any more then. I tried to tell him there wouldn't be enough to keep him for the rest of his life but he'd got this fixed idea in his head and he thought I was deceiving him. He was very nasty in drink. He got violent. He knocked me about and he got a month in jail for clouting a chap at his work. He was all right for a while when he came out and then it all started again, losing jobs, drinking, carrying on with women. We had blazing rows nearly every day. In the end he walked out and went off with his current fancy woman. I've never heard of him again – apart from a few vague rumours from his brother when he called – till this letter came.

'When my mother did die she left me enough to buy this place and a bit over for a nest-egg. Nobody knew me round these parts and when they took me for a widow I let 'em go on believing it.'

'And you never made any attempt to divorce him?'

'No, I never did.'

'You know that once he gets inside this house you may lose your chance?'

'Yes, I can see that.'

'Well, for God's sake, Poppy, send him away. Don't let him get inside. Now you know where he is it's your chance to be free of him for ever.'

'I can't do that. He's in trouble, with nobody to turn to. I've got to give him a chance to show he's changed.'

Wilf looked at her. He was conscious of staring. He was revolted by the thought of Poppy, his Poppy, and this man she'd described together. Her eyes slid away to the fire. There was that shifty look again. It was almost as though she was conscious of some compelling vice. He knew that he'd lost her. He couldn't compete with this. He was out of his depth. She suddenly wasn't his Poppy any longer, but more like a stranger. There was that look in her face and a queer light in her eyes among the reflected firelight.

'He always had a way with him,' Poppy murmured, watching the fire. 'I'm as excited as a young lass at the thought of seeing him again.'

He picked up his glass and emptied it at a gulp. Then he looked at it in his hand and he tightened his grip as though he would crush it by the force of his fingers.

Marguerite had *hors d'oeuvres maison*, minestrone soup and a slice of York ham with a green salad. Here she capitulated and sat back, sipping at the Chablis Stephen had ordered while he, a huge rump steak already inside him, pressed on with an almost boyish concentration through an ice-cream sundae and cheese and biscuits. The sun was going down outside, striking a last golden glow from the diamond panes of the leaded windows, and laying long tree-shadows across the lawn behind this wing of the building. Table lights were switched on and the daylight receded to linger in glimpsed fragments of fading yellow sky. After drinking coffee they danced to the quartet of piano, bass, drums and saxophone on the floor along whose perimeter was a staggered double rim of tables. At one place, near the band, several tables had been pushed together to seat a party of about a dozen people who were having a celebration of some kind and were laughing and flushed with both the occasion and the wine from some half-dozen bottles that stood up among the wreckage of their meal. Later on the saxophone-player made an announcement: 'Ladies and gentlemen, we have with us this evening a happy couple who are celebrating their twenty-fifth wedding anniversary with their friends. I won't embarrass them by pointing them out (some scattered laughter) but I'm sure you'll wish to join with the management and myself in wishing them many more years of married bliss.' The band began to play and the party to sing '*For they are jolly good fellows/for they are jolly good fellows . . .*' while the husband and wife, a thin-faced bespectacled man in a navy-blue suit and a silver-grey tie and a plump woman in a coral-pink evening frock that didn't suit her, grinned sheepishly at each other, finally exchanging a rapid kiss under persuasion from their friends.

Something, some perverse masochistic instinct she told herself as she watched him in brief conversation with the saxophone-player, made her ask Stephen to request the band to play *My Funny Valentine*. It was one of Floyd's favourite tunes. He had three different recordings of it and wherever they had danced or dined to music he had asked for it. Then as she and Stephen danced to the number she found herself at first listening to it, then humming it, without heartache but with a melancholy that, while linked with regret for a happiness suddenly snatched away, was also partly the blue mood engendered by any romantic melody when you were in love with love and without a man.

Stephen? Clean cut, good looking, well off, eminently eligible and obviously interested in her. Brenda's dream, and an opportunist's. But she wasn't in love with him, nor was she an opportunist. He'd give her an evening that was all any girl could ask for; an evening that had everything – except magic. So magic faded, couldn't by its very nature be expected to last; and marriages were held by fond 'togetherness' as the Americans called it. And togetherness could grow out of mutual eligibility and respect, often more successfully than out of the disillusionment of fading magic. But magic was what she had to have. Everything in her cried out for it and now more than ever, after Floyd, she couldn't deny it.

She could sense, as any girl could after a time, a man's assessment of her. She had no doubts that Stephen and his friends had gone out with girls for no other reason than that they were good for a laugh and a romp at the end of the evening. But she realised quickly enough, if she hadn't known it before, that this wasn't his assessment of her. There had been in his conversation no risqué humour, none of the sexual innuendo usual as a preliminary testing of promising ground before an attempted seduction. His manner throughout had been attentive, courteous, irreproachable and it had all served to confirm that flash of intuition which had hit her in the bar before dinner. Stephen was a confirmed member of the old-fashioned middle-class and a subscriber to the double standard of morality. There were girls you slept around with as opportunity arose and there were those you might marry. He might sleep with the girl before the ceremony but he would expect it to cost him an engagement ring and involve manoeuvring to ensure no loss of respect for her. She thought that he wouldn't be shocked to know about her and Floyd and the confession of it, at the right moment, mightn't do her any serious harm. But it would inevitably tarnish slightly his image of her.

She turned all this over as he drove her home at approaching midnight and was amused to recall her first arrogant impulse to lead him on then rebuff him. She'd not only misjudged him but underestimated herself. No fighting off of hot groping hands tonight. Everything clean-cut, gentlemanly, above board. In fact, she thought for a time after he'd stopped the car in the street opposite the house that he wasn't even going to try to kiss her. Then he finally leaned over and touched his lips to her cheek. Nothing more.

'Thank you very much for coming.'

'Thank you for asking,' she said lightly. 'It's been lovely.'

'I take it another invitation will be in order, then?'

'Why not try it and see?' She hated herself for her mill-girl coyness but she couldn't help it coming out that way. She opened the door and put one leg out.

'I'm sorry I can't ask you in for a cup of coffee or something.'

'That's okay. I understand. Perhaps you could come to my home for supper sometime. Meet the rest of the family.'

Something like panic smote her. God, so soon? She said, 'That would be nice,' and slid out of the car. 'Good night, then.'

He was leaning right over to look up at her and then he turned the other way and wound down the window on his side as she walked round the back of the car and into the road.

'Good night,' he called, and she waved to him as she crossed to the other side. 'Don't be late in the morning.'

She laughed. 'Cheeky!'

He waited till she had opened the door with her key before moving off in a sudden exuberant open-throttled roar that boomed in the sheltered quiet of the street.

The tune was in her mind as she closed the door and stood in the dark hall. The house was quiet but she had seen light behind the drawn curtains of Wilf's window. He was perhaps reading or working late, the novel suddenly going demandingly well. The intermittent melancholy of the evening came over her in an enormous nostalgia. She felt utterly lost, devoid of roots. She seemed deprived of identity, so that she didn't know who or what she was. How could she exist if she had no identity in the minds of other people, people who *cared*? She shivered as if touched by the cold breath of a legion of lost souls, and she was afraid.

She wondered if Wilf would let her in if she tapped at his door; if he would let her sit and be comforted by his presence and the sound of his dry West Riding voice. Then it occurred to her that Poppy might be with him, lying with him in his single bed or embracing him in the depths of the big wing-chair, and when she heard the sounds of movement in the room she fled for the stairs.

The landing was in darkness too. She had reached it when the door of the bathroom suddenly opened and Poppy came out, startling her so that she stood transfixed.

'Oh, it's you, Marguerite. I thought I heard a car go off.' She pressed the switch for the landing-light and turned off that in the bathroom, pulling the door shut behind her. She looked quite splendid in her pale-green dressing gown, her face flushed with colour after her bath.

'What's wrong? Did I make you jump?'

'I thought everybody was in bed except Wilf. I noticed the light in his room.'

'He might be up for a while yet,' Poppy said. 'His brother turned up not long since.'

'His brother?'

'Yes, Harry.'

'It seems a funny time to come calling. Was Wilf expecting him?'

'No. The doorbell rang about half-past ten and when Wilf went to answer it, there he was. Still, he'll get over it. He's had one or two surprises tonight,' she said mysteriously. 'Have you had a nice time?'

'Lovely, thanks.'

'Nothing like doing it in style when you can, is there?'

'No.'

'Sure you're all right? You look a bit pale.'

'I've a headache. Perhaps too much wine.'

'You can be forgiven once in a while. Have you got some aspirin?'

'Yes, in my room.'

'Well, you take a couple, they'll help you to get a good night's sleep. Would you like me to pop downstairs and make you a cup of cocoa?'

She was inordinately touched by Poppy's kindness. She turned her face away. 'No, I'll be all right, thanks.'

Poppy came closer. 'Hey,' she said softly, 'you haven't been having any trouble with that young feller, have you?'

Marguerite shook her head. 'No.'

'Sure?'

'Yes, really.'

'Something's upset you, though.' Her hand was on Marguerite's shoulder.

'You mustn't mind me,' Marguerite said. 'I'm a damned cry-baby, I'm sorry to say.'

'Nowt wrong with a woman havin' a cry now an' again,' Poppy said. 'It's her safety valve.' She slid her arm round Marguerite's shoulders. 'You come on in here for five minutes. It's nice and warm. We'll have a little chat.'

Marguerite let herself be led into Poppy's room. 'A little chat.' Oh, how she wanted to talk to somebody. God, how she wanted to talk!

14

Neither of them had spoken for some time. Harry lit yet another cigarette from the stub of the last and looked round once more for the ashtray before lounging back moodily in his chair.

'I think I'll have a cigarette,' Wilf said, breaking the silence.

'I thought you said you'd stopped.'

'I have. I just feel like one now.' He caught the twenty-packet of Senior Service and the box of matches which Harry tossed to him. He lit one of the cigarettes and took a long pull, inhaling deeply. He was like a schoolboy having his first grown-up drag. The smoke seemed to curl upwards inside his skull and turn his brain to jelly. For a moment he couldn't see straight.

'Christ!'

'Don't make yourself sick, will you?' Harry said dispassionately.

The next pull was more cautious. He held up the cigarette and looked at it without enthusiasm. 'It makes you wonder what you ever saw in them.'

'Try it for a couple of days,' Harry said, 'and you'll be back smoking as much as ever.'

'We'll see.'

Harry's eyes roved over as much of the room as he could see without moving his head.

'Not a bad little place you've got here.'

'I like it.'

'Just the job. Come an' go as you like without people watching you.'

'Yes, you can live your own life; up to a point.'

'Up to a point?'

'Well there are always restrictions wherever you go.'

'I suppose so . . . That landlady of yours, Poppy, she's very attractive for a woman her age – well preserved.'

'Yes, she is.' He couldn't keep a touch of dryness out of his voice. 'I reckon you'll have had enough of attractive women to last you for a bit, though.'

Harry said, 'You're not bloody kidding, mate.'

'You say Mam doesn't know where you are?' Wilf said.

'No, I told you. I went into Calderford and had a couple of drinks, then I saw a bus coming this way and hopped on it. It took me long enough to find where you lived. I couldn't remember your address at first, and then some silly sod in the bus station sent me the wrong way altogether.'

'She'll wonder what the hell's happened when she finds your bed empty in the morning.'

Harry moved restlessly in the chair. 'I can't help that. I had to talk to somebody, and not in Bronhill, either. It's too good a tale to keep to yourself. Mention it to the wrong bloke and it'll be all over the village in twenty-four hours. Anyway, me mam'll know about it now – or some of it – if he's kept his word.'

'D'you think he really meant it?'

'He meant it when he said it, all right. If wishing could have done it I'd have dropped down dead on the spot. God, I've not seen anybody as mad as that in a long time.'

Wilf said, 'Y'know, I don't like to say this, old lad, but I warned you what sort of a bloke he was.'

Harry spread his hands. 'Well, I mean, Wilf, any bloke would ha' been mad, wouldn't he? You can't blame him for that.'

'I know, but another bloke would probably have taken a swing at you and settled for that. Trust Ronnie to think of bringing a charge.'

'Aye, an' any other bloke would ha' got to wondering afterwards just how much encouragement *she'd* given.'

'Well, he's had time to think it over a bit now. Maybe it's done some good.'

'I wish I thought so. He can be a nasty sod when he gets crossed . . . Aye, I know you told me so. Well I'm not daft altogether and I had him pretty well weighed up for meself. I just thought this was dead safe, that's all.'

'If only we were on the 'phone at home . . .'

'What for?'

'I could ring Mam up and tell her you'd come over to see me, had a few drinks and missed the last bus. That'd settle that unless they'd had a copper up, and she'd tell me about that quick enough. As it is, we don't know anything and neither does she. She'll probably think you've had an accident.'

'Or done meself an injury.'

'Don't talk wet, man. In any case, I'm betting Ronnie's thought better of the whole thing since you saw him.'

Harry shrugged gloomily and stubbed out his half-smoked cigarette. Wilf had already disposed of his.

'I dunno,' Harry said. 'I've been thinking about it all last night and today. I can't think any more. Me mind's in a whirl.'

'Just how far had you got when he came in?'

'All I can say is it's a bloody good job he wasn't ten minutes later, that's all,' Harry said.

'Tell me about it again, from the beginning this time. You say you didn't know Ronnie was out?'

'No, I hadn't heard about it. You know I pop round mebbe once a week and sit and natter with 'em. It varies. I haven't a regular night. Well last night I went out and had a couple of halves at the Welfare. There was nobody in I wanted to talk to so I thought I'd go round to Ronnie's.'

'You mean you were feeling a bit randy so you thought you'd go and sit and look at June.'

'All right, have it like that, if you like. Anyway, she

answered the door when I got there, and let me in. She didn't tell me till we were right inside that Ronnie was off on some sort of union business and he wouldn't be back that night. She asked me if I wanted to see him about anything in particular and I said no, I'd just popped round for a natter. She said there wasn't any need for me to rush off, was there, and I could sit down for five minutes seeing as I was there. Well apart from anything else, it was raining out and she'd a nice fire going in the lounge and the telly switched on, so I let her take me coat and hang it in the passage.'

'What time was this?'

'Oh, it must have been getting on for eight. June was all tidied up herself. Y'know, washed and made-up and her hair brushed. I told her I didn't want to keep her in and she said she wasn't going anywhere and it was such a miserable night, chilly and raining, she was glad she hadn't arranged to go over to her mother's in Calderford like Ronnie'd suggested.

'I was glad the telly was on because I didn't really know what to talk to her about. She never says a lot when Ronnie's around and it was the first time I'd really been on my own with her. So we just sat and watched the programme, her curled up on the couch and me in an armchair.'

Harry offered the packet of cigarettes to Wilf, who shook his head. 'No, thanks.'

Harry lit one for himself and looked at his wrist-watch. 'Is it twenty past twelve already?'

Wilf checked his own watch. 'Twenty-five past, I make it.'

'You're sure your landlady doesn't mind me kipping down here tonight?'

'No. She gave us the blankets, didn't she?'

'Aye. She seemed all right about it but I wouldn't want to get you across with her. Y'know, queer your pitch.'

'My pitch with her was queered before you got here,' Wilf said. 'Not in the way you mean, though. I'll tell you about it sometime. Go on with your tale. You say you didn't talk. There must have been some kind of conversation.'

'Oh, you couldn't call it conversation. She'd say something about Ronnie while the commercials were on, or ask me something about meself. She asked about you, one time; how you were getting on. We smoked a lot. I'd have one of her cigs then she'd have one of mine.'

'Did you get the impression she was keyed-up or nervous at all? You know, a bit excited because you were on your own together?'

'No, I don't think I did. She said things about the programmes while they were on. There was a bit of a play on and she passed remarks about the characters like a kid might do. "He's a cheeky devil," and "she'd better watch out." Things like that. I thought that was a bit funny.'

'Could be she's just not very bright.'

'Tell you the truth, I don't think she is. 'Course, it never was her brains I was interested in.'

Wilf laughed at Harry's sour expression.

'It's all right for you, mate,' Harry said. 'You're not in this lot.'

'Sorry,' Wilf said. 'Carry on.'

'We went on like that till about ten and then she asked me if I'd like a cup of coffee. I said yes and she went into the kitchen to make it.'

'I suppose you were thinking by now how to lead up to making a pass at her.'

'I'd been thinking about it all night, man,' Harry said with a frankness that made Wilf smile again. 'This was the sort of chance I'd been waiting for and I didn't know when it might come again.'

'But all this conversation, what there was, had been quite proper? No suggestive remarks or anything like that on either side?'

Harry shook her head. 'No, nowt at all like that. She even kept her skirt right down over her legs while she was on the couch. No, things started moving a bit when she'd made the supper. I thought she was a fair time just making a couple of cups of coffee so I went into the kitchen to see what she was doing. She'd set a tray out with biscuits and buns and made some little sandwiches with boiled ham in them.

' "I thought you were just making coffee," I said.

' "I'm hungry," she says, "and I expect you can eat something. You can carry the tray in for me. Get that little stool out from under the television set and put it on that."

'I did this and sat down on the couch next to where she'd been. When she came in with the coffee-pot she said, "Yes, that's right. I can see to you better if you're there." I thought of a very suggestive remark I could have made to that but I let it go and she said her and Ronnie often had their supper off a tray like that and I said summat about the joys of married life and she said had I never thought of trying it.

'I said I expected I'd get round to it in time but I wasn't thinking about it at all serious yet. So she said it was all right for men, they could go around having as much fun as they liked but when they got married they expected the girl to be absolutely untouched. I said I didn't think all men were that way and anyway most lasses weren't too much bothered about that sort of thing till they did get married.

' "Perhaps they're not," she says, "but some men are very good at persuading them."

' "Oh, you've got to use a bit of persuasion," I said; "that's part of the game."

' "I'll bet you're good at it, too," she says.

'Well, you can imagine how I was feeling by this time . . .'

'Perfectly,' Wilf said. 'Carry on.'

'I said I'd had me moments like, but I didn't want her to think I was out with women every night.

"Oh no," she said, "she didn't think that, but when

you'd been married a while you forgot what it was like when you were single and men were attentive and paid you compliments. In fact," she said, "even though you were perfectly happy with your husband there were times when you thought it'd be a pleasant change if another chap did make advances." '

'And this was when you kissed her?'

'Aye. The next thing I knew we were sprawling across the couch and she was ruffling my hair while I kissed her. She said when we came up for air, "You've been wanting to do that for some time, haven't you?" I said how did she know and she said women could always tell. Then she said we were going to knock the tray over if we didn't watch out and she got up and took it into the kitchen. When she came back she sat down next to me again and reached for a cigarette. I took it off her and pushed her back down again. She didn't hold me off at all and when I thought it was time, I started to unfasten her blouse.'

Harry stopped and looked at Wilf. 'Are you getting a second-hand thrill out of all this?' he said, almost accusingly.

Wilf grinned. 'I must admit I'm a bit envious.'

'You won't be in a minute,' Harry said. 'I'm sorry to disappoint you but there's not much more to it. The telly was still playing and we were both busy with what we were doing, not expecting anybody. We didn't hear anybody come up the path and the first thing we know is the back door opening and Ronnie shouting hello. I suppose it takes above five seconds to shut the door and walk nice and steady through their kitchen and two seconds after Ronnie shouts June's pushing me off and shouting herself. "Get off, get off! Leave me alone!" Then she's on her feet, breathing heavy, her face red, her hair mussed up, and somehow her blouse is torn. And Ronnie's standing in the doorway gawping at us.

'He can't speak for a minute, but June's saying plenty. Thank God Ronnie's back, he's just come at the right time. Another minute later and she doesn't know what might have happened. Then she turns away and fastens her blouse and reckons she's sobbin' like. Ronnie drops his case and starts on me. His face is red at first and then it goes white and his eyes stare as if they'll pop out of his head. I'm a dirty sneaking bastard, supposed to be a friend of the family and the minute his back's turned I sneak in there and try to rape his wife. And so on, while I try to gather me wits and get over the shock of Ronnie coming home and the way June's turned round on me.

' "You don't mean you really think I forced her to it, do you?" I say to him. "All right, you caught your missis havin' a cuddle with another bloke, but that's all it was an' she wasn't pushing me off a minute since."

'June turns round on me, her eyes flashing. "You're a rotten liar," she says. "You know very well how it happened." An' y'know, she's so bloody good in the part I can nearly believe her meself.

'So I say all right, then, if that's her story I suppose she'll stick to it and there's nowt much else I can say. I'm keeping one eye on Ronnie all this time, y'understand, because I'm expecting him to come for me any second. But he doesn't. He stands still, kinda frozen to the spot with rage. Then he starts again. Some blokes would punch me face for me, he says, but that's too good for a lousy, two-faced underhand bastard like me. He'll show me up good an' proper for what I am. He'll lay a charge against me for criminal assault and I can think about it while I'm doing time.

'Then he goes over to June, who's got her back turned doing the sobbing act again, an' says to me, "You'd better clear off, mate. You've done enough damage here tonight. But don't think you've heard the last of it, because you haven't. Not by a long chalk. By the time I've finished with you your name'll stink with every decent man and woman in the village." '

Harry gave an expressive lift of his shoulders.

'And that's where you swep' out,' Wilf said.

'Not so much swep' as crawled. Christ, what a bitch!'

'Come to think of it, you can't expect her to admit straight out that she encouraged you.'

'No, mebbe not, but it's a bit thick coming the assault business.'

'You said you went to work yesterday as usual?'

'Aye.'

'And there was no whisper of it about?'

'Not a breath. An' I was waiting for it, believe me.'

'I wonder if he's been to see a solicitor.'

'Oh Christ, man, you're Job's bloody comforter, you are!'

'I'm only examining the possibilities. If he goes to the police it might not be possible for him to change his mind later. In some cases the police themselves prefer the charges and this might be one of them.'

'You do think I can be had up for it, then?'

'I sure do. I most certainly do. If Master Ronnie and his missis really feel malicious they can make you sing.'

There was a sense of baffled outrage about Harry. 'But I mean,' he said, 'I only kissed her and put me hand inside her blouse, and she practically invited me to do that.'

'Society always believes the woman, Harry, even if her name might suffer a bit in the process. Look, you're sitting in a non-corridor railway carriage minding your own business. You're alone with a woman you've never seen before. She pulls herself about a bit and at the next station she accuses you of interfering with her. You haven't a leg to stand on. Or you take a bird out in a car and stop somewhere and put your hand on her knee. She's one of these young teasers who panic easy and haven't the gumption to say no. She screams. You're in trouble. Technically you've assaulted her.' Wilf shook his head. 'You can't win, old lad.'

Harry was silent. He'd come to him to talk about it (which flattered Wilf) and derived some comfort from recounting the episode. Now, if anything, he was more scared than when he arrived. It hadn't been Wilf's purpose to make him so, but there was nothing to be gained by avoiding the facts.

Harry cleared his throat. 'What sort of sentence can they give you for this kinda thing?' he said.

Here Wilf began to play it softly; there was no use panicking Harry altogether. It was curious, Harry's fear. Wilf thought that his being wanted on an ordinary charge of assault or even a crime such as breaking and entering wouldn't have affected him in the same way. But there was this shameful taint about cases of sexual misdemeanour which for a person of Harry's straightforward masculine pride was particularly hard to take.

'In your case I should say fairly light. Three months, perhaps only probation. They deal very severely with really serious cases, of course.'

He didn't add that he had an uneasy suspicion that Ronnie, if really vindictive (and if he could get June to tell the right story), could make a charge of attempted rape.

'Anyway, it won't happen to you.'

'I wish I'd your confidence, mate.'

'You should have. Have you forgotten you've a joker up your sleeve that neither Ronnie nor June knows about?'

'What's that?'

'The photograph of June in the raw.'

'Oh, that.'

'Yes, that. Don't tell me you've burned it, or something.'

He had a moment of near panic himself before Harry said, 'No, it's still in the case at home.'

'That's okay, then.'

'I don't see what good it is, though.'

'Well, use your loaf and think, man.'

'You mean because she's had her picture taken in her pants she can't be assaulted? Why, you can be pinched for raping a prostitute if you do it when she doesn't want you to.'

'Yes, but your defence would be a sight more convincing than if it was an ordinary decent housewife who was charging you.'

Harry shrugged. 'I dunno. I suppose so.'

Wilf said, 'Look, if June thought Ronnie was going to get to know about the picture she might talk him out of going ahead with his revenge. Or if Ronnie saw it he might realise that June could have given you some encouragement after all. And there's always the fact that it could become public property. If nothing else that would show that perhaps Mrs Ronnie Betley isn't all she seems and you're not quite the rogue they're making you out to be.'

'You mean you'd show the photo round?'

Wilf looked at him. 'If this thing goes wrong, Harry, and they get you put away, I'll print so many copies of that picture they'll fall on Bronhill like confetti at a wedding.'

Harry regarded Wilf wonderingly. 'You're a bugger when you get going, aren't you?' he said finally.

Wilf was on his feet, going towards the folded blankets that lay on his bed. 'It all depends how hard I'm pushed,' he said over his shoulder. He half unfolded one of the blankets and threw it over the arm of his chair. 'Those two chairs won't be as comfortable as a bed, but you'll manage.'

'I'll manage all right.' Harry rubbed his eyes and yawned. 'I could sleep on a clothes-line right now.' He stood up and started to unfasten his tie.

'Maybe Poppy'll know where you can get a room if you want to stick around here a while. Anyway, we'll talk about that when I get back from home tomorrow.'

'Are you goin' tomorrow?'

'First thing. Somebody's got to go and tell Mam where you are and see the Betleys as well. If I'd known about all this last night I'd have been over today. Let's hope it won't be too late, that's all.'

'Oh hell!' Harry said in exasperation. 'I don't know

where I am with you. One minute you're saying it'll be all right and the next you're on about it being too late.'

Wilf stood with his hands on his hips and watched Harry unbutton his shirt and pull it free of his trousers. 'Y'know, you're like a bloody little boy, Harry. You've got to face the facts.' He sat on the edge of his bed, still watching his scowling brother. 'All my life, Harry, you've been there, three years older than me, the leader, the bloke who knew what was what. The man who did a man's work while his kid brother pushed a pen and messed about with writing in his spare time. Now here you are, coming to me because there's nobody else you can talk to. Coming to me for advice.'

'Don't bloody rub it in,' Harry said.

'No, I like it, Harry. If nothing else comes out of this I'll always be pleased you came to me.'

'You've got all the friggin' brains in the family,' Harry said; 'you might as well use 'em now an' again.'

Wilf was grinning as he unfolded the second blanket. 'Bog's to the left on the first landing,' he said. 'Don't wake the house up.'

15

He set out straight after breakfast, having asked Poppy to phone his office to say that urgent personal affairs at home forced him to take the day off, and reached Bronhill about noon. There was no direct bus service and he had to change several times, his progress occasionally halted by the necessity of waiting for connections which were not arranged to facilitate his particular journey. He wondered that Harry had reached him at all last night.

He left the last bus on the high road and walked the remaining mile to the village, skirting the fenced-off mine premises, the coal-dust-surfaced yard, the piles of rusting ironwork, the litter of grimy surface buildings and the wheels of the headgear which seemed to quiver against the summer-blue sky, and emerged into the belt of farmland beyond. The sulphurous stink of the pit-heap lingered in his nostrils till he had gone a considerable way along the beaten colliers'-path. Then the village came into view, the houses straggling along a low skyline, rows of vile plum-red boxes that had held all his childhood and that of hundreds like him. Before him the village, behind him the pit. He walked the trodden colliers'-path and his mind's ear picked up the scuff of the thousands of pairs of boots and clogs which had walked there before him. It could so easily have been his destiny, and the blessed rightness of his escape so suddenly filled him that even the seriousness of his errand couldn't stop the buoyant lift of his heart. There on the path he seemed in possession of a sure clear knowledge of what he was and what he would become. It was a certainty of knowledge he had never experienced before and it lasted only a few moments. Then he was sobered by remembering the reason for his journey and he began to think over what he would say to his mother. Before going to bed he had phoned a telegram to be delivered first thing this morning and taken advantage of its acceptable brevity to make the message vague: 'Harry here overnight. Will be home about noon.' He knew it would be Harry she would be expecting, not him, but he had a satisfactory story to cover that. He would have avoided sending the telegram if he could – to his mother their rare arrival inevitably meant bad news – but there was no other means of communicating with her and he knew the agony of worry she would have suffered after finding Harry's bed empty and unslept in. She would have had to go to the police, and he wanted no contact with them just now. This was assuming they hadn't already been to find Harry.

When the square tower of the Norman church, a beautiful old relic of feudal Bronhill, standing aloof in parkland beyond the mining township, came into view he had reached a narrow connecting path along which he struck to get to the road. He came in then past newish grey section-built council houses before reaching the yard of old Armitage's smallholding which had previously marked the termination of the village proper on this side since he could remember. In a few minutes he was passing the school, surrounded by asphalted playground, with newly painted green iron hand-railings on the steps which led up to the two doors. One had carved over its lintel BOYS, the other one GIRLS. Boys and girls mixed in classes often to the extent of sharing double desks but those who built the school had frowned on fraternisation during entry and exist. His leaving there at eleven marked something of a dividing line in his overall memory image of his childhood. He could recall clearly many of the doubts and fears of grammar school, but was life before that really the uncomplex thing it seemed to him now to have been? There were guard-rails on the pavement-edge immediately opposite each of the two gates into the yard. He couldn't remember any accident resulting from their absence in his own time, though it was, later, a child's death under the wheels of a bus that was the direct cause of their erection. Through the open tops of the tall windows came the chant of children's voices reciting in unison some piece of verse he felt he ought to remember, but couldn't. He glanced at his watch. They would be out before long.

Going round the corner he had to step off the narrow pavement to avoid three or four people queuing outside Collinson's fish and chip shop. Collinson's was no more than a painted shed fitted out with frying equipment. Bottles of fizzy lemonade, lime-juice and soda, and dandelion and burdock stood across the bottom of the small four-paned window overlooking the pavement and in the window's two upper corners were, as in all the past years he could remember, a notice of some church activity and a bill showing the current programme at the Star Cinema, Ashfield. Housed in the least imposing premises, Collinson's sold the best fish and chips for miles around. Old Collinson must be nearly seventy now but he showed no sign of relinquishing his hold on the little gold mine he'd worked for the past forty years. People said he was tight, but if he nibbled at the portions he never varied his quality. And his stuff was clean.

Wilf hesitated when he had passed the little wooden building and stopped to turn and look back. His mother usually kept the main meal of the day until his father and Harry came off shift in the early afternoon and he wondered if he should take some fish and chips in with him. He had decided to wait until he'd seen his mother and come back if necessary, when a girl came out from among the six or seven people crowding the tiny interior of the shop.

Wilf said, 'Hello, Glynis.'

Glynis Wardle raised her head and looked at him. 'Why, hello, Wilf. What are you doing here?'

'I was just standing here wishing I'd a bob for every mixed I've had from Collinson's.'

She smiled pleasantly. 'Yes, they are popular, aren't they?'

She was carrying a newspaper package of fish and chips; just enough for one person by the size of it. 'I thought you stayed in Calderford for lunch,' he said.

She walked with him along the street.

'I'm not at the shop any more,' Glynis told him.

'Oh?'

'Haven't you heard about me mam?' she said. 'She's been poorly for about a month now. It's some sort of growth on her kidneys. They've had her into hospital and operated once, but they say there's nothing much more they can do.' Glynis's face was clouded over by an expression of long-maturing concern. 'She just lies in bed getting thinner every day. You wouldn't know her now. I gave up me job when they brought her home, so that I could look after her . . .'

He felt a spasm of compassion for her, but over his murmured 'I am sorry, Glynis' she said, forcibly erasing the look of worry and summoning a smile for him, 'Anyway, you don't come home to be met with other people's troubles. Have you been here long?'

'I'm just arriving. You're the first person I've run into.'

'And how is everything with you? Have you got a nice place to live?'

'Yes, I've a very comfortable room and a landlady who looks after me hand and foot.'

'What about your writing? Any more successes yet?'

'Not yet. I'm working on a novel. It's a long job.'

'Yes, it must be. But are you pleased with it? Do you think it's good?'

'Sometimes I do and then sometimes I don't.' He laughed.

'But you do know really, don't you? I mean inside you?'

'Yes, Glynis, yes I do. It's all right.'

'You'll be famous yet. I can see it coming.'

He laughed again. 'One of these days.'

They stood at the corner for a moment and as Glynis faced him, the packet of fish and chips held up against her breast, the sun caught the cluster of tiny diamonds in the ring on her left hand.

He said, 'Ey, ey, ey! You'd have left me without mentioning it, wouldn't you?'

She coloured faintly with pleasure and glanced quickly down at the ring.

'When did all this take place? Is it anybody I know?' He found that he was genuinely pleased for her, smiling widely.

'I don't think you will know him. He's a Calderford boy, a joiner. His firm did some work in the shop. That's how I met him. We've been engaged a fortnight.'

Impulsively he took her free hand in his. 'And are you happy about it?'

Her eyes clouded again and he felt the stupidity of his question.

'It seems wrong to be happy about anything with me mam the way she is.'

'I know.' He squeezed her hand and released it. 'It was a damn' silly thing to say.'

'I know what you mean,' Glynis said. 'Don't apologise. I am happy about it. He's a lovely boy, Geoff. He's so understanding. It can't be much fun for him, me not being able to get out much, but he comes over nearly every night on his motorbike and sits in the house with me.'

He said quietly, 'We were right about us, you see, Glynis. It's come out right in the end.'

She nodded. 'Yes. I know what you meant now.' She had coloured faintly and her eyes were downcast.

Yes, it looked as though she'd found what she wanted. A decent, sober, probably rather undersexed young chap who would cherish her and give her children to whom she would be a warm, flexible, if rather unimaginative mother. Glynis would be all right.

'How's your dad?' he said. 'It must be a strain for him.'

'He just doesn't seem to be able to understand it,' she said. 'He goes to his work and comes homes and mopes about not saying anything and not doing anything.'

'Ah, well . . .'

She squeezed the packet. 'I shall have to run or these'll be cold.'

He said, 'Give him my regards. And all the very best to you, love.'

'I'm ever so glad to have seen you,' she said. 'Best of luck with the book.'

He watched her go, then went on himself, unable now to repress a small nag of self-criticism – that somebody else had come to terms with Glynis when he could not; succeeded where he'd failed. He was only a few minutes from home now. He went through the entry and in at the back door. The house was quiet, clean as a scrubbed pan, a small hot fire burning in the blackleaded grate. He called out 'Hello!' and heard the tread of feet on the bedroom floor overhead. His mother called from the stairhead 'Who's there? Is that you, Harry?' He heard her begin to come down and he stood with his hands in his trousers pockets on the hearth-rug till she appeared through the door.

'Well,' she said, 'here's a stranger.' She gave not the slightest sign of being glad to see him. But since expressions of emotions other than impatience or bad temper had always been unusual in the house he thought nothing of this. He knew she was pleased he was here though she would hold against this his absence for so long.

'You haven't forgotten your way after all, then?' she said.

'But I was here only the other week,' he protested without conviction.

'Five weeks ago,' his mother said. 'Six weeks this coming Saturday. For a couple of hours. Three visits in the seven months you've been away.'

'Well I do write as well, don't I?'

'Aye,' she said, 'you do write. When you've time.'

She looked across the room into the scullery. 'Where's our Harry? Haven't you brought him with you?'

'Well no. He's not feeling too good. I think he might have a touch of 'flu. I made him stop in bed this morning. He'll be okay in a day or two.'

She grunted. ' 'Flu. I'll bet you two were on the beer last night, weren't you?'

'We did have a couple,' Wilf lied.

'An' then he gets a thick head an' has to stop in bed and break his work. What was he thinking of to go off all that way from home without telling me, and then miss his last bus?'

'He came on the spur of the moment.'

'Aye, an' me worried out of me wits when I find his bed empty and a telegram lad banging on the door at the crack o' dawn, coming with I don't know what manner o' news. He ought to show a bit more consideration, that's all I can say.' Her face was severe, disapproving. She said, 'I reckon you'll have had to break your own work to come over here today.'

He shrugged. 'Oh, it'll be all right.'

'Aye, it'll be all right. You young fowk, you think you can come an' go as you please.' She came towards him and pushed him away from the fire. 'Sit yersen down now you're here. You're no good as a draw-tin.'

He sat down by the table and his mother bent and opened the oven door, releasing a delicious odour of cooking into the room.

'Is that a meat and potato pie?'

'It is.'

'I nearly brought some fish and chips in with me.'

'A good job you didn't, then. I'm making this now an' it'll warm up for your dad when he comes in.'

'How is me dad? All right?'

'Like he allus is: quiet as an old sheep when he's well an' as bad tempered as an old billy goat when he's off it.'

Wilf smiled. It must be all right, he thought. She could be holding out on him, deliberately testing his patience. But that was not her way. If she knew anything she would have spoken by now.

'I've just been talking to Glynis Wardle up the street,' he said. 'It seems her mother's very poorly.'

His mother straightened up, shutting the oven door and draping over the fireguard the cloth she had used to protect her hands from the heat of the pie-dish.

'Aye, that poor woman. They say she can't last much longer. She's just wasting away. That lass has learned a lot o' things the hard way this past few weeks.'

'She's engaged to be married.'

'So I hear. Still, you shouldn't be surprised at that. You had your chance with her and you can't expect her to wait about. She'll make him a grand wife, whoever he is.'

'Young feller from Calderford,' Wilf said, ignoring the provocative part of his mother's comment. 'A joiner, she says.'

'It'll be a funeral followed by a wedding, from the look of it. And there's her father to think about; she can't leave him to fend for himself.'

'She can stay at home when she's married. It'll save them the trouble of looking for a house.'

'Ah, but to be saddled with a widowed father. It's not right. A young couple want privacy, some life on their own before they start with a family.'

He had a sudden wild notion of his mother's upholding the right of a young married couple to run naked about the house in idyllic bouts of newly granted sexual licence, making love on the rug in front of the fire if they wanted to. And, of course, in a way this was true though his mother's mental image would be more of a vaguely generalised picture of the intimacy of married life and the right to adjust to it, enjoy the novelty of it, without a third person around to distort the process.

'Love conquers all,' he said idly. He drummed the finger-ends of his right hand on the table top. He was pleased to see his mother but rather bored. Five minutes in the house and he was bored, restless, wanting to be off. It wasn't that he wasn't fond of her, didn't love her, but the contentment in her company that a simpler man than himself might have felt was something he could not summon up. And he couldn't help it. He was slightly ashamed of it, but he couldn't help it. He moved his hand. He could try not to show it, anyway.

His mother laid the table for the two of them. There was nothing fancy about it. A knife and fork at each side of the table, on a clean cloth. The cruet in the middle: salt, pepper and empty, never-used mustard dish in a nickel-plated stand with 'A present from Morecambe' and the town's coat of arms on the base. He couldn't recall who had brought them that back but they'd had it for years. She put two dinner plates to warm in the recess over the oven then fetched a glass of water from the scullery tap and set it by his place. She opened the oven door and inspected the pie again. The smell of it set the saliva running in his mouth.

'We'll give that just another minute.' There was nothing else for her to do so she stood with folded arms, the oven cloth in one hand, and regarded him. 'Well, what have you got to say for yourself now you're here?'

He shrugged. 'Nothing much.'

'Well you're a poor affair. You might as well have stopped away for all the good you are. Is that Mrs Swallow still looking after you well?'

He prepared himself for the usual run of questions. Did he get enough to eat? Did he change his underwear regularly and get his socks mended? He didn't seem to be putting much weight on. Was he sure he was getting his meals? Missing meals was easy when you didn't live at home; but silly. It meant you became a prey of every infection going about.

'It's about time you treated yourself to a haircut as well,' she said, eyeing him critically. 'You look like a spring poet.'

He fingered the thick hair at the back of his head. Yes, he had let it go a bit too far. He liked his hair to be short and easily manageable, tidy when he couldn't be bothered to comb it, but he'd been on his way to the barber's for the past two or three weeks now and hadn't got there yet.

'An' haven't you a better pair o' shoes than them to walk about in?' she went on, looking with distaste at his greasy suèdes with the sole on the right one coming away from the upper.

'My others are ready for the cobbler's,' he said.

'Well I don't know what they can be like then, because these're ready for the rag and bone man.' She turned to take the pie out of the oven, talking over her shoulder. 'I could do with all these fancy ideas about living away from home if they showed any improvement in your position, but when you come back looking as if you're ready for the poorhouse I think it's time you revised your ideas a bit.'

She stood with the pie in her hands. Gravy steam rose up through the slots cut in the crust. 'Just pop into the scullery and get me something to stand this on.'

He hurried through and brought a big table-mat and his mother set the pie-dish on it in the middle of the table.

'That looks marvellous,' Wilf said, the juices running in his mouth. 'I'm famished.'

'Didn't you get a good breakfast afore you set off?'

'I had bacon and egg, but that was four hours ago.'

She served him a large helping, spooning a smaller portion on to her own plate, and they sat down to eat.

'Careful with the salt,' she warned. 'I should try it first.'

He dug in. Ah! his mother's meat and potato pie . . . the tasty slices of potato, the tender chopped mutton, and the crust, not too short but not stodgy either –

perfect! He wolfed it down and she watched him, a flicker of pleasure in her eyes as he sat back behind his empty plate.

'Well, it didn't take you long to shift that. D'you want a bit more?'

He held out the plate with both hands. 'Please.'

'Doesn't your Mrs Swallow make you meat an' tatie pie?' she asked as she served him.

'Sometimes. She's not a bad cook, Poppy, but she hasn't your touch with a pie.'

She almost smirked with pleasure!

'You can't have everything, can you?' she said. 'You can't have your independence, as you call it, and your mother's pies as well.'

There was no sweet. She made a pot of tea and they moved away from the table to drink it. As if to show still further what he was missing of home comforts she cut into a fruit cake she'd baked yesterday and he ate three slices under her approving, self-satisfied gaze.

'I'm really happy living as I am,' he told her.

'Well then,' she conceded, 'a mother can't keep her lads at home for ever.'

'And you've still got Harry,' he pointed out.

'Aye, till he bethinks himself to get wed.'

'He's not even courting, is he? He didn't say anything to me about it.'

'He hasn't said owt to me but he'll be dropping it on us one o' these days. I expect.'

Wilf set aside his cup and leaned back in his chair. So she really didn't know anything. So far, so good.

16

He went round to the Betleys' house that afternoon when his father had come home from the pit. He thought it the most likely time to catch Ronnie in, though it was hard to be sure because he didn't stick to the usual hours. The pit managers let union officials come on and off at irregular times to avoid the inconvenience of being plunged into the middle of the men with their petty grumbles and grievances at the conventional shift changes. He sat with his father while the latter ate the rest of the pie, washing it down with long draughts from a pint mug of heavily sweetened tea. There was not much in the way of conversation between them. His father asked him how he was keeping and gave the reply of 'fair to middlin'' when asked the same in return. He was a distant man with a deep reserve, hard to get to know. Wilf felt that he had never got to know him. He was *shy*: shy with his wife and children, with his workmates and with everyone he knew. He had no real friends, only acquaintances. And underlying the shyness was the personal bitterness that Wilf had always perceived yet never understood. It came from somewhere far back, deep in the roots of his early life. It was as though, somewhere far back there, he had suffered a stupendous disappointment from which he never recovered, a gigantic shattering of his faith in life itself, so that ever after he had cultivated a quiet resignation that left him only in rare moments of rage. He was really, Wilf thought, an exemplary husband, always the steady provider, never given to excessive drinking or gambling, never a fancier of women. But a dull dog, unable to share his children's pleasures and now, with one of them at least, beyond the effort of understanding.

He would have to leave early after tea, he told his mother, but in the meantime he thought he would have a stroll round the village. There were a few of his personal belongings left in the room he'd shared with Harry and these gave him the excuse to go upstairs and get the photograph out of his brother's case. On the way he tried not to rehearse the coming interview in his imagination; he might be thrown off balance if he had his own lines off pat and the other half of the dialogue didn't come out as expected. He reflected instead on his attitude towards Betley in general, and what he stood for. He decided that he both disliked and feared him. His dislike was the dislike he felt for the apostle of any creed which was based on the humanities and which violated those humanities in the furtherance of its ends. Jesus Christ had taught the humanities and through century after century since men and women and children had been butchered, tortured, and put to death in grisly ceremony for the sake of lip service. God for the sake of God. It was better that you were a sinner and believed than that you were upright, kindly, humane and did not. But death in agony could redeem you. Communism had grown out of an exile's passionate sense of injustice, a burning desire to see a fair apportioning of the world's wealth so that the paradox of the inordinately rich and the pitifully poor might be resolved for ever. And the churches had never done this: it was, all evidence showed, in their interest to foster ignorance and superstitious fear, and humble acceptance of one's lot in the world. And now? The cause for the sake of the cause. So you fostered what you were ostensibly out to banish. Industrial unrest was bad for the workers as well as the industrialists themselves, but to foster it under capitalism was to bring closer the day of triumph for the cause.

A means to an end, when in fact there would never be an end, all means being ends in themselves, and corruption in their every perversion. And the fear he felt for Betley was the fear he felt for anyone who was single-minded enough to be able to say, in a word, I am a—, I believe in—. Because what was he himself? A vague, woolly minded semi-intellectual with liberal leanings. And what did he believe in? There were so many things he did *not* believe in. But what *did* he believe in? What was he ready to stand up and shout for, or to plot secretly for? What? . . . A couple of hours in bed with Poppy?

He wondered if June would be there and couldn't make up his mind whether he hoped she would be or not. As it happened, she was not.

The Betleys lived in a two-bedroomed bungalow on a small new development at the upper end of the village. The houses hadn't been up long and although the grey concrete kerbstones were in position the street itself was still an unsurfaced rubble track that must knock hell out of Ronnie's secondhand Morris Minor which was parked outside the house as Wilf went along the unmade pavement. The ingrained custom of a lifetime took him to the back door when he felt that better tactics should have made him choose the front. But there was some sense of feeling exposed while standing on the front step waiting for an answer to his knock that he didn't like; as though everyone along the street was in the know and awaiting developments.

The back door stood wide open and he knocked on that, wondering why, even in normal circumstances, you felt slightly foolish knocking on an open door. He looked at what he could see of the small neat kitchen with built-in cupboard units, painted lilac and pale grey, and the stainless-steel fittings. A big new refrigerator stood against the wall, very near to the door.

He started as he was hailed from behind, and spun round to see Betley coming out of the shed that stood at the far end of the garden past the recently sown square of lawn where the young green shoots of grass stood delicately proud above the hard greyish earth. He watched Betley come down the path towards him, a smallish dapper man of about thirty in a brown wool sports shirt and belted slacks. His strong straight black hair was brushed along his neat skull. He had a good complexion and as he drew nearer Wilf saw that he needed a shave and was beginning ever so slightly to run to fat along his jawline and round his middle.

Wilf said, 'Hello, Ronnie.'

'Now, then, Wilf,' Betley said. 'Long time no see. How's tricks?'

'Oh, not so dusty . . .'

Ronnie fished out a packet of cigarettes, darting little glances here and there and at Wilf's face. He remembered to offer the packet to Wilf after he'd lit a cigarette for himself. Wilf refused with a shake of his head.

'I wanted to have a bit of a chat with you,' he said. 'I reckon you'll know what about.'

'I can make a good guess.' Betley drew deeply at the cigarette. 'Well then,' he said abruptly, 'come on inside.' He led the way in through the kitchen, still talking. 'No use entertaining the neighbours.'

'There'll be nothing to see anyway,' Wilf said. 'I haven't brought me gun this time.'

'Voices carry on a quiet afternoon,' Ronnie said. 'I never did believe in letting everybody know me business.' He opened the sitting-room door. 'We can go in here.'

Wilf followed him in. Immediately facing him across the blue fitted carpet was an open bureau with papers in the pigeon-holes and on the writing surface. Signs of a man of affairs, he thought, and sat down on the deep sofa, trying to look as casually at ease as possible. As he sat back and crossed his legs he reflected that he was occupying the very spot where, two nights ago, Harry had clasped Betley's wife in a passionate and long-wished-for clinch. Betley sat forward in an armchair by the low blue-tiled fireplace. Someone round here was very fond of blue, Wilf thought. The firegrate was empty, with a folded newspaper propped up in it but the window caught the sun and the room was full of light and warmth. Ronnie smoked in silence for a few moments, flicking ash on to the tiled hearth. Finally he said curtly:

'Come on then, say your piece.'

'Is June in?'

'No, she's at her mother's for the day.'

Wilf settled himself more comfortably on the sofa, thought of the photograph in his pocket, and said:

'Harry's at my place. He came over last night and told me what had happened.'

'I heard he hadn't been at work today,' Betley said. 'What's he doing skulking out there?'

'He was a bit off it this morning so he stayed in bed.'

'And he let his kid brother come to plead for him.'

More sharply than he intended, at this stage of the conversation anyway, Wilf said, 'Pleading wasn't exactly what I had in mind, Ronnie.'

'Oh?' Betley let his eyes drift sardonically to Wilf's face for a second. 'What then?'

'A bit of reasonable talking to a man who's used to it.'

'And he has to send you to do it for him.'

'I can't imagine you and him talking reasonably any more, can you? Anyway, he didn't send me. I took it out of his hands and came. I knew we could talk, because you've got no quarrel with me. Have you?'

Betley went on smoking. 'Well, go on. I'm listening.'

'According to Harry there was some talk of bringing a charge for assault.'

'That's right.'

'It struck me that he'd misunderstood in the confusion of the moment. I thought he'd misheard.'

'He heard, all right.'

'You really did threaten to have him charged?'

'I did.'

Wilf pursed his lips and appeared to think for a moment.

'Well, of course,' he said then, 'Harry was in the wrong to some extent, but a charge . . . that's going a bit far, isn't it?'

'To some extent?' Betley said. He sat further forward. 'That bloody brother of yours has shown himself up for the biggest bastard for miles around. He's come here without hardly missing a week for months past and he's always been made welcome, treated as a friend of the family. We've sat in this room for hours on end, the three of us, talking about everything under the sun. And when he's gone home June and I have remarked to each other what a grand bloke he was, and we've wondered when he was going to find himself a nice young woman and settle down.'

Wilf looked at Betley, nodding gravely at the image of clean wholesome friendship he was conjuring up.

'And then what?' Betley cried. 'When we've got to a stage where I'd trust him with anything I've got, then what does he do? He takes the first chance of finding June on her own and tries to rape her!'

'Oh, come on now, Ronnie,' Wilf said. 'That's a bit strong, surely.'

'Strong? Strong, y'say? The only bloody thing that stopped him was me walking in when I did.'

'I should have thought that June was capable of holding him off if she wanted to.'

Betley's head jerked round. 'Now just a minute, mate. This is my wife we're talking about. What d'you mean "if she wanted to"?'

Wilf met Betley's look with one of innocence. 'It was just a slip of the tongue, Ronnie. A figure of speech.'

Betley jabbed the air in front of Wilf with his forefinger. 'I'd just like you to be clear how much this has upset June,' he said. 'It's a wonder she hasn't had a breakdown.'

'Well, naturally, I'm more concerned for Harry,' Wilf

said. 'He's my responsibility in this affair, as I might say. Still, I can understand the feelings of any decent, unsuspecting young woman when something like this happens. And honestly, in your shoes, Ronnie, I'd think for a long time before I prolonged it for her and possibly made it a good deal worse.'

'What d'you mean?'

'Well, to bring a charge against Harry would mean her going through the ordeal of testifying about what happened – and in detail. And then there's the publicity to think about. I certainly shouldn't want a wife of mine to have her name bandied about on every street corner and in every bar in the village.'

'No, and you don't want Harry's name bandied about either, eh?' Betley said.

'Of course not. But you know how it is – a man; they nudge one another and wink and say hard lines, he didn't get away with it, and they wouldn't mind having a crack at the same target themselves—'

'Now look here!' Betley's throat and cheeks flushed with sudden violent colour. Wilf saw him tense himself as if to rise from the chair and he quickly uncrossed his legs and leaned forward, lifting both hands, the palms turned towards Betley as if in supplication.

'Let's have no illusions about this, Ronnie. You know what people are and you know what they'll think and say if this gets noised about. Everybody knows that June's an attractive woman.' He swung his hands and for a moment placed his palms to his chest, his eyes widening in an expression of disarming candour. '*I* know it, Ronnie; I've always known it. And you know what minds they have, these people, and how they fasten on to a nine-day wonder. They'll start to fancy things. They'll begin to say things like "Ah, it's all very well them shoving that young feller in jail but she must have given him some encouragement, if the truth be known. Hadn't he been visiting them regular for months? Thick as thieves, they were. Never off their doorstep by all accounts. And for why? Because she must have been making up to him when the husband wasn't looking. If you ask me she can't be any better than she should be . . ." '

Wilf stopped and looked at Betley who sat very still, his elbows on his knees, hands clasped before his mouth.

'Can't you imagine it, Ronnie? All of 'em, the women and the men at it: the women looking at June and the men looking at both her and you because you're a man they've always respected, a man who can talk to them, a man who's going a long way before he's finished. Nobody'll hold anything against Harry for long. If he doesn't want to stay in Bronhill he can get a job somewhere else. It doesn't matter to him: he's a nobody. But you're not a nobody, Ronnie. Everybody knows you. You tell people what to do . . .'

He leaned back, as though finished, and looked at his hands. When he judged that Betley was about to speak he said, almost casually:

'Something I've always admired about you is the way you can influence the men here. Cuthbert was one of them but he couldn't do it like you can. And you're both one of them and a cut above them. They know you're a cut above them but they respect you because you're not just a bloke who shoots his mouth off. You've earned your living the same way they do and when you talk it makes sense to them. You know what these men are as well as I do. Better, in fact. They work hard and they play hard, and they know how to handle their women. And a man that can't handle his woman in his own way without calling in the police . . .'

Wilf stopped with a shrug. Betley got up and went into the kitchen. Wilf heard a tap running. He thought that Betley was having a drink of water, and would have liked one himself. He came back and lit another cigarette. He didn't sit down. There wasn't much more that Wilf could say. He waited. He felt he'd gone as far along that particular line of cant and humbug as he cared to.

Perhaps that was why he wanted the water: a physical symptom of the mental desire to clean his mouth.

'Well I thought I was a good talker,' Betley said, 'but you're a bloody expert yourself.' He brushed ash from the front of his trousers. 'How many people has Harry told about this?'

'Only me. And I've said nothing to anybody else. I hope,' he said without looking at Ronnie, 'that June's going to her mother's doesn't mean she wanted to confide in her.'

'She won't be doing any confiding,' Betley said with harsh assurance. 'I've told her I'll break her neck if she breathes a word to anybody about it.'

It was like a glimmer of new daylight breaking in Wilf's mind. He wondered why he should have overestimated Betley so mucn in the past. He said carefully, 'You've got my solemn assurance that it won't get out from either Harry or me.'

Betley almost snorted. '*Your* solemn assurance! That's rich. Thank you very much!' he said with heavy irony. 'You don't have to reckon to be protecting us when all you're doing is looking after that bastard brother of yours.'

'You're all three in it together,' Wilf said evenly. 'What affects one affects you all.'

'I don't know what the hell you're talking about,' Betley said. 'To listen to you you'd think we were all accomplices in something; but in fact it's Harry who's for the high jump, and we're the injured party.'

'And June's ready to swear in court that she gave him no encouragement, not the slightest sign that a pass wouldn't be unwelcome?'

'She's ready to swear to the truth. And before you go any further on that line, mate, just remember what I told you – it's my wife you're talking about.'

He was on the frontier, the line between reasonable, restrained argument and open conflict. He hesitated to cross because once over there was no way back, no alternative for him but to drive as hard as he could with the one real weapon he'd got.

'What I'm trying to say is that in all fairness you should make June realise that Harry's lawyer would be sure to try to discredit her either by trying to break down her story or digging back to try to uncover some evidence that would reflect on her character.'

'I've told you once,' Betley said, his face red again; 'you'd better watch that kind of talk.'

'I am trying,' Wilf said with heavily assumed patience, 'to show you what will happen. Harry won't give up without a fight and I'll stand by him and do anything I can to help him. The world's full of stupid people who'll cut off their nose to spite their face. I never thought you were one of them.'

He pulled himself up off the settee and stood upright, as though to mark an end to the discussion. He said quietly, 'Harry's done you a bad turn, Ronnie; but it's nothing to the one you're going to do yourself. Right now the decision's in your hands, but turn it loose and you've lost control of it. You'll be at the mercy of public opinion and God help you when you are.'

'I'll have to think about it, then, won't I?' Betley said.

'I'd like to know what you're going to do before I go.'

'I've told you – I'm going to think about it.'

So he was going to let Harry sweat. He'd listened to all Wilf had said and surely seen the sense in it. He wasn't going to jeopardise his own standing for an act of vindictiveness. He must have thought all this out for himself before Wilf came. But he'd let Wilf go on talking, and for nothing. And now Harry could stew in his own juice for a few days until it became clear that nothing would happen. This was how it surely must be, but Wilf couldn't risk going away without leaving Betley in full knowledge of what he was up against.

He said, 'Harry will be at my place for a few days. If you, or anybody else, wants him you can contact him there.' He was taking out the bundle of odds and ends that accumulated in his inside pocket: a couple of letters, a pocket diary, a notecase, a folded sheet of paper with jottings for the novel. He slipped the photograph out and put it face down on top, holding it with his thumb, and rummaged for his ballpoint. 'I'd be grateful if my mother weren't bothered for the time being; she'll be upset enough when she knows about it.'

'A bit late for the sentimental approach, isn't it?' Betley said. 'Harry should've thought about that before he attacked June.'

One more try, Wilf thought. Just one. And then he would punch this very stupid clever-dick right where it would hurt. He said, 'Y'know, Ronnie, you think too much in terms of black and white, both with politics and with people; and things are never as simple as that. Are you sure you know all there is to know about this business?'

'I know what June told me and what I saw for myself,' Betley said levelly; 'and that's good enough for me.'

'And you won't say here and now that you're going to drop this thing for the sake of everybody concerned?'

'I've told you,' Betley said. 'I'll think it over.'

'And that's the message I'm to give Harry?'

'Tell him what you like,' Betley said contemptuously; 'I'm sending him no messages.'

Wilf's gaze stayed on Betley's face for a long moment after the other had finished speaking. Betley eyed him in return. There was lofty contempt in his expression. It stung Wilf. He looked at the white, slightly soiled back of the photograph as he wrote on it. He held it out to Betley, face down. His heart was beating faster.

'There's my address, then.'

Betley took it in his fingers and looked at it idly. 'Thanks, I'll keep it in a safe place.' He turned it over, just as casually, standing swaying slightly backwards and forwards, his heels on the tiled curb, his toes in the thick pile of the powder-blue half-moon hearth-rug. He stopped moving all at once, his height dropping by a couple of inches as his heels slid down to rest flat on the rug. Wilf watched his face pale. His throat seemed to clog with phlegm through which his voice came half strangled.

'Where did you get this?' Betley's hand was trembling visibly.

'Does that matter?'

'I'm asking you where you got it,' Betley shouted, his voice suddenly breaking through harsh and strong. He lifted his eyes for an instant from the picture of his wife, almost naked in the chair, cupping her breasts as though offering them and smiling into the camera-eye.

'Harry picked it up in Sheffield some time ago.'

Wilf took a step forward, reaching out to pluck the photograph from Betley's fingers. He pushed it back into his pocket. 'Perhaps I'd better put my address on a less interesting document.'

'You bastard!'

Betley turned away and stood leaning forward, both hands on the upper edge of the fireplace, his head down between his shoulders.

'I didn't want to bring it out,' Wilf said, talking to Betley's back; 'but you forced my hand. You'll have noticed that it was taken a long time ago, before she knew you. Harry hasn't spoken about it to anybody but me.' When Betley neither moved nor spoke, he went on, 'You can't crucify a girl because she posed for a pin-up picture once. It doesn't have to mean anything. Except that this business with Harry isn't quite as black and white as you thought.'

'D'you think I don't know?' Betley burst out with sudden savagery. 'D'you think I could get her to go to court and say that Harry tried to rape her? All that time he was coming here, and I thought we were friends, he had that photo. He thought she was fair game and he was waiting for the signal. Then she gave it to him. What did he need the photo for? Couldn't he tell without it? That bloke in Calderford hadn't any photo but he got the message. And *he* had her. It wasn't just a couple of kisses and a feel inside her blouse with him. He got the bloody jackpot on the back seat of his car . . .'

He lifted his head and turned to face Wilf, seeming to pull himself together, to realise that he'd revealed more in his outburst than he'd meant to do.

'You'd better bugger off back to your brother and tell him he's won.'

'Nobody wins in a case like this, Ronnie. Everybody ends up a bit sadder and wiser, that's all.'

'Shit,' Betley said savagely. 'Don't spout your tuppence-ha'penny philosophy at me. Save it for your writing.'

'You have my word that what you've told me won't be repeated.'

'There's a good little boy scout,' Betley sneered. 'You'll just gloat over it in idle moments.'

Wilf took the photograph out of his pocket again. 'And I don't think we'll need this now.' He struck a match and held the flame to the corner of the photo.

'How do I know you haven't got some more prints?' Betley said.

'You don't.' The flame took and worked its way across a quarter of the photograph, then went out.

Betley said, 'Here, give it to me.'

He went on his knees on the hearth-rug, tore the newspaper in the grate into pieces, dropped the photograph on top and applied a match. They watched it burn, Wilf looking down over Betley's shoulder. When it was over Betley broke the ashes small with the end of the poker. Then he stood up.

'Now f—off,' he said. 'Get out of my sight.'

Wilf left without speaking. He walked out and left Betley with his thoughts. Afternoon school was out and children were playing along the street. Their cries punctured the quiet of the little backwater. A small boy rushed blindly out of a gateway and bounced back off

Wilf's legs. Wilf bent down and set him on his feet again and brushed him down. Then he went on.

He got home about nine. Harry shot up out of a chair as he went into his room. He was in shirtsleeves, without a tie. His eyes as he looked at Wilf were narrowed as though the evening sunlight was too strong for them.

'I was expecting you to ring up.'

'Were you?'

'Well there was no bloody need to keep me in suspense, was there?'

'Perhaps I didn't want to give you bad news.' He took out of his raincoat pockets the two pint-bottles of beer he'd called at the Tower for and put them on the table. He glanced at Harry whose face was set in a serious grimace.

'It's like that, is it?'

Wilf said wearily, 'No, it isn't like that. He's dropping it. You can sleep easily tonight.' He pulled off his raincoat and walked across the floor to drop it on the foot of his bed.

Harry stared at him, his face going through an almost comical slow-motion change of expression to unbelieving eagerness. 'By God, you mean you've pulled it off? You wouldn't kid me, would you?'

Wilf shook his head. 'No.' He slumped down into the big wing-chair and threw one leg over the arm. 'Go and get a couple of glasses so's we can have some beer. If I go Poppy might keep me talking.'

Harry looked for a second as though he was going to object; then he almost ran out of the room.

'Well, come on, then,' he said when he came back. He unscrewed the top of one of the bottles, poured into both tumblers and handed one to Wilf; 'let's hear all about it.'

Wilf took a drink from his glass. 'I went round to see him this afternoon when he came off shift.'

'Was she there?'

'No. He said she'd gone to her mother's. We talked for

about three-quarters of an hour. I told him I didn't see what good it would do anybody for them to bring a charge. People were sure to gossip and start wondering if June hadn't given you the come-on when he wasn't looking. He turned a bit huffy when I got on to that tack but I said I was just telling him what people would think. I also told him that the men wouldn't have much respect for a bloke who couldn't keep his own house in order without bringing the police in to help him. I laid it on as thick as I dared.'

Wilf yawned. 'Gosh, I'm tired. I feel as if I'd done a really heavy day's work.'

'You've done a bloody good day's work,' Harry said jubilantly. 'I've been walking about here all day biting my nails and wondering what was happening.'

'Haven't you been out anywhere?'

'No. I've hardly moved from this room. Poppy brought me my dinner and tea on a tray and didn't ask any questions. She's a bit of all right, that one.'

'So you said before.'

'Aye, well, it's what I think. Anyway, you're a rotten sod for not phoning. I've been expecting a call all day.'

'Oh, I hadn't time. I had a bus to catch.'

'What did me mam say?'

'She was a bit peeved, but it's nothing. I told her you'd probably got a touch of 'flu.'

Harry grinned. 'By God, Wilf, but I won't forget this, lad. The way you've helped me out . . . Anyway, what did Ronnie say to all that?'

'Well, we argy bargyed back'ards and forrards a bit. I let him give vent to his indignation and then, to cut a long story short, he admitted that all I'd told him he'd already thought out for himself. He also dropped a hint, without coming straight out with it, that June might have given you the wrong idea without meaning to, and she wasn't at all happy about making a fuss. That's the impression I got, anyway. He must already have decided to let it drop and hope you'd be sweating it out for a day or two.'

'Did you take the photo with you?'

'Yes.'

'But you didn't have to use it on him?'

'No.'

'A pity, that, in a way. I'd ha' loved to know what his face looked like when he saw that . . . Have you brought it with you or did you put it away again?'

'Neither,' Wilf said. 'I tore it up and burnt the bits.'

Harry stared at him. 'What did you do that for?'

'It's had its day. I thought that leching over it had got you into enough trouble, and it could cause a lot more if it went astray. So I took it upon meself to destroy it.'

Harry reflected. 'Aye, I suppose it's as well out of the way.' He opened the second bottle of beer and filled his own empty glass and topped up Wilf's. 'It's funny, y'know, to think how long I'd been aching to make a pass at June, and then I could have had a first-class red-hot affair with her if things had turned out just a bit different.'

Wilf waved his glass at Harry. 'Now don't start weaving fantasies along those lines again. My bet is she'd have stopped you at the waistline herself even if Ronnie hadn't turned up. She's a teaser, Harry. You've always said so yourself. And think how much worse it'd've been for you going up there afterwards, looking at her and knowing you'd had your hands on her, and wondering if there'd ever be another chance. Out of sight, out of mind. That's my prophecy for her, as far as you're concerned.'

'I suppose I'll bump into her again, though. I shan't be able to help it.'

'Well that's another thing. Take my advice and you'll get away from Bronhill as soon as you can. Get a job somewhere else.'

'Y'mean leave home an' live in digs?'

'Yeh, why not? You were telling me how lucky I was last night. Now's your chance to sample the life.'

'It'd be a change, I suppose. But I like living at home.

It's cheaper an' you get looked after better, pandered to a bit, y'know.'

'All I'm saying, Harry, is that Ronnie's not going to forget all this and if he sees a chance of getting back at you he'll take it. You're too big a target where you are, that's all.'

Harry looked at his hands. 'I suppose I can get a job easy enough . . . Plenty more pits.' He sighed. 'Aye, I think you're right again. It'll be better to get away.'

They drank beer in silence for a time.

Wilf said eventually, 'You must have been bored stiff stuck in here all day.'

'Oh, I dunno. I had a nap this afternoon. Slept for a couple of hours. Apart from that I've been scrounging round your bookcase and reading. I allus did like reading, anyway. 'Smatter of fact, I've been dipping into that book you're writing.'

Wilf sat up. 'Have you been rummaging among my papers?'

'No, I just picked the folder up with your novel in it. What you've done of it. When you gunna finish it?'

'When I can find time off from looking after other people's affairs,' Wilf said.

'You want to get stuck into it,' Harry said blithely. 'It's not bad; not bad at all.' A sly grin crept over his face. 'A bit warm in parts.'

'Warm?' Wilf said, pretending not to know what Harry was talking about.

'The sexy bits, I mean.'

'I take it there was nothing you'd have found offensive in anybody else's book?' Wilf said loftily.

'Oh, no, no. You know me, I'm as broadminded as they come. If fact I've read some pretty crude stuff in me time. Enough to turn you over, some of it. But you say a lot without actually using the words, and get it across all the same. Better, in fact.'

'I take that as a compliment.'

'It's meant to be. I've told you, it's good. You want to get it finished and sent off to a publisher. Has anybody else read it?'

'No,' Wilf said, 'and you wouldn't have if I'd thought to put it out of the way this morning.'

'You don't have to be so bloody touchy about it. You're writing it for people to read, aren't you?'

'But it'll be finished then. It seems to be a practice for some American writers to hawk books about for any Joe Doakes to make suggestions about the writing, though how the hell anybody can criticise chapter two when they don't know what chapter ten's going to be like is beyond me. But to me a book's a private thing until it's finished. Parts of that book are hopeless even if you didn't notice them.'

'Not being a literary genius, eh?'

'Oh, bollocks.'

'With knobs on,' Harry said.

Wilf grinned. 'Let's change the subject. I'm hungry.'

'I'm a bit peckish meself.'

'There's a fish and chip shop up on the main road. I thought you might like to show your gratitude by popping up for some.'

'Let's both go and have a pint at the same time.'

Wilf wasn't enthusiastic. 'I'm a bit done in.'

'Oh, come on; it'll take you out of yourself. I could do with a breath of air.' Harry was already looking round for his tie. 'What about asking Poppy to go with us?'

'You haven't been up to anything with Poppy today, have you?' Wilf said, and Harry stopped looking for the tie to gaze at him.

'Well you're a suspicious bastard, I must say. Just because I've been in one scrape with a married woman doesn't mean I go round makin' passes at every attractive bint I meet. Anyway, she's not like that, is she?'

His glance slid off Wilf's face, lingering for the last second necessary for detecting any flicker of response in Wilf's expression.

'No, she isn't,' Wilf said blandly. 'And her husband's coming home before long.'

'I thought you said she was a widow.'

'I always thought she was, but it turns out she's been separated from her hubby and now they've decided to have another go.'

'And bloody good luck to him. I wouldn't mind coming home to her meself, but I can enjoy her company for its own sake.'

Wilf went out to see Poppy and fifteen minutes later, after she'd been upstairs to change her clothes, they set off to the Tower. In the forty-five minutes left before closing time they shifted a fair number of drinks, Harry organising a string of gin and tonics for Poppy which, surprisingly soon, had her laughing like a young girl. Harry splashed on a bottle of whisky to take home and when they could stay no longer they went across the road and bought a parcel of fish and chips with which they returned, a little tipsily, to the house. Poppy made some coffee and filled a plate with bread and butter. After supper they sat on in the kitchen, drinking the whisky and talking, till after midnight. Wilf was tired and infinitely depressed. He wished he could go up with Poppy to find the oblivion of her body and pillow his head between her breasts while she comforted him to sleep. Instead, he drank more whisky than he wanted, knowing he would regret it in the morning. Eventually, while Harry and Poppy were still chatting, he dozed off to sleep and Harry had to wake him to get him to his room and into bed.

17

Summer died, after lingering on into a golden early October. The city became a place of sodium-lighted rainswept canyons, of blazing shop windows, of shopping crowds in crisp Saturday afternoon air, a city that sprawled out on all sides of its tightly knit centre in a web of access roads and dark back streets glimpsed mostly from the interiors of swaying buses. Marguerite had almost forgotten the near-total reliance of a provincial city on its bus services. In London she had used the Underground and hardly travelled on a bus at all. Before that, in Amhurst, she had seemed always to have access to private transport, either Uncle Edward's car or those of friends, and she had followed the local fashion in using a bicycle for errands about the town. Now she had to get used to buses all over again, and she disliked them, especially after dark when they brought back lingering symptoms of a childhood tendency to travel-sickness.

It was this tendency which led, towards the end of November, to a rather curious incident. On the infrequent occasions when it showed itself it affected her no more acutely than as a sense of restlessness, an inability to relax on a bus which, if it began early enough in the journey, could grow into an apprehension of sickness rather than a real attack. This one time, though, on a crowded night-time bus pulling up out of the city centre, full of damp raincoats and the day's acrid fug of stale tobacco smoke, she actually broke out in a sweat of nausea and knew that if she didn't get off quickly she would vomit helplessly on the floor. She left her seat and pushed to the platform where she clung to the rail and took deep breaths of the damp air, feeling it strike coldly on her hot face. She got off at the next stop, thankful to have escaped without disgracing herself, and set out to walk the remaining mile to home. The homegoing traffic sizzled by on the wet road as her stiletto heels clicked along the pavement. Now she quickly felt cold as the heat of the sickness left her and she walked briskly, pushing her gloved hands up under the wide collar of her coat to adjust it more closely to her face. She was crossing the opening of a side road, apparently no different from several she had passed already and, automatically, she glanced along it to check that there was no vehicle bearing down on the intersection. And she stopped, struck by a memory of an occasion far back in her childhood. There was a woman with a hawk-nosed aristocratic face and thick wavy grey hair, almost white it was, and faintly yellow in the roots. There was a room, three or four steps up from the pavement in a small house and a little boy with one leg in irons playing on the floor in front of the fire. Visually, this was all. But overlaying the visual images was the smell of ointment, not the smell itself but the memory of it, a pungent, penetrating odour which permeated the whole house, as though someone were boiling ointment in the kitchen. She was obviously recalling a visit paid with her mother but she couldn't remember who the people were or recall having been in this part of the town, on foot, as a child. The square stone-built villa on the corner was a dentist's premises. She could see the arm of a drill above the frosted lower half of one lighted window. Beyond that stone-fronted semis with heavy square bays gave way to more modest houses in what were conveniently described as 'superior terraces'. She looked at them without recognition, unable to recapture the fleeting something that had triggered off the memory, or any more details of the memory itself.

The first few weeks of her return to the city had been full of the strangeness of half-remembered things. Where people were involved the memories were mostly confined to the cottage on Thompson's Row and the streets around. In the city centre they were a recurring sensation of 'I have seen that in just that way before and yet it was somehow different.' These impressions were felt only in those parts untouched by the extensive redeveloping going on, and gradually they had become overlaid by the fresh associations of current living. She had seen no one she knew or who knew her. It wasn't surprising. One could live continuously in a city of a quarter-million and miss seeing certain people for years. And since most of the faces she remembered were those of children she could well have passed some of them on the street without recognising them, or they her.

The old life was gone. She was a stranger to it, to all intents and purposes five months familiar with a town she had never visited before. Thompson's Row, to which she never went back, could have been two-hundred miles away. It was people who bound you to a place and her associations were through people she had met during the last five months. One thread remained to connect her and the town to the childhood she had spent here, and this was her father. And still she had made no effort to find him, to learn whether or not he was still here, or even if he was alive or dead. She had instead, at the back of a mind pre-occupied with a new life, sensed without positive formulation a wish to postpone knowledge of him until she had established herself in such a way that, whatever form that knowledge took, it would have no power to hurt her.

She had left Hollis's by now. Going out occasionally with Stephen and working so near to Brenda had created a situation which the job itself couldn't compensate for. Stephen himself had been maddeningly insensitive to it and she had once had to refuse an invitation of his, because of a previous engagement, in Brenda's presence. It was too much to sit within six feet of her for eight hours a day knowing that you could have, and didn't want, what she was eating her heart out for. It was better too that she should make herself less accessible to Stephen. She liked him well enough and enjoyed her dates with him. She liked the kisses he gave her in the car at the end of these dates as she might have liked the kisses of any attractive man, and she knew that when she pulled away from him with a gentle 'that's enough. Time to go' she was both carefully checking his ardour and increasing his respect for her. In her response to the kisses there was always something of reserve, a physical expression of the distance she kept between herself and him. She hoped he didn't think of her as what men called a 'teaser'. She let him kiss her because he wanted to and she gave as much as she was prepared to give. She was in no sense baiting a trap, because she didn't want the catch. If she could imagine him discussing her with her friends it was in tones of some puzzlement. She felt that she was something of a mystery to him; there was a good deal about her that he couldn't fathom. It was as she wanted it to be.

She had heard about a vacancy for a typist with a small advertising agency in the city, and got the job. It was, at present, little more than routine secretarial work but she was fortunate in having a sloppy predecessor so that the partners were astonishingly grateful for her competence. Here, with Maple and Adderley, she felt in the presence of opportunity of a kind woefully lacking at Hollis's. She felt she could make an increasingly important place for herself in an organisation sparked by two clever youngish men who were on their way up and could be painlessly persuaded to take her with them. If she wanted to stay in the town . . .

Did she want to stay or was it rather that there was nowhere else she particularly wanted to go? She felt that she was living through an interlude, that her present life – in the kind of image Wilf might throw up – was a stretch of quiet narrative in a novel, between big dramatic scenes. Behind her was the diminishing heartache of Floyd and his deceit. Thoughts of that could still give her an occasional stab, but she knew now that she'd been as much in love with love as with Floyd himself, living in the intoxicating atmosphere of her first all-out, grown-up love affair. She should in fact be grateful to him. He had shown her what a wonderful thing the act of love could be. Trembling she had gone to him to be soothed and reassured in his arms. Floyd had soothed away the harshness from the memory of her painful defloration at seventeen in an Amhurst hayloft. She had given herself to what she saw as a wounding impalement not in passion but in defiance against her aunt and transformed a harmless flirtation (an undesirable liaison in her aunt's eyes) into a disgusting, humiliating episode that she had thought afterwards would mark her for ever.

There had been some changes at the house. Mr Mostyn, to whom she'd hardly spoken – or for that matter rarely even seen – had left. It seemed he'd been courting a widow on the other side of town for years and they'd finally got round to getting married. You hardly noticed he was gone and Poppy hadn't let the room yet so his departure had made no noticeable difference to the routine. More important, before this, was the arrival of Poppy's husband. It had been strange at first to see Swallow's bullet head – shaved high at back and sides to a slickly brilliantined patch on top – bobbing up all over the place. Stranger still to go into the kitchen and see that head behind an upraised newspaper, its owner occupying a place of intimacy with Poppy, who had always seemed so sturdily independent. Swallow was one of the most unself-conscious men Marguerite had ever met. His bright blue eyes seemed always to be appraising people, weighing them up, sorting them out, putting them into categories. He liked at odd moments to talk and he had confidently-stated opinions on all manner of subjects. He was reticent about himself but he was, he liked to tell you, a man who'd knocked about a bit and he knew the ways of the world. He brought out all the dry irony in Poppy. How they behaved in the privacy of her room, which Swallow shared, she had no means of knowing, but in the presence of herself or Wilf Poppy's attitude was one which seemed to voice an unspoken 'I've seen this one before.' To this Swallow seemed oblivious. His manner was full of an almost old-world courtesy, even-tempered, untroubled. To come into the house and meet them for the first time you might have thought that he, like Mr Mostyn, was a late starter, who had courted Poppy for years in a placid, dignified way and finally slipped into a quiet middle-aged marriage.

But from the first Marguerite had sensed something in Swallow that she didn't like. She found his courtesy not reassuring but almost sinister. There were times when she had to admit to herself that she was afraid of him. She felt that under the calm exterior he was capable of atrocious outbursts of passionate rage. Between the bouts of talkativeness there were periods of an almost brooding silence, when Swallow seemed to be always watching, never sleeping. Then you couldn't move in the house without coming across him. On two occasions she had come in late at night to a dark hall and been frightened by his sudden materialisation along the kitchen passage. Another time, queasy in her stomach from something she'd eaten, she had got up in the night to go to the bathroom and been struck with a shock of terror as she opened her door to find him standing perfectly still at the landing rail, his back to her. She had nothing on over her pyjamas and when she'd turned back for her dressing-gown only her own urgent physical need had forced her out of her room again. He was gone, which was worse than if he'd stayed there and spoken to her. Coming out of the bathroom was another test of her nerves. The landing was still deserted but when she heard a tread on the stairs she dashed in panic into her room and locked her door behind her. She got into bed and lay awake, ears strained, her skin crawling with the fright of her experience.

For a time Swallow had worked in some kind of unskilled capacity at a local mill but in November he either lost the job or gave it up to hang about the house all day. Poppy explained, in a manner of attempted justification that made Marguerite squirm, that the dyes gave Swallow dermatitis of the hands and he would take other employment when he found something suitable. It was about this time that Marguerite began to notice their relationship deteriorating. There was not much to see on the surface, though it couldn't be missed. Poppy's affectionate irony had given way to barbs of bitter comment which Swallow took in cold silence. At night, in their room, the acrimony would sometimes flare into open dispute, its virulence evident to Marguerite from the rise and fall of the wordless voices. She got the idea, she didn't know from where, that Swallow had been in prison and she had tried once or twice to draw Wilf out, to discuss Swallow with him, to find out if he knew more than she did, which was basically what he had told her before Swallow came to the house: that it seemed Poppy wasn't a widow at all but was separated from her husband who had been working in the south and now wanted to give their marriage another try. But Wilf didn't follow through, the reason being, she knew, that he couldn't discuss Poppy and her husband except from the stand-point of an intimacy she wasn't supposed to know about.

Poor Wilf . . . to be deprived of Poppy's favours by a man like Swallow. Had she liked Wilf a lot less and Swallow a lot more she could have found it amusing. She wondered how long he'd known about Swallow. He was decent enough to be glad for her sake. Fond of Poppy as he obviously was, he couldn't have seen any future for them together and it was better that it should end like this than continue until the time when Wilf couldn't walk out free without hurting her. He was young enough to throw it off. She supposed that most men would have remedied the situation by moving out. The effect on Wilf had been to drive him in on himself so that he became lost in his writing. There was a serious determination under his humour, a concern for his talent, that she liked in him. There were a great many things she liked about Wilf. She had experienced a steady deepening of regard for him; so much so that even though after a couple of promising dates she'd lost him to the book she could find in herself the hope that, if he wasn't aware of it himself, his staying had been partly because of her. There were signs now that he was coming out of his pre-occupation. He chattered more when they rode into town together. His sense of humour had quickened again. She waited for him to ask her out once more.

He had finished the novel in a two-month burst of energy, working solidly almost every evening from seven till midnight, and sometimes into early morning, regretting the daylight hours spent earning money in someone else's employ. But he was adept enough by now at living the double life, at keeping the never-sleeping writer's mind ticking away behind the daily routine of time cards, piece-work, bonuses, overtime rates, National Health deductions and PAYE. He knew that his employers were satisfied with him and he was conscientious enough to want to keep things that way. At night . . . It was as though everything that had gone into the novel up to then was like water building up behind a dam until, at last, the floodgates opened under the pressure and the torrent poured through, so fast that he had to abandon his hampering two-fingered typing for a ballpoint pen with which he filled page after page in a longhand scribble that even he sometimes found hard to read later. Then he went back to revise and rewrite, the creative energy of the final section reaching back to re-galvanise the earlier material. God! but he was elated.

And no company for anybody outside the nine to five-thirty stretch when he was forced to come to terms with the world beyond the pages of the book. He had taken Marguerite out once or twice earlier on, but lately he'd seen little of her except on morning walks to the bus, when he was often withdrawn, his mind working, making use of every last minute before the day's confinement. He knew that she was bright enough to understand his pre-occupation: her conversation and her tactful silences all showed that. It was Poppy who, he thought, might have got hold of the wrong end of the stick, interpreting his withdrawal as sulkiness because he couldn't share her bed any more. Of course he missed what he'd had, but not as much as when Swallow first came to the house. Then it had been so intolerable seeing the position of authority and intimacy the infuriating bastard casually assumed that he'd thought of moving elsewhere. He realised that he'd been clinging to the hope that Swallow wouldn't turn up after all and it wasn't till he actually arrived that Wilf had come fully awake to the end of his relationship with Poppy. And lying awake at night, wanting her, he remembered her beside him, the unencumbered softness of her, her movements of love and the words their contact drew from her. He couldn't bear to wonder if Swallow had these things, if Poppy could give them as readily to him as she had given them to himself. He reappraised their relationship and acknowledged that he might have deluded himself. There was no denying the hold Swallow had over Poppy, the fascination he held for her. She could have rid herself of him years ago, and with justification; but she had held on to the legal tie despite all he'd done to her and all the years he'd been away. He could only imagine that she'd hoped he might eventually turn up again; and with this thought came suspicion of himself as a substitute, a shadow of Swallow, the boy hearing words of love meant for the man.

So he had turned to the novel. He had been grateful before to Poppy for giving him the contentment in which to work; now he was thankful for the work's capacity to dull the edge of his losing her. He knew once again, as he'd found when it had helped him fly beyond his environment, the consolatory power of his writing. And then it had happened: the renewed determination with which he had approached the work had led him to the moment when it all came to life, when he was no longer feeling his way forward but knew clearly and certainly where the book was going. He'd had periods of optimism before when things were going well, but never anything like this. This was a new-found impetus powerful enough to sweep him on to the end of the book. He'd become (he hated the term but had to use it) inspired. He remembered things he'd long forgotten about the life he'd known. He saw his material with fresh eyes and saw the logical and inevitable way it had to be developed. He found new significance in passages he'd written months ago and enthusiastically rewrote whole sequences, cutting here, adding there, injecting fresh life into passages of pedestrian dialogue.

Until it was done and he sprawled in the big wing-chair, legs stuck out before him, and looked in a kind of exhausted trance at the three hundred and seventy-two pages of double-spaced typescript sitting on his table. There was so much of what he knew in it he wondered if he would ever be capable of writing another word. But this was good. It was good because it was real and true – true in the sense of Lewis's 'ten thousand unconscious associations of living'; true in the sense of Hemingway's iceberg, one ninth above the surface, the rest instinctively felt, solid and real, below the words themselves. But would they have it? There were welcome signs that the novel and the drama were moving out of London and the Home Counties, and of course regional novels had been published before the war. But he hadn't the flaming genius of a Lawrence on the one hand; and on the other his was an authentic world, his people harsh and dour, without the comic idiosyncrasies designed to appeal to the illusions of people who never travelled north of the Trent. But it was *good*. He jumped up and began to walk about the room, casting little glances at the manuscript. He couldn't keep a foolish little smile of happiness off his face.

18

She was sitting in a corner of the big lounge bar of the Prince of Wales Hotel with a gin and bitter lemon, from which she'd taken a few sips, on the table in front of her. It was Wednesday evening, and quiet. The small bar next door was doing better business. Here the big overhead lights blazed down on an almost empty room. There was a tarty-looking middle-aged blonde with a big bust sitting with a weedy, dark-jowled man at a table in the middle of the floor. Rings flashed on her fingers as she moved her hand to flick ash from her cigarette. Four boys of eighteen or nineteen, two in duffel coats and one wearing a scarf with the green and yellow colours of the technical college, sat with glasses of beer against the far wall. From the way they all leaned in across the table then sat back in simultaneous laughter she guessed they were swapping dirty stories. The two portly men in expensive overcoats standing at the bar seemed to be transacting some kind of business together. They were talking intently, but not furtively, to each other and one was producing sheets of paper that looked like lists from his pocket for the other man to examine. After she'd watched them for several minutes they seemed to come to a decision. The second man stuck his hand into a front trousers pocket and dragged out a well-filled notecase. He began to count out banknotes on to the bar counter and Marguerite counted with him. Fifteen. They looked liked fivers. The first man had produced a pen which he handed to the man with the money. While the latter scribbled on a slip of paper the first man pocketed the cash. When his pen had been returned to him the first man wrote something, presumably his signature, on another piece of paper which the second man took and put into the notecase before jamming it back under his paunch. The first man put away the wad of lists and they both straightened their jackets and settled their coats more comfortably on their shoulders before picking up their glasses of whisky to drink. The second man finished his drink quickly, said something to his friend before touching him lightly on the upper arm and walking out of the room. Left alone, the first man looked round the room before moving down the bar to engage the barman in conversation while his glass was replenished. Marguerite was still reflecting in a dreamy, imprecise way upon the philosophical and economic aspects of the monetary system when, a few minutes later, Wilf came through the doorway from the lobby.

He raised his hand in greeting when he saw her, then pointed to her glass, his eyebrows raised in an expression of query that looked both clownish and lovable. She lifted the glass, smiling, to show how full it was and he waved his hand at her again before turning his back and making for the bar. She watched him get a glass of beer and come towards her with it. He was looking unusually smart, in his grey raglan overcoat with under it a new suit in a soft dark green tweed that he'd bought in the January sales.

'Hello, love.'

'Love.' It was his favourite form of address, bestowed carelessly on bus conductresses, barmaids, shop assistants and probably every girl at the shirt factory with whom he came in contact. She wondered what special term of endearment he reserved for a woman he loved. He wasn't a 'darling' man. Perhaps it was all in the tone and intensity of the voice. He took off his overcoat and slung it carelessly over a chair before sitting down.

He looked at her over the rim of his uplifted glass.

'Cheers.' He drank and put the glass down. 'Been waiting long?'

'Only about ten minutes. I didn't get away from the office till nine.'

'They're pushing you a bit hard, aren't they? Working over three nights a week till half-past eight or nine.'

'It's only for a while, until we get on top of the rush of work. Anyway, I like the job and overtime's all extra money at the end of the week.'

'Yes, the lolly's always handy.'

Marguerite took cigarettes from her handbag and offered Wilf one. He shook his head. 'No, thanks.' He was smoking on and off nowadays but it hadn't become a regular thing again yet. He watched her go through the motions of lighting up, then as she put the spent match in the ashtray he said impulsively, 'I think I'd like a cigar.'

She was surprised. 'Sorry, I'm afraid I haven't got one on me.'

'I'll get one.'

He pushed back his chair and set off purposefully to the bar. In a minute he was back. He stripped the cellophane off a long panatella. She struck a match for him and breathed in through her nose as he got the cigar going and released a cloud of fragrant smoke.

'That smells lovely.'

'It ought to,' Wilf said. 'That's a tuppenny sniff you've just had.'

'Are you celebrating something?'

'No, I just had a sudden urge.'

'That's a good enough excuse.' She smiled. It amused her to see him flourishing the long cigar.

'Y'know' – he was puffing away appreciatively – 'I could acquire a taste for these things.'

'You'd better wait until you're a celebrated author.'

He pulled a face. 'That'll be the day.'

'How did the meeting go?'

He gave a disdainful shrug of his shoulders.

'Are they going to form a club?'

'Oh, they'll form a club, all right, but I shan't be in it.'

'As bad as that?'

'Just put me down as naïve. I expected too much, that's all. They're just scribblers,' he went on. 'A guinea for a letter here, a chatty little article on window-boxes there – you know. One or two of them seem to have done quite well out of the woman's short-story markets and they could probably make the few quid I've picked up look sick. Still, there isn't a real writer among them. Not one.'

'Were they mostly women?' Marguerite asked, and Wilf nodded.

'How did you guess? Housewives young and old, dashing off hospital stories among the washing-up and the nappies. Oh, don't get me wrong: there are plenty of good women writers and I don't give a damn what a person does for a living. He can empty dustbins for all I care. But that lot simply haven't got the approach. They just don't know what real writing is.' He took a drink. 'Hell, I couldn't find one person in the room who'd *read* anything! I started talking to a cove in the corner about Lawrence and he just looked blankly polite. Then all at once his light came on and he went rambling off about the Arab situation and the trouble in the Middle East. It was so damned disappointing. I went expecting to find some kindred spirits and felt as out of place as if I'd blundered into a meeting of a sewing circle.'

'Did you tell them what you'd done?'

'Well, they kind of went round everybody to find out what they were interested in and when they got to me I said I was doing a novel and they said Oh, what kind of a novel? and I said Oh, just a novel. So they asked if I'd had anything published and I told them about the broadcast stories and the piece in *Etude* and they said Hmm! and looked impressed, and that was it. Then a smart-looking bit sitting next to me and showing a lot of knee said she'd sold half-a-dozen stories on the trot to *Gay Girl* for fifteen guineas apiece and that was where I went into eclipse. If there are any real writers in this town they must be at home slaving over their hot typewriters and come to think of it that's the best place for them. All this talking about your work – it doesn't do it any good. It's getting it written that counts, and you're on your own with that. Nobody can help you.'

'But talking to people with similar interests and problems can stimulate,' Marguerite said, 'and that's where it helps, in encouraging you to go on and get the work done.'

'These people couldn't stimulate me to write a laundry list,' Wilf said.

Marguerite said, ' I do think, you know, that you're being rather intolerant and arrogant about it.'

'Yes,' he admitted, 'perhaps I am. It's like I've always said: it's failure that breeds arrogance and intolerance. Only successful people can afford to be magnanimous.'

She was stung to quick impatience. 'How can you talk about failure at this stage? At all? You've had your short stories broadcast and printed and you've written a full-length novel that's as honest and powerful as anything I've read in a long time.'

'Aw,' Wilf broke in facetiously, 'you know you wouldn't say that if you didn't love me.'

She looked quickly down at the table. She wanted to say 'Yes, I do love you, you silly fool,' but she kept quiet. The trouble was that their relationship had deepened into a kind of platonic intimacy that seemed to fix them in its own course. She wondered if there was something in her manner which, without her knowing it, kept Wilf at bay. Or was it simply that he just didn't see her in any way other than as a pal who happened to be of the opposite sex? Why, he'd never even kissed her. There had been one or two occasions when she thought he looked as though he might try; but that was all.

'I'm simply telling you what I'd tell anyone else,' she said, lifting her face. 'I know I'd practically to scratch your eyes out before you'd let me read the carbon of the manuscript, but that doesn't mean I'd feel obliged to praise it if I didn't think it was worth it.'

Wilf shrugged and sucked at his cigar. 'You know I do value your opinion, Marguerite,' he said.

'Thank you,' Marguerite said. 'How long is it since you sent the novel out now?'

'Eight weeks. Eight weeks and three days, to be exact.'

'Well it shows at least that it's getting a good reading. You should be hearing from them any time now.'

He rolled cigar ash into the ashtray, his face gone sombre for a moment.

He said suddenly, 'Oh, hell, I can't hold out on you.' He pushed his hand into his inside pocket and took out an envelope. 'This came today.'

She unfolded the letter. It was headed 'Thomas Ransome Ltd, 14 Copeland Street, London, WC1.

'Dear Sir, We have read the typescript of your novel "Bitter Dawn" with considerable interest and feel that this is a well-written, carefully-worked-out story which shows a good deal of ability, particularly in the dialogue passages. After careful consideration, however, we have come to the conclusion that the subject matter, the setting and the characters are such that they are likely to appeal to only a limited audience. We are, therefore, unable to make you an offer of publication. Your manuscript, which we thank you for giving us the opportunity of seeing, is being returned to you under separate cover.'

She didn't know what to say so she read the letter a second time.

'So there you are,' Wilf said after a time.

'But it's not so bad, is it?' Marguerite said. 'At least they do say some complimentary things about it.'

'Oh, they can see that it's literate so they do me the honour of writing to me instead of sending a rejection slip. Then they have to make some kind of comment so they say it shows ability and the dialogue's good. But the point is how much ability and is the dialogue good enough.'

'It must be rotten to have this happen to you,' she said. 'I don't think I could take it myself.'

'Who says I'm taking it?' Wilf said with a wry laugh. 'I'm bloody low, I can tell you.' He sat forward and put his elbows on the table. 'Oh, I know what it is . . . You spend a couple of years putting everything you've got into a book and when you've finished you just know it's good. You just know it's the best thing you've ever done. You send it out with visions of a telegram arriving three days later. Instead you hear nothing for eight weeks, and then this.' He flicked the letter with his finger.

'Why did you send it to Ransome's?'

'I wanted them to have it. They're a smallish house but they have some good writers on their list and their books are well produced.'

'You could try one of the bigger firms. They'd have more resources and probably be more inclined to take a chance on an off-beat novel.'

'You're probably right. Still, any firm'll take a chance on an off-beat first novel if it's good enough. But nobody wants watered-down Lawrence.'

'It isn't watered-down Lawrence,' Marguerite protested. 'It's full-strength Wilf Cotton. Anybody can see you've read Lawrence, but what serious English novelist hasn't? You know the book's good. You know it *will* be published sooner or later, so why act as if this is the end of the world? You're not the only writer this has happened to and you won't be the last. You're asking for publishers to be all of a piece, infallible, all thinking alike, when in fact they're human just like anybody else. How do you know that Thomas Ransome aren't stretching their budget as far as it will go with first novels this year? And how do you know the next publisher you send it to won't be *looking* for promising new names? All that's happened to you is you've lost eight weeks, and what will that matter in ten years' time? So choose yourself another name and wrap it up and send it off. And stop weeping in your beer.'

He brooded for a moment over his half-smoked cigar. Then he said, 'I think I'll send it to an agent.'

'I don't know much about agents,' Marguerite said. 'Does it cost money?'

'Not until they sell the work. Then they take a commission. Ten per cent, I believe. You see, you're right about publishers. I could go on sending it to the wrong places. But an agent knows them all and what they're looking for. And besides, it's probably the quickest way of getting a professional opinion on its chances.'

'Well then, send it off to an agent. Do it tomorrow. Have you got a list of them?'

'Yes, in the *Writers' and Artists' Yearbook*. I'll choose one when we get back tonight. In fact, I'll do better than that – I'll let you pick one for me.'

'But I don't know which are good and which aren't.'

'Neither do I; so we'll rely on feminine intuition.'

'I ought to tell you that I'm not a very lucky person.'

'But you might be lucky for me, like the chap who gave his friends good tips all the time but could never back a winner himself.'

'All right.'

'God! it's like a brick wall in front of you and you're trying to punch a hole in it, make a breakthrough.' She saw the hard, set line of his mouth and his clenched fist on the table. She reached out to him.

'It'll come,' she said. 'Don't worry. In a couple of years' time all this will seem like a distant dream.'

He looked at her hand covering his fist, then lifted his eyes to hers.

'You really do believe that, don't you?'

She nodded. 'Yes.'

He went on looking at her. He seemed to be looking straight into her. She felt like blushing at the thought of what he might find there.

'I'm glad that woman across the road didn't have a room,' he said.

'So am I.'

Opening her bag and pretending she needed a handkerchief gave her the excuse to move her hand and look away from him.

'Would you like another drink?'

'I don't think so. You have one.'

'No, I'm not bothered. I'm a bit peckish, though. Have you ever been to that Chinese restaurant down the road?'

'No.'

'Care to join me in a bowl of chop suey?'

She laughed. 'What is chop suey, the dish that international adventurers eat in old American films?'

'I always thought it was something Cecil B. De Mille invented in one of his spare moments from writing the authorised Hollywood version of the Scriptures.'

He pushed back his chair and stood up. Marguerite followed, thinking how almost childlike was the swiftness of his moods. A moment ago he'd been downcast, gloomy with thoughts of failure; now he was suddenly as high-spirited as she remembered seeing him. As they walked out of the hotel he was improvising aloud a parody of the dialogue in biblical films: ' "Say, Plutonius, who's dat bum walkin' across the lake?" "It's dat troublemakin' Jew-boy dat raised the guy from the dead last week." "Why cain' he hire a boat like anybody else?" "Like I told ya, he's a trouble-maker, an' he's makin' a heap o' trouble for himself, or I ain't no seventh-generation citizen of Imperial Rome!" '

A strong rain-carrying wind buffeted them along the street. It swooped on them in sudden powerful gusts, carrying them forward in little trotting bursts of speed. Wilf took Marguerite's hand in his and they ran with the wind, laughing, the last hundred and fifty yards to the house. They stood in the hall, smiling breathlessly at each other, Marguerite pushing back her hair.

'Phew!'

He opened the door of his room. 'Would you like to come in for a while?'

'I ought to go upstairs and change my stockings; they're wet.'

'You can dry them in front of my fire.'

'All right.'

She went in and he helped her off with her coat. He switched on the electric fire and pulled the two armchairs forward. She sat down and ran her hands along the damp backs of her legs.

'Would you excuse me for a second?'

'Sure,' he said, 'I'll look for that Yearbook.'

She drew back her skirt and unclipped her suspenders to roll her stockings down. He turned from the bookshelves and looked at her sitting with her legs outstretched, her feet raised off the floor, the soles held up to the bars of the fire.

'Are they cold?'

'Like two blocks of ice.'

He dropped the book into the other chair and went down on his knees. 'Let me rub them for you.' He took her right foot in his hands.

'Ugh! they are cold.'

'Your hands are lovely and warm.'

He began to massage her foot with slow firm strokes, smoothing out from ankle and heel as though drawing heat from the rest of her body and persuading it, urging it, through her foot to force out the cold through the extremities of her toes. She lay back in the chair with her eyes closed, feeling soft vibrations of excitement inside herself.

'That better?'

'Lovely.'

He released the right foot and she lowered it to the floor as he began to work on the other one.

'I usually think that feet are rather disgusting things, but yours are pretty.'

'Thank you.'

He went on, easing golden warmth into her foot until she felt the pressure of his hands relax. Her leg was still supported and she thought – could she possibly only have imagined? – that she felt the quick light touch of something else. Then the pressure of one hand returned and her eyes flickered open to see Wilf crouching quite still, his cheek pressed into the curve of ankle and foot. She closed her eyes again. Her heart seemed to tremble. She hardly dared breathe. She didn't know how long they stayed like that before her leg was lowered gently and she felt him near her.

'Marguerite.'

She opened her eyes and looked into his face.

He said again, 'Marguerite,' looking back at her.

She murmured, 'Stone-cold sober?'

'Stone-cold sober.'

Then she reached out to put one hand behind his head and draw him to her. Their kiss was long and gentle, without passion. It tapped the deep well of her tender feeling for him and she let it flood up unchecked, pouring out to him through the soft, trembling union of their mouths. She held him, prolonging the unbearable sweetness and mystery of their first kiss, until at last he drew away.

'I hate to be unromantic,' he said, 'but I'm going to fall over.'

She turned sideways in the deep, broad recess of the chair. 'Come here.' He slid in beside her and they half lay together, arms round each other, very close. She smiled, her face buried in his neck, as his hand moved over her back.

'Just listen to that wind!'

'Mmm.'

'There'll be some slates off in the morning.'

'I shouldn't wonder.'

Great waves of wind dashed against the house. The building quivered under their impact. A heavy thud on the floor of the room above made Marguerite lift her head.

'What was that?'

'Poppy's just pushed Swallow out of bed.'

'I can't joke about that man,' Marguerite said. 'Have you heard them quarrelling?'

'Yes. The second honeymoon's over there, I'm afraid.'

'Poor Poppy.'

They lay with their heads resting on the back of the chair, their faces a few inches apart.

Wilf said, 'I can't be interested in anyone's unhappiness tonight.'

She traced with her forefinger the lines of his eyebrows, then his mouth. 'Don't you think it's time you kissed me again?'

Now she strained against him. Her moist flesh throbbed in slow pulsing shocks of ecstatic feeling, as though he were already fused into her. Spiritually too she wanted badly to submit, to plunge at once into the unplumbed depths of their relationship as though to ensure everything by this immediate act of faith.

The front door opened, then crashed shut again. A gust of cold air poured under Wilf's door and spread across the floor. She shivered as it touched her bare feet.

'Cold?'

'A draught on my feet.'

'Just a minute.'

He wriggled out of the chair and got the day-cover off the bed to wrap round their legs.

'You'll be all right now.'

She moved her lips across his cheek to murmur in his ear: 'Wouldn't it be simpler to get in?'

He was a moment before he answered. 'You know what you're saying?'

'Yes . . . I'm not a wanton. It does mean something to

me. It's just . . . just that I love you so very much I want to prove it to you. I want to be more to you than any woman ever has been.'

'Oh, my love; my little love.' He took her face between his hands. 'Do you think I don't want you this very minute? I do. I do. I want all that you can give me. But slowly. I don't want to spoil a single moment of it. I want to walk about remembering the kisses we've just had. I want the excitement of just holding your hand in a cinema, of seeing you look at me when other people are there and knowing that what your eyes say is just for me. I want all of you, but I want the promise first as well.'

She hid her face a little.

'You know you won't be the first.'

'Neither will you.'

'No, I know that.'

'You mean about Poppy and me?'

'Yes.'

'I wondered if you did know . . . It wasn't anything like this.'

'I knew it couldn't have been or you'd have left when Swallow came back . . . It wasn't like that with me. I don't suppose it ever is for a woman.'

'Were you in love with him?'

'I thought so at the time . . . Oh, yes, I was. Only, he was married and I didn't know.'

'Was that why you came back here?'

'Yes. I was very upset and confused. I had to run somewhere and I thought I might sort myself out here, find new bearings. Before I went to London I lived I suppose a rather sheltered life. My aunt and uncle, who took me in when I was nine, they were very quiet people, very genteel, with no children of their own. It was a big thing for them to take in a child at their time of life. Especially a child like me. I was rather rough and uncouth. I swore when I felt like it. I'll never forget that first day when I got off the train with Uncle Edward at Amhurst. I got the feeling he wanted to get me home and under cover before somebody saw me. The blossom was out on the roadside trees. It was beautiful and I was so desperately lonely I wanted to cry.'

He stroked her hair. 'Weren't they kind to you?'

'Oh yes. They did all they could for me within their means and their understanding; but we never really became intimate. When I think back I seem to always have been in revolt. I went through a period when I wanted to be a boy. I used to associate with a gang of boys, rough boys, on the quiet. There was one called Dave – Dave Summers. He was the leader. I idolised him. His father worked in the glassworks. A great big thickheaded oaf of a man. He used to knock Dave about. I met Dave one summer afternoon. I was in the house on my own and I heard a noise downstairs and when I went to look I found Dave. He'd just walked in through the french windows and was opening drawers to see what he could steal. He'd have run away but I told him I was alone and on his side. I gave him a pound out of Uncle Edward's box and took the blame for it myself.'

'What happened to him?'

'He was caught stealing and put on probation. Then he was caught again and sent to a reform school. I never knew what happened to him after that. But I desperately wanted to be a boy like him. I remember the first time I had a period I was so disgusted and ashamed I hid the sheet off the bed and they had to stop all my privileges to make me tell where it was. I settled down a bit in my teens, but this was the time when everything started to get on top of my aunt. She got worse and worse until she couldn't cope with the simplest job without doing it six or seven times. They were both elderly. Uncle Edward started to fail in health so they took my aunt away to a home. I'd left school and had a job in an estate agent's office by this time. He had a woman in mornings so we managed for a time. Then he got a really bad attack of bronchitis and that finished him.'

'That's when you went to London?'

'Yes, a friend of my uncle's in Amhurst – the manager of the bank where he worked actually – gave me a letter of introduction to a business friend in London when he knew I was planning to go there. Then when I'd been in London for a time I met Floyd.'

'Floyd? Was he an American?'

'Yes, which was how he managed to keep his wife and family a secret for so long. I suppose if he was looking for a young girl to have an affair with he found me at just the right time. I needed love and I had a lot bottled up to give in return . . .'

And still needed it, and still had so much to give. He asked her about her life before Amhurst and held her protectively close in the chair while she told him about her father and Laura and the children: an appalling, hair-raising story which she told in a quiet almost childishly solemn voice completely free of self-pity. And he marvelled that behind the cool, composed exterior of this young woman was a girl looking for love in a world which had so often denied it to her. It was the girl whom he held, the child in the innocence of her need. She filled him with an almost uncontainable joy and at the same time a stupendous sense of wonder. She wanted him . . . *him*!

'Will you come home with me this weekend?' he asked her. 'I'd like you to meet my mother.'

He wanted to walk into the house with her and see the pleasure in his mother's eyes; to let Marguerite bask in its reflected warmth.

'Is she fierce?'

He laughed. 'She can be. But she'll love you. Just don't go all cool and lofty on her, that's all.'

'Am I cool and lofty?'

'Not really, but you have a very effective daughter-of-the-earl air which you switch on when you think people are getting at you.'

She giggled. 'Yes, I know. I watch myself doing it. It's a defence mechanism I developed at school in Amhurst. I didn't exactly fit in there at first, you see, and I found out straight away that I'd either have to stand up for myself or become a mouse. They used to mimic my accent and for a while I was too proud to copy theirs. But time took care of that. After eighteen months I was indistinguishable from the rest of them and I only switched back to Yorkshire occasionally to make people laugh.'

'Do it now,' he said.

She put her hand to his cheek and looked at him with her lovely eyes. 'Ah luv thee, lad,' she said.

He was suddenly inexpressibly moved. He took her hand and pressed his mouth into her palm. 'Darling. Darling Marguerite.'

She had closed her eyes and her lips were smiling.

A long time later she turned his wrist to look at his watch.

'What time is it?' he murmured.

'One o'clock.'

'Time all respectable people were in bed.'

'Are we respectable?'

'I'm containing myself with difficulty.'

'Compromised in his bachelor quarters by an abandoned young woman.'

'Please don't feel hurt about that,' he said. 'I haven't gone all high principled and moral on you. It's just that I know the moment, the right moment, will come soon.'

'Yes, I know what you mean.'

'We've got a long time.'

She looked at him. 'Have we?'

'Yes. And you can't imagine how much I want you.'

'I know . . . I know. Will you think about me when you're falling asleep?'

'I don't know if I will sleep, I've got so much to think about.'

'I'll think about you. And in the morning, in that tiny moment between sleeping and waking, I'll open my eyes and think that nothing's different, that everything's like it was this morning. And then I'll remember. It'll all come rushing in . . .'

He kissed her gently before struggling up out of the chair.

'What's wrong?'

'Cramp. Plain, bloody unromantic cramp.'

He hobbled about in front of her, getting the circulation going in his leg. She got up, putting her hands to her hair and pulling at the hem of her sweater. Then suddenly she was clinging to him, her arms round him, squeezing and squeezing with surprising strength, her face pressed to his chest.

'What is it, Marguerite? What's wrong, love?

'Nothing,' she answered in a small voice. 'I'm just being silly.'

'Are you scared?'

She nodded against him.

'So am I, a bit. I always told Poppy I didn't want to be saddled with a woman, but I didn't count on anything like this happening. Now I know it's just the opposite. When it does happen everything seems to fit into place.'

She squeezed him again then moved away from him and stepped into her shoes. 'You'll send the novel off again, won't you?' she said as she bent to pick up her stockings.

'Yes.' He reached for the Yearbook. 'Come on and do your stuff.'

'I can't imagine this is a very good way.'

'Let's try it and see what happens. Here . . .' He handed her the book already open at the page.

'Ooh, what a lot! They can't all be good.'

She looked down the list, one hand lifted to cover a huge yawn. 'Gosh, I'm tired now . . . What about this one?'

He put his arms round her shoulders and looked where her finger was pointing.

'Okay, it goes there as soon as I get it back.'

'When will that be?'

'Tomorrow, I expect. Parcel post takes a bit longer than letter.'

She got her coat and they went to the door. There she looked at him with eyes that were sleepy but still held enough light of love to make him feel twenty feet tall.

He took her wrist and put his clenched fist into her hand. 'That's the world,' he said, 'right there in my fist.' He opened his fingers across her palm. 'You look after it for me.'

'For how long?'

'For as long as you like.'

'You know what *you're* saying now?'

'Yes, I know.'

They clung together again. Oh, it was so wrong that they had to part just now, yet so necessary that they should.

'I must go.'

'Yes. If you don't go in a minute it'll be too late.'

'Good night, then . . . darling.'

He opened the door for her.

'Oh, I was going to put the light on for you but it's already on. I'll leave it till you get upstairs.'

He reached forward to kiss her again but their lips had hardly met before she pulled back and turned her head.

'What's wrong?'

She held up her hand. 'Listen.'

'What is it?'

'I thought I heard something.'

'It's only the wind.'

'No.' She was straining her ears to the stairs. 'There was something else. Listen.'

He listened with her to the intermittent crash and roar of the wind. It rattled the front door in its frame and poured in cold floods across the tiled floor. What a gloomy place this hallway was, with the cold light from the naked bulb, whose shade Poppy had broken weeks ago and not bothered to replace, and the dark paint on the doors and banister rail. They would have to get away from here now, together. He could think about it in bed. So many plans to make, so many possibilities in this glorious new world!

He was about to say something when Marguerite's hand grasped his forearm.

'There it is again. Can't you *hear* it? It's coming from upstairs. It's . . . it sounds like somebody *moaning*.' She shot an uneasy glance at him. 'What can it be?'

He smiled in fond condescension. 'Honestly, I haven't heard a thing apart from the wind. Perhaps it's the bathroom pipes.'

Her fingers were still tight on his arm but she released their pressure as he took a step towards the stairs. She moved with him, sliding her hand into his.

'It isn't there now,' she said.

He squeezed her hand and walked to the stairs. 'Wait here.'

He started up, steadily and quietly. Damn it, Marguerite had put the wind up him now. He'd have to find some reasonable explanation for whatever it was she'd heard before she would go easily to her room.

The landing light was out but the door of Poppy's room stood ajar and a light was burning in there. He stood in the middle of the landing and listened. Up here, away from any immediate outside wall, the wind wasn't so noisy. With the door open and the light on Poppy must be awake. But where was Swallow? There was nobody about downstairs. He had taken the few paces to Poppy's door and lifted his hand to knock when he heard unmistakably the sound that Marguerite's ears had picked up downstairs.

His heart was thudding as he pushed open the door and stepped into the room. It looked empty, the bedside lamp burning on the cabinet, the bed turned down but empty. The candlewick bedspread was half-dragged on to the floor on the far side. *Half-dragged*. In an awful instant of comprehension he knew what he was going to find as he stepped forward to see beyond the bed. He tried to say her name but uttered no more than a croak as he stared, frozen with horror, at the desperate clutch of the hand on the dragged bedspread, the pink flush of her body in the nylon folds of the nightdress and her averted face. And the blood . . . oh, God, the blood.

His brain was swimming as he reached the top of the stairs. He clutched at the rail to steady himself. He never knew how he got down without falling. On the bottom step he sat down and shoved his head between his thighs as Marguerite spoke to him.

'The phone,' he said. 'Dial 999.'

'But what . . .' she began. Then he felt her leave his side.

In a moment he was recovered enough to stand up again. He crossed the hall and took the receiver from her hand.

'Emergency. What service do you want?'

He forced his brain to lucidity. He said clearly and distinctly, 'This is Cross Park 587. I want medical help and the police, at once . . .'

They all sounded so maddeningly calm and methodical. When he'd finished he replaced the receiver and turned to look at Marguerite. 'It's Poppy. For God's sake don't go up there. There's nothing we can do. They'll be here in a minute.'

She was turning fluid before his eyes. He said, 'I think I'm going to be . . .'

He made for the front door and opened it. The wind tore it out of his hand and slammed it back on its hinges. He lurched on to the step and held himself up against the wall. He leaned out over the soggy earth of the flower-bed, retching helplessly, and then as he vomited he thought foolishly, 'Golden dragon chop suey . . . "Who's dat bum walkin' across the lake?" '

19

There was a hole in his sock which was doing its best to amputate his big toe. He stopped to stand on one foot against a lamp-post and take off his shoe.

'Have you got a pebble in your shoe?' Marguerite asked.

'No, a hole in my sock. A whopper.'

'You should have told me.'

'Oh, I'm careless about these things. Anyway, you can't be spending your time mending for me.'

He pulled the sock forward on his foot, leaving it loose at the toe. It would work its way back in a short time, but that couldn't be helped.

'You know I don't mind,' she said.

'Time enough for you to do it when you have to.'

She slipped her hand into his as they walked on. He pressed it reassuringly, sensing the nervousness which had grown out of her earlier indecision. He thought that without him she wouldn't have gone through with it. He hoped he was right.

He was checking off the intersections and side streets on a street map which he pored over under the sodium lights.

'It can't be much farther now,' he said. 'No, look . . . Two more streets, then we're there. Watch out for the church.'

'I can see it now,' Marguerite said.

'Yes. Well it's almost dead opposite there.'

They were on the ring road, no specially built highway

here on the south side of the city, but a marked route through a warren of drab residential streets with corner grocery shops and small mills and warehouses, where, here and there, the destruction of the very oldest property for redevelopment left gaps which opened up unexpected vistas of the lights of the city in the basin below. The road was in its quiet period of the day, the business traffic ended, the evening's pleasure traffic not yet fully begun. Lighted buses swayed by with frequent regularity, dropping off and picking up passengers in ones and twos at the stops.

'We could have ridden a bit farther on the bus if we'd known,' Wilf said.

'I don't mind,' Marguerite said. 'Anyway, we're there now.'

'Yes. Are you all right?'

'Yes.'

'Butterflies in the tummy?'

'A bit.'

They stopped under the lighted window of a public house and looked along the street, stretching away into darkness pricked by dim lights.

'Here we are. It can't be far along.'

'Which side is it on?'

They walked along until they could make out the number on the first door in the terrace. It stood up five steps from the pavement.

'Number three,' Wilf said. 'Must be even numbers on the other side.'

He took her hand again and they crossed the street diagonally, reaching the pavement only five doors below the one they were looking for. A lamp on an old-fashioned iron standard threw its light on to the front of the house, showing clearly the number on the door.

'The steps are clean and the front door's been painted recently,' Wilf said. 'And there's somebody in.' He pointed to the light behind the drawn curtains.

'Here goes, then,' Marguerite said. 'Where will you wait? In the pub?'

'Sure you don't want me to come in with you?'

'No. I think I ought to be on my own first.'

'Okay, I'll be in the pub on the corner. Just whistle when you want me.'

How pale she looked in the lamplight! He put his hand under her chin and bent his head to kiss her.

'Good luck, love.'

He walked away from her, looking back after some twenty paces to wave. She was already standing on the steps by the door and as he looked the door opened and she turned her head away from him.

In a period when pubs were being renovated in their hundreds that on the corner looked as though it hadn't been touched for thirty years or more except for an occasional repapering and new varnishing on the woodwork.The bar ran in one length through the saloon and the adjoining taproom which were separated by a wood partition with ornamental glass above shoulder height. Plain, worn lino covered the floor and the round-topped tables had ornate cast-iron legs. The saloon was empty but the voices of a group of youths reached Wilf from the other room. They seemed to be playing darts. He wasn't familiar with the brand of draught beer offered so he bought a bottle of Guinness and stood at the bar to drink it. The publican rang up the money in the till and gave him his change.

'Is it still fine out?'

He was a short, paunchy man with grey hair brushed straight back, and glasses. His shirtsleeves were rolled up above tattooed forearms and his waistcoat hung unbuttoned.

'Yes, it is,' Wilf said.

'Cold, though?' the publican said.

'It's none too warm.'

One of the youths called from the other side of the

partition, 'Same again, please,' and the publican walked away to serve him.

Wilf took out the agent's letter and read it for the sixth or seventh time, looking for subtleties of meaning behind the obviously routine words.

'Dear Mr Cotton, Thank you very much for sending me the typescript of your novel "Bitter Dawn" and the letter from Thomas Ransome Ltd, which I return herewith. I do agree that your novel shows a good deal of talent, and I must also agree with them that the setting, characters, theme, etc., may limit the book's appeal to some extent. However, we mustn't worry overmuch about that at this stage. Your novel is well up to publication standard and I propose to show it to one or two publishers straight away. I'll write to you again as soon as I have some news for you.'

Fair enough . . . No, bloody marvellous, really. Only he didn't feel like dancing a jig about it. The trouble was that you lived your life waiting for tomorrow to bring you something more, and what you were asking for was tomorrow's promise in today's context. But tomorrow was another day. Life had a way of alloying one's joy. But Marguerite . . . would his happiness with her ever diminish till it was no more than the measure of the sorrow he would know if he lost her? He couldn't imagine it.

'Make your peace with it, love,' he'd said to her. 'Lay the last of the ghosts and then we'll go away.'

'Yes,' she'd said; 'you're right. I'm not afraid any more now I've got you.'

But in the evening hours they had spent in the reference room of the Central Library he'd known that a part of her was hoping their search would prove fruitless. And he himself, in quiet moments of reflection, pondered on the wisdom of what they were doing. The old wounds still occasionally smarted. Could he be sure that in trying to heal them for good he wouldn't end in re-opening them even more painfully? On the fifth evening he had pushed the papers away with a sigh. The names of the town's citizens and the streets where they lived danced in bewildering variety before his eyes. Turning to Marguerite he saw her sitting quite still, the point of her pencil resting on the sheet before her, her eyes lifted to stare into space.

'No luck,' he said in a low voice. 'Gosh, what a job! The trouble is, you can't be sure you haven't missed it in a careless moment . . . How're you doing?'

She spoke without turning her head. 'I've found it.'

He scrambled to his feet, the rasp of the chair legs on the floor sounding shockingly loud in the quiet of the room, and looked over her shoulder to where her pencil was pointing.

'You're sure?' he said.

'Absolutely,' Marguerite said.

The publican came into view again and looked at Wilf's empty glass.

'Same again?'

'Please.'

The publican reached behind him for a bottle of Guinness, removed the cap in the opener attached to the bar counter and filled Wilf's glass for him.

Wilf paid him. 'Have one with me?'

The publican said thanks very much and drew himself a half-pint of bitter, raising the glass to Wilf.

'All the best.'

'Cheers.'

They set their glasses down.

'Is it always as quiet as this?' Wilf said.

'Oh, there'll be a few more in later on. Weekend nights are busiest: Friday, Saturday, Sunday. It's week-ends when they have all the money round here.'

The publican stood with his arms outspread, hands resting on the counter as though waiting on a vacillatory customer.

'Do you know a Walter Fisher, lives up the street?'

'Who? Walt Fisher? Aye, he comes in now an' again.

Quiet feller. Brings his missis in on Saturday night sometimes, when they can get a sitter for the kids.'

'A family man, is he?'

'Oh aye. A wife an' a couple o' bairns.'

'Is that tonight's paper?'

He didn't want to look at it but it drew him.

The publican passed over the folded newspaper and Wilf opened it and looked at the front page.

'I see that bloke that did that woman in over in Cross Park says he doesn't know why he did it.'

'Yes.'

'Anyway, he's admitted to it so it'll save 'em a lot o' bother and expense when he comes up for trial.'

'I suppose it will.'

'Looks as though he'll swing for it, though. He took some money belonging to her.'

'Yes.'

'I don't know what she was thinking about to take him back. It says she'd been separated from him for years and then she took him in when he came out o' jail. Strikes me she should have had her head seen to.'

'She got it seen to,' Wilf said.

'What? Oh, aye, you're right there.'

Oh, the blood, the blood. Would he ever forget it?

'Well, they want to get him strung up. Buggers like that are no good to nobody.'

'I don't believe in capital punishment,' Wilf said.

The publican shot a quick glance at him. 'I don't see why we should all have to pay to keep a bloke like that in jail.'

'Do you really measure a man's life against what it costs to imprison him?'

'He took her life, didn't he?' the publican said. 'That woman. And what for? Fifty quid.'

'There was more to it than that.'

'How d'you mean?'

'They were man and wife. They were living together.'

'Aye, well, happen you've got summat there. There's times when I don't see eye to eye with my missis . . . But I don't clout her over the head.'

'Perhaps you don't want to badly enough.'

'Oh, come on now . . .' The publican looked embarrassed by having to disagree with a strange customer, especially when he was drinking his beer. 'I know the difference between right and wrong, which is more than you can say for that chap.' He jerked his thumb at the newspaper which Wilf was still holding.

'Hanging him won't teach him.'

Oh, why the hell was he talking about it? He didn't want to. He wanted to forget it, if only everybody would leave him alone. But they wouldn't. He was involved . . . And he couldn't forget it anyway. Perhaps he'd learn to live with it one day . . . The way he'd run away from her like a scared kid. He'd held her naked, listened to her moan in the act of love. And when she needed him he couldn't touch her. He'd backed away from her. He wanted to vomit at the sight of her. Eight minutes it had taken for the ambulance to arrive. Then she was dead, and nobody near her. He'd never know if she'd known he was there, what he'd done.

The landlord was saying something about teaching others. He heard him through a mist. He closed his eyes and concentrated on himself, who he was, what he was doing there. He opened his eyes and looked round.

'Where . . . ?'

'Through that door, in the yard.'

He went out into the cold air of the yard. He didn't really want the gents', only fresh air, but he went into the brick building and stood over the drain. 'Always game,' he thought. 'Never at a loss.' He felt as though he'd drunk several pints of beer. All depended upon the mood you were in. He went out into the yard again and looked up at the sky. It was beautifully high and clear. A line of O'Casey's swam into his mind: 'What is the stars?' and he answered himself out loud: 'The stars,' he said, 'is bloody indifferent.' He decided all at once that he would have Marguerite tonight. Why wait? What was he doing – acting in a pornographic novel? Will I, won't I, sometime, never? Who knew that they'd be here tomorrow? Perhaps he'd get knocked down by a bus. Perhaps somebody would beat her on the head like that maniac had done to Poppy. The odds were against it. So were the odds against his ever being so near to violent death of that kind. 'Do you appreciate, Mr Cotton, just how valuable such an experience is to you as a writer?'

You never knew anything, not a thing. But you had to act as though you did. By God, yes! Or you might as well pack it all in. A low wall bounded the yard on the far side. He went and looked over it. He found himself looking across steeply falling ground at the city. It was all spread out before him. Two hundred and fifty thousand people. He thought God bless us all, here and now and evermore, Amen.

He went back into the pub. Marguerite saw him as soon as he came through the door. There was a man with her and the publican was talking to both of them. He wondered why he'd been carrying the image of a tall man. He could have read all kinds of things into the tight little smile on Marguerite's face. There were two patches of colour high on her cheekbones and her eyes glittered strangely.

She said, 'Here he is now,' as he crossed the room, and the two men looked at him.

She stepped to one side and the man turned from the bar to face him. Marguerite said, 'This is my father, Wilf.'

As he felt a hard hand thrust into his he thought: She's done it the wrong way round. She should have introduced me to him. Aloud, he said, 'What are we all drinking, then?'

'No, no, this is on me.'

As the drinks were being ordered he looked into Marguerite's face. She nodded almost imperceptibly and tears formed in her eyes as he looked at her. He reached down and felt for her hand.

THE END

Just You Wait and See

Stan Barstow

'Mr Barstow's strength is in the resolute honesty of his depiction of how people feel. He is a writer you can trust'
The Scotsman

Set in a closely-knit industrial community at the beginning of the Second World War, Stan Barstow's novel tells the story of young Ella Palmer and her family. Ella wants to marry, but her affections are torn between the solid, dependable, qualities of Walter, a local butcher, and the romantic enticements of Mr Strickland, a visiting tradesman with knowledge of the world beyond the village. But there are conventions to be obeyed, and with the onset of war Ella finds she cannot delay much longer.

Against this background, Ella sifts through the vagaries of her physical and emotional needs and weighs up the value of two different kinds of love. The circumstances in which Ella makes her final choice provide a poignant and fulfilling conclusion to Stan Barstow's perfectly crafted novel, which is sure to win him new readers.

'A simple tale, told with great clarity and never a wrong note struck'
Hilary Bailey, The Guardian

0 552 99341 7

BLACK SWAN